Someone to watch over her . . .

Her life in beautiful Arrowhead Bay seems like paradise. But for former CIA operative Marissa Hayes, it's a deep cover she's forced to live under after daring to take down a powerful enemy with strong terrorist ties. Out of necessity, she keeps her emotions as guarded as her life, even as she finds herself drawn to Justin Kelly, the most arousing man she's ever met. But when Marissa must find a new place to hide, the able-bodied Vigilance agent is the first man she turns to . . .

Justin can't get close to Marissa, if he hopes to keep her alive. Which only makes sharing a villa with her at a remote island resort all the more challenging. The passion rising between them is exquisite—and excruciating. Even more so when terrorists infiltrate the island, putting Marissa in the crosshairs. Now Justin will do anything to protect the woman he cares about more deeply than he dares to admit. . . .

Visit us at www.kensingtonbooks.com

Books by Desiree Holt

Finding Julia

Game On Series
Forward Pass
Line of Scrimmage
Pass Interference
Fourth Down

Vigilance Series
Hide and Seek
Without Warning
A Deadly Business

Published by Kensington Publishing Corporation

A Deadly Business

A Vigilance Novel

Desiree Holt

LYRICAL PRESS
Kensington Publishing Corp.
www.kensingtonbooks.com

Lyrical Press books are published by
Kensington Publishing Corp. 119 West 40th Street New York, NY 10018

First Electronic Edition: August 2018
eISBN-13: 978-1-5161-0369-0
eISBN-10: 1-5161-0369-6

First Print Edition: August 2018
ISBN-13: 978-1-5161-0372-0
ISBN-10: 1-5161-0372-6

Printed in the United States of America

I have a lot of people to thank for the creation of this story. First and foremost for the real Justin and Marissa, for letting me borrow their names. And to Justin himself for all the help with Marissa's CIA assignment and personality. To those who requested anonymity but were incredibly helpful: my doctor who answered my questions about Justin's wound and his hospitalization; the customs officer who was so helpful with information about declarations in Nassau and on the way to private islands; to my always dependable police officer, Joseph Patrick Trainor, who was a great resource about anything to do with the police. And last, but far from least, my incredible editor, Paige Christian, who is sharp, savvy, so good at her job and pushed me hard to get the desired results. Without you, Paige, this story would not sing. Thank you, everyone, for helping me bring this story to life.

Author Foreward

Writing a book is a solitary experience but it never comes to the bookshelves, virtual or other, alone. For me it starts with my treasured friend and beta reader extraordinaire, Margie Hager, who has the best eagle eye in the world. Thank you, Margie for your friendship and for all the hours you put in to help me bring my stories to life. Thanks to Joseph P. Trainor for letting me pester him with a million questions and for keeping me honest and providing me with invaluable information on all things law enforcement and military elite. To my family, who believed in me from the beginning and are my biggest promoters: my daughter Amy and Suzanne, my son Steven and my granddaughter Kayla. And of course, to you, my readers, without whom none of this would be possible.

Desiree Holt

Chapter 1

"Thank you for dining with me, Miss Masters. It is always such a great pleasure."

Valentin Desmet, the man who carried the trash for London billionaire Stefan Maes—her target—stepped out of the limousine and straightened the jacket of his suit. He smiled and gave a slight bow before holding out his hand to her. Others might consider him a sophisticated continental gentleman, but his elegant suit, his linen shirt, and silk tie couldn't hide, to her, the slimy weasel he was.

Lauren Masters gritted her teeth as she put her hand in his, allowing him to help her from the vehicle, doing her best not to show her distaste.

God. She couldn't wait to get away from him.

The streetlamp cast its light on his longish, slicked-back, dark brown hair and his tall, slender body. If vampires were real, she would have said he belonged to a family of them. Spending time with him creeped her out, a feeling that had stayed with her from the moment of that first *accidental* meeting.

The most distasteful part of her job had been establishing the relationship with Desmet. Polished and urbane on the surface, he had a cruelty in his eyes that nothing could hide. Pulling out all the stops before he'd finally referred her to Maes had often turned her stomach. But an assignment was an assignment, and she'd known when she accepted it the kind of people she'd be dealing with. So, she had dazzled him with her knowledge of the financial markets and how to squeeze every extra nickel out of investments, selling him on why he should recommend her to his boss.

Dining with him once a week had become silently mandatory since she'd snagged Maes's account. She had told the CIA that yes, she'd do whatever was needed to bring down the man who funded terrorists and fomented revolutions in Third World countries. She just hadn't expected it to include weekly dinners with a man who made her want to take a bath every time she left him.

Sometimes she wondered how she'd managed to do this for three years—playing a part, cozying up to Desmet, but in a very professional way. Dealing with Maes, who was evil personified. But now, at last, it was all paying off.

She gave Desmet her best fake smile. "The pleasure was mine, Mr. Desmet."

She hoped she didn't choke on her words. She should get an award for acting.

He continued to hold her hand even after she exited the vehicle.

"Come, come." He shook his head. "Mr. Desmet? I keep telling you we're past that. After all this time we should be on a first-name basis, no?"

No! She'd call him a slimy piece of shit if she could.

"I try to keep business and pleasure separated. You know that."

He gave a soft laugh. "One of the many things I admire about you. All business, and exceptionally good at it. Mr. Maes is very pleased with your work. I still consider the day we met one of my most fortunate."

"Thank you. I do my best." She eased her hand from his as gracefully as possible.

"Well, enjoy your weekend." He took a step back. "Plan on meeting for lunch next week. Mr. Maes has some additional assets he needs to deal with."

More assets? This could be the last piece of the puzzle she was looking for. Among other things, they still had no information on the other men Maes had dealt with, men who colluded with hm. Maybe whatever Desmet had would lead her to them. Then maybe she could get the hell out of here before it all fell apart.

"I look forward to it. And again, thank you for dinner."

She tamped down her need to hurry as she mounted the steps to her building, turned once to wave at him, then let herself in. And leaned against the door, drawing a breath, and exhaling slowly. A ribbon of excitement curled inside her at his last statement.

After three years of swimming in the high-energy financial waters of London's Canary Wharf district, she had almost enough for the CIA to drop the net on Maes, but there was one piece of the pie she was still missing. She prayed that what Desmet had for her was that piece, because she needed to get the hell out of London. Lately she'd had the itchy feeling she was being watched. And was there a slight change in Desmet's attitude at dinner, or had she just imagined it?

She checked her watch, realized she was running late for her meeting with Craig Joffrey, and raced up the flight of stairs to her flat. The man had been her handler from day one, and she both liked and respected him. Tonight, she had two things for him: a flash drive with more critical information on Maes's accounts, and the tidbit Desmet had teased her with.

One good thing about a small flat was you didn't have to look a lot of places for things. In less than ten minutes her business look was gone, replaced by jeans, sweater, and battered boots. A worn jacket and a watch cap pulled down over her distinctive auburn hair, the flash drive slipped into a hidden pocket in her sleeve, and she was ready.

Downstairs again, Lauren pressed a hidden button that opened a panel at the back of the foyer. In seconds, she was racing through a tunnel connecting to the house behind hers. After exiting the other building, also CIA-owned, she hurried to the corner and turned right. She always used this method when meeting Craig. Anyone looking for her would be watching the front of her known address.

She loved the fact the Kensington area was convenient for transportation. The Tube was only two blocks from her flat, and with her Oyster card she could travel anywhere in London and be as anonymous as possible. Even if someone followed her, getting lost in the station and on the train was old hat to her by now.

But no one followed her on the street, and nothing tickled her senses at the station. On each new train, she changed cars to see if anyone followed. If only she could get rid of that damn itch between her shoulder blades. Nothing had happened to put it there, but she'd been at this for three years now. The shelf life of safety was about to expire, and she knew it. If she could just make it through next week.

She had no qualms about what would happen to her if Maes knew what she was doing. When Brian Gould had recruited her, he hadn't pulled any punches describing the man.

"He's a vicious bastard with no conscience and no soul. He destroys lives as easily as some people squash bugs. He kills as easily as some people brush their teeth. He's not too particular, either. If someone gets in his way, they and anyone connected with them become his victims."

"Nice guy," she'd commented, and shivered.

"Not," he'd snapped. "He's the quintessential Croatian thug, growing up on the streets of Zagreb where the biggest requirement was a lack of conscience. He has a hit squad recruited from the gangs he ran with, and inflicting unbearable pain is only one of the weapons in their arsenal."

"If you're trying to scare me," she'd told him, "you're doing a good job."

"I just want you to watch your step, but we'll have your back all the way."

It still amazed her that for three years she'd walked this tightrope without falling off.

Two Tube transfers later, she entered the Dirty Dog, a pub in a dingier part of Kensington whose dark interior provided the perfect environment for her meetings with Craig. She found him waiting in their usual booth, two beers sitting on the table. He always ordered to keep the waitress from pestering them, but they only pretended to drink, taking a sip for show now and then.

She slid in across from him and pulled off her cap.

"Safe for another week." It was her standard greeting, only tonight it sounded hollow to her. More than at any other time since she'd stepped into the role of Lauren Masters, financial wizard, she felt uneasy.

Craig scowled. "Don't joke about that, kiddo. Any op can turn sour in a minute. And you've been on this one for three years. That's a long time in anyone's book."

"But it's worked so far, right?" Joking was one way she dealt with the tension of her situation. She never forgot for one minute the dangerous game she'd agreed to play.

"So far." He frowned. "I never did cotton to the idea of the CIA taking untrained people and putting them in dangerous jobs. I just wish I didn't have this feeling we're pushing our luck."

Lauren tensed. So, he felt something, too? Should she forget about next week, and have him pull her out now? No. She didn't want to leave feeling her job wasn't finished. Surely, she'd be safe for one more week. Right?

"I was trained," she reminded him.

He shook his head. "A degree from the London School of Economics isn't much good in a firefight."

"But it's what you needed to put someone in place to handle Maes's financial accounts. Besides, you've done this long enough. If you thought there was imminent danger, we'd flip the kill switch now. Right?"

"Right, I just..." He shook his head. "I haven't because I think you're the most focused agent I've ever worked with. And doing a damned good job."

"I think that's a compliment."

"It can be good and bad. Never mind. Just be alert. How was your dinner with Desmet tonight? You watch your back with that slimy bastard. He'd cut your throat and not turn a hair."

Lauren nodded. "I agree, but I've learned how to handle him over time." She hoped.

"Just be on your toes, please. You've done a great job for us and I'd hate to see anything happen to you."

Lauren grinned. "Aw. You like me," she teased. "You really like me."

"Don't joke, Lauren." Craig's tone was dead serious. "I told your boss we needed to wrap this up. Stefan Maes trusts no one, except maybe Desmet. He's been known to set traps for people—both real and electronic—just to set his mind at ease that nothing wonky is happening. I want you out before he decides you're next up."

"I am being very, very careful," she assured him. "Believe me, I don't want to be the object of his wrath."

She didn't want to tell him she'd been feeling uneasy lately. That she looked constantly to be sure no one was following her or checking her computer work. If she did, he would pull her out right now. Maybe he should, but there was that little tidbit Desmet had dangled in front of her tonight. It could be the final nail in Maes's coffin.

Still she couldn't help sliding glances toward the door, checking people who entered.

"Just don't forget where that asshole came from." Craig growled. "He's a soulless bastard."

"We still have eyes on Adrian McCormack, you know." Craig shook his head. "He's a loose cannon and I don't trust him."

McCormack was the account specialist whose firm had previously handled everything for Maes. Until Lauren became the shiny new penny at Heath Financial, got close to Valentin Desmet, and swiped the account from under McCormack's nose. He continued to badmouth her, even after all this time.

"He can't still be on a tear over what happened." She frowned. "I thought he got over the whole thing. As he loves to say, it's just business."

Craig shook his head. "You grabbed a major account from him. From his firm. You think they would ever forget something like this? Or let him forget it? He's been doing his best to find out whatever he can about you. I worry that he'll somehow manage to turn up something and take it to Maes to expose you."

"Expose me how? He doesn't know a damn thing about me." She scowled. "Right? My cover is still in place? Isn't it?"

God! Was he trying to tell her something?

"Of course. But you and I both know if someone pays enough money to the right people, no information is sacred."

"Wait. Are you saying there's a leak somewhere?" Butterflies began dancing the tarantella in her stomach. Damn! She'd been warned from the very first day there was always a remote possibility her cover might be blown, but she had been assured ten times over the percentage of that happening was very small.

Craig shook his head. "No. I'm not saying that. But I am telling you there's always that possibility. If McCormack is bitter enough, if his life has been destroyed enough, there's always the chance he'll find a way to make this whole thing blow up."

"The escape plan is still in place, right?"

He nodded. "We can activate with one phone call. I promise you that. Your safety is a primary goal."

She blew out a breath. "Good. I know, but it helps to hear you say it."

"We don't want anything to happen to you," he assured her. "Like I said, I just have a funny feeling." He studied her face. "I expect you took the usual precautions getting here tonight?"

"I did. Just like always."

"Good." He leaned toward her. "Tell me about tonight's dinner with Desmet."

She told him about her dinner and what the man had said about next week.

"I've a feeling about this, Craig." She couldn't keep the edge of excitement from her voice. "This might be information that leads me to other men he did business with. He's been scrupulous about not leaving any trail, even in his secret accounts."

"If that's so, you need to be doubly careful," he cautioned. "Especially with McCormack out there."

"I hear you."

"And if we don't get these men this time, Lauren, the CIA will keep trying. But Maes is the big fish they want."

She nodded. "Let me just see what Desmet hands me next week and how I can use it. Then, if you still have this feeling, we can roll it up."

She'd spent months in place establishing herself, to reach a point where people stopped checking everything she did. It had taken a while, but at last she felt comfortable using the program Craig had given her. It blocked her digital fingerprint on the mainframe at Heath Financial, so no one could track what she was doing. She might have an itchy feeling, but after all her hard work and living on the edge for three years, she didn't want to quit before the end. She was determined to get every last scrap of information she could before leaving Lauren Masters behind.

"All right. What else?"

She fished a thumb drive from a hidden pocket in her jacket sleeve. Craig's hand covered hers on the table, and that quick, he had it and stashed it away.

"Not much, but every little bit helps, right? I hope whatever I find out next week closes the books on Maes."

"And good riddance," Craig said. "The man's a blight on the world."

"Amen to that."

They sipped a bit from their drinks, always scanning the pub to see who might be suspect. Lauren had learned by now what signs to look for.

Craig checked his watch. "We need to wrap this up. You have the other phone I gave you?"

"I do." She patted her pocket. "Always carry it with me."

"Good."

At their first meeting, he'd given her two burner phones. One was used to set up their meetings as well as for any conversation they needed to have between those meetings. The other only had one number programmed into it. His. If she ever had a real emergency, if her work was discovered and a trap set, all she had to do was press one button. Conversely, if he ever called her on that phone it meant the operation was shut down, and she was to get the hell out of Dodge to the prearranged meeting place for extraction.

"Okay." He leaned back in the booth. "Call me next week after you find out what this latest with Maes is about and we'll set up a time to meet. Be prepared to be pulled out right after that."

"I will." She tugged her hat down on her head and was sliding from the booth when Craig reached out and grabbed her wrist.

"I can't stress this enough. Be careful, Lauren. My Spidey senses are tingling."

"I will. I promise." She had no wish to get crosswise with Stefan Maes.

As she exited the Dirty Dog, she pulled her jacket tighter around her body and turned up the collar. The temperature had dipped again while she was inside and there was a sharp nip in the air. Craig's words echoed in her brain and she felt as if she had a target painted on her back. She walked with rapid steps to the closest Tube station. A mob still crowded the sidewalks despite the temperature, and she had to fight her way through it, all her senses on high alert.

Even when she reached the station she scanned every area the way she'd been trained. Nothing seemed out of the ordinary. Just the usual

Friday night late crowd, everything from singles and couples heading home after a night out to the usual lowlifes who seemed to spend their lives in the Tube stations.

She was smart and savvy enough, however, to know that didn't mean anything. At each station she was careful to choose where she stood to wait. She changed trains twice, and damn it, why did it seem as if all the cars on the three trains she rode were full past capacity? She had that familiar twitchy feeling between her shoulder blades, as if someone was watching her. Or worse yet, aiming a gun at her.

Her eyes never stopped moving. Did that guy in the black jacket look at her strangely? Was that a gun in his pocket? Maybe it was the woman watching her from the corner of her eye. At one station she boarded a train then just before it took off, leaped out, and waited for the next one. But that twitchy feeling was still there.

She hadn't tripped any wires. She knew she hadn't. And Craig was just being his usual old lady self. That was what he got paid for. So why had she been feeling this way all week?

From the beginning, she'd been able to play her part because she knew her handler had her back. She just hoped that neither of them was overreacting.

She was exhausted by the time she exited the final stop of the night. Again, she searched the streets as she hiked from the train to the building where she entered the tunnel. Were those footsteps she heard behind her? A man was out walking his dog, and she closed her hand over the gun in her pocket, just in case.

Tap, tap, tap.

When she looked over her shoulder she saw an old man walking with a cane. What on earth was he doing out so late at night? She walked faster, hurrying down the familiar street. Maybe she should have stayed at an all-night place until it was light before heading home.

She raced up the stairs of the building behind hers, let herself in, and hurried to the tunnel, following it to her building. At last she climbed the inside stairway to her flat with weary steps. She had just pulled her key out to unlock her door when the special phone buzzed in her pocket. Her stomach knotted, knowing this meant something serious. She pulled it out and pressed the button to answer.

"Craig?"

"Get the hell out of there. Don't pack, don't do anything. You know where to meet me, and I'll have everything you need. Just get going. This minute."

Then he said the three words no covert CIA agent ever wanted to hear.

"Your cover's blown."

Chapter 2

Arrowhead Bay, two years later

"That's it, Marissa. Foot sweep. Just like that."

Marissa Hayes extended her leg and swept her foot as instructed, almost, but not quite taking Justin Kelly to the floor. Sweat dripped from her as the former SEAL, wearing protective gear and a big grin, moved just out of range. The protective gear she wore didn't help her movements, either.

"Damn!" She swiped her forearm across her forehead, catching the drips of perspiration. "You do it every time."

"That's what I get paid for. Don't tell me you're ready to quit."

She glared at him. "Not even for money. Bring it on, mister."

Justin grinned at her, a curve of his lips that made her body want something other than kicks and jabs and punches.

"Okay, then."

This was the fourth lesson she'd taken from him. When Vigilance, the elite private security agency that made its home in Arrowhead Bay, began offering both group and private classes in certain forms of self-defense, Avery March, the owner, had urged Marissa to take advantage of it.

"You never know when you might need it," she'd cautioned.

And in Marissa's situation, that was more truth than poetry.

When one of the most dangerous men in the world had you at the top of his hit list, you never had the luxury of relaxing. Stefan Maes's reach, even after losing so much of his empire, was still extensive. And she knew, without a doubt, he'd never give up.

In the two years since her job with the CIA had ended so abruptly, she'd fit herself in to the slow pace of life in Arrowhead Bay, which really suited her. She could be as anonymous as she wanted. For the most part she'd isolated herself from social situations, reminding herself she wasn't in a position to develop a relationship. Not now. Maybe not ever. Her situation could blow up in her face any time. She never stopped looking over her shoulder. Always double and triple checking locks. Never parking her car in dark places. Ever alert to her surroundings and strangers who could bring danger to her. Never getting too close to people.

She didn't think she'd ever be able to let her guard down again. She'd always be looking over her shoulder, but that was the tradeoff.

Reluctantly she'd let Avery talk her into these classes.

"You know Justin," the woman reminded her. "You'll be comfortable with him."

That was true. He was an unexpected and unplanned bright spot as she crafted a new life for herself for the third time. She'd also begun to think of him as her safety net. Not only had he been with Vigilance for five years but he was also a former SEAL. She couldn't get better protection than that if she needed it.

Maybe because of that he was one of the few people here she could relax with.

Sort of.

Because he was also a man who lived in her dreams almost every night. Who woke up parts of her body she'd thought frozen. It didn't help that she sensed she was having the same effect on him, from the way he looked at her and the tentative signals he'd floated. But he would never make any kind of move unless she indicated she was open to one. It both excited and scared her.

She couldn't relax too much.

She had to keep repeating that to herself on a daily basis. Letting down her guard could prove fatal to her. Something she never forgot. When she took the CIA assignment, she had suppressed any need for sex, buried any desire for a relationship. She couldn't do that and her job. Something like that softened her edge, could destroy her, could distract her senses and expose her secrets.

Taking these classes had been a bad idea. Temptation wasn't something she needed, even if sometimes alone at night she was desperate for the comfort of another human being. And too often, Justin Kelly was exactly the comfort she craved. How she longed to lean into that toned body, feel those muscular arms around her, press her mouth to his lips that looked so firm. At just over six feet, his lean body was solid, toned muscle. Short-cropped light brown hair accented a sculpted face with a square jaw, high cheekbones, and dark brown eyes that reminded her of melted chocolate.

She hadn't been with anyone for so long she'd almost forgotten what it was like. But, if she was honest with herself, she hadn't ever felt that same crackle of electricity with any other man. That same hunger. That same throbbing in every one of her pulse points.

And beyond that, he made her feel safe. With Justin, more than with anyone else, she felt one hundred percent protected. Knew if danger came calling, Justin would be there helping her.

She was sure Avery hadn't clued him in on her real situation. One of the reasons her former boss had sent her here was because Avery had a zipped lip, knew the meaning of security, and had top-of-the-line protection available. To Justin, she was just someone who had moved to Arrowhead Bay, ran a small art gallery, and basically avoided the mainstream of life.

She had no idea what to do with this hot sexual attraction growing between them, an elephant in the room they both were ignoring. Not that he was overt about it. No, that wasn't his style. But he left plenty of openings for her to send him signals. She saw it in his eyes when he was teaching her certain moves. Or when he helped her to her feet and held her hand just a few seconds longer than necessary. Or removed the protective pads she wore during class and let his hands linger on her skin.

Twice he'd asked her to go for coffee after class. At first, she'd said no, but then she'd thought, *I want this. What harm can coffee do?* Except, even with a table between them, and casual conversation, the electricity in the air surrounding them was so strong it was almost visible.

Then last week he'd been teaching her a kick maneuver and swept her legs out from under her, taking her to the floor. They lay there for an endless moment, neither wanting to break the intense gaze they were locked in.

Yes! She wanted to shout. *Kiss me.*

And she was sure he would have, except Avery had come into the room to tell Justin he had a phone call. Her brain told her that was for the best, but the rest of her body had yet to catch up.

Marissa was so busy letting all these thoughts dangle in her brain that she missed it completely when Justin executed a perfect kick to her knees and took her to the mat.

"Hey!" She pushed herself up so she was leaning on her elbows. "That's supposed to be my move."

That tantalizing grin flashed again. "Then you best get to it. Come on, or I'll think you're a quitter."

It continued to amaze her the way he could tease her into putting all of herself into this very physical exercise.

"Marissa?" Justin's voice broke into her tiny reverie.

She blinked and shook her head. "Sorry. Didn't mean to let my mind wander again. Let's get to it."

He cocked his head, studying her. "You sure? We can quit for the day. The hour's almost up, anyway."

"Quit? Hah! You wish. Come on, show me what you've got."

She skillfully parried and blocked every move of his, answering with one of her own. When the alarm on Justin's watch sounded, letting them know the hour was up, she was again dripping in sweat and breathing hard, but she felt exhilarated. She'd had greater success blocking his moves then previously, and got in a few hits of her own.

"You did great there at the end," he told her, helping her out of the pads. "One of these days you'll kick my ass but good."

"Oh, right." She snorted. "As if."

"Seriously. You picked this up quicker than most people. You're my star pupil."

"I bet you say that to all your students," she teased, grabbing a towel from the bench and mopping her face and neck.

"Not quite." He checked his watch. "Listen. It's eight thirty. You don't open until ten. Want to grab a coffee and muffin at Fresh from the Oven like we did the last couple of times?"

Yes!

She was playing with danger here. Her life could blow up at any moment, dragging Justin in with her. But despite all her discipline, she couldn't say no.

"You've got plenty of time." He tapped his watch. "An hour and a half. Come on. You know what they say about all work and no play. Besides, you always end up having fun." He cocked an eyebrow. "Right?"

She had really enjoyed the last two times. What could it hurt to do it again?

God, she certainly didn't want to answer that question. But wasn't she entitled to a little pleasure? As long as she kept remembering it was just coffee. Do not pass Go. Do not collect two hundred dollars or anything else. Suppress all those tantalizing feelings. It was becoming harder and harder to do that, but...

She blew out a breath.

"Okay. Sure. That would be nice."

He burst out laughing. A deep, warm sound that tickled her nerve endings. "Not the enthusiastic response I hoped for, but I'll take it."

Heat suffused her cheeks. "I'm sorry. I—"

He waved a hand at her. "Just kidding. It's fine. Meet you there in about a half hour? That will give you plenty of time to relax with coffee and a roll before you open the gallery."

"I— Yes. That works out fine. Thank you."

It might have been her imagination, but she was sure she could feel him staring after her as she walked out of the room.

The gym was housed in a long building next to the renovated Key West house that contained the Vigilance offices and electronics setup. She had just unlocked the door to her car when she heard a woman calling her and turned to see Avery standing on the porch.

"Hey, Avery." She waved back.

"Come on in for a minute, can you?"

Marissa's stomach knotted. This had to be bad news. And just when she was finally drawing a full breath and thinking she was safe.

"Sure."

When she reached the porch, Avery gave her a hug. Marissa wasn't sure if it meant the woman was glad to see her or was setting the stage to drop a bomb.

"Is everything okay?" She hated to ask the question.

"What? Oh, sure." Avery grinned. "I just wanted to chat with you a little bit. Come on in for coffee."

"Um, the thing is, I'm meeting Justin for coffee in half an hour and I still need to shower and change."

Avery's smile got bigger. "That's better than a cup with me. You go on. I just wanted to check up on you. We've been a little busy lately and I haven't had as much time to stop by the gallery."

"No problem. It's—I'm actually doing okay there. In fact, better than okay. Traffic is steady and I'm starting to show more local artists."

"Glad to hear it." Avery studied her face. "You've done a great job weaving yourself into the fabric of life in Arrowhead Bay without being front and center."

Marissa squeezed the other woman's hand. "Thanks. I feel good here, and I appreciate your concern. Not many people would have done what you did—taken in a complete stranger and helped her build a new life."

"Brian Gould is a longtime friend," she told her, referring to Marissa's former boss at the CIA. "I owe him big time on a lot of fronts, so I was glad to do it." She grinned. "The fact that you turned out to be someone I could really like and be friends with has been a bonus."

"I don't know what to say except thank you, to both you and Sheri." She checked her watch. "And now I'm going to be rude and say I have to run."

"Go ahead. Have a little fun." Avery winked at her. "You could have a *lot* of fun with Justin."

Marissa shook her head. "I—No. It's nothing like that. He just wants to have coffee."

"If you say so. But, Marissa? He's safe, and you know what I mean by that. He's also a really nice guy and you couldn't ask for better protection if you need it." She held up a hand. "Not that I expect you will. We've got you sewed up nice and tight down here. I just think you need to cut yourself a break now and then. I, of all people, wouldn't encourage it if I didn't believe you could have complete trust in Justin."

Safe. Trustworthy. What dull ways to describe someone. But right now, it was what she needed.

"At least we're having coffee," she pointed out.

Avery started back into the building then turned. "I forgot to ask. Are you going to the Fourth of July boat parade and barbecue? I understand why you didn't want to last year, but now it would be nice for you. Meet more people, promote the gallery a little."

Marissa shrugged. "I haven't given it much thought."

"Well, let it roll around in your brain a while. I think you'd have a good time. At least meet me for lunch at the Driftwood on Friday. I'd be happy to pick you up."

"Thanks. I'll let you know."

She climbed in her car, cranking the engine so she could turn on the air conditioning. She hated to throw snow on Avery's obvious determination to help her lead as normal a life as she could, but she wondered if normal would ever be possible again.

Getting ready took little time. In her previous life, she'd learned to be a quick-change artist, so despite the few minutes she spent with Avery she was showered, dressed, and heading to Fresh from the Oven at five minutes until nine. One nice thing about Arrowhead Bay, nothing was very far from anything.

The gallery was only two blocks down from the café, so she parked in front and walked down. There was a decent parking lot in the back, but Marissa had learned to avoid places she couldn't exit from quickly, as well as places where she was hidden from the public. After two years, she was *almost* sure every trace of her last identity had been wiped from the earth. *Almost* sure that even the most sophisticated computers couldn't find her now. That the CIA had done a very good job of burying her.

And she prayed that was only a figurative expression.

She had woven herself into life in Arrowhead Bay, but her socializing was limited. She often had lunch with Avery and her sister, Sheri, the Arrowhead Bay chief of police. Sometimes one of the female Vigilance agents joined them. Sheri was the only person in town who knew who she was besides Avery. After all, who could be safer than a cop, right? She was grateful for both of them, and the way they had eased her into life in this little town.

On occasion, Avery invited her to join a group of people hanging out at the Purple Papaya or having dinner at the Driftwood. It was fun, and she appreciated being included. Avery had pointed out if she became a recluse not only would the gallery suffer but she'd cause more gossip, which was not what she wanted. Still, old habits died hard, and she was always so careful to watch everything she said and how she said it.

In many ways it was like being back in London, when she had to watch every word and walk a tightrope to do her job. But in London there was an escape plan when her job was completed or if her cover was blown. Once she'd been extracted, every trace of her London identity had been wiped away. Now she was living as yet another person in this unlikely place, hiding from the very man she'd brought down. Arrowhead Bay was her safe hidey-hole, as long as she kept her guard up.

She hadn't been attracted to a man in longer than she wanted to remember. Yet here she was, having coffee with one. And a man who made her hungry for intimacy, for the connection she hadn't craved until Justin came into her life.

Did he feel the same way?

She needed to quit dithering and go meet him. Nothing was going to happen at Fresh from the Oven. Anyway, it was not an invitation to get naked, just to have coffee.

True, but coffee sometimes led to a meal and a meal to—

Jesus. It was just coffee.

She swallowed a sigh and pushed open the door to the coffee shop, her senses immediately assaulted by the aroma of fresh baked cinnamon rolls and orange scones. Maybe she could bury her hormones under a ton of calories.

She scanned the room the way she always did, searching for anything that might set off her antenna. But nothing and no one seemed out of place. She spotted Justin waiting for her at a table against the wall, out of direct line of the window and still in a position to take in the entire place. She was sure his line of work had him choosing seats like that all the time, just as she had learned to do in London.

A tiny flicker of nerves raced over the surface of her skin when she saw him chatting with a man she did not recognize. She hesitated before approaching the table, wondering if she should just turn around and leave. But Justin saw her, smiled, and motioned her forward, and the knot of tension that was her constant companion eased a bit.

"Say hello to one of our local celebrities. Marissa Hayes, meet Blake Edwards."

Edwards turned and gave her a warm smile. "I don't know about the celebrity bit, but I am local. At least part of the time."

She relaxed a fraction. "Nice to meet you. As a matter of fact, I'm reading your latest book and really enjoying it."

"Thanks." He chuckled. "I'll take all the compliments I can get."

"I don't think you're lacking," she joked. "I know you've had several number one best sellers in a row." She frowned. "Wait. Didn't I hear or read something about a threat to your life? A stalker or something?"

"Yeah, but thanks to Vigilance it's over and done with."

Justin chuckled. "Thanks to Vigilance, he's now a married man."

Marissa looked from one to the other, puzzled. She paid little attention to local gossip unless it pertained to her.

"He married his bodyguard," Justin explained. "Can't get more successful than that."

Marissa stared at him. "You did?"

"Yes, but there's a little more to it than that. We grew up together in Arrowhead Bay, so we knew each other before."

"That's the sanitized version," Justin joked.

"And we won't be discussing any of the details," Blake warned.

"So, you guys in town for a while?"

"About a week," Blake told him. "We decided to buy the cottage Sam was renting and keep it as our get-away-from-it-all place."

"Good deal."

"Yeah. I'm getting ready to tour for this latest book," Blake explained, "and we wanted to get this done while I had a break. Then while I'm on the road, Sam's taking a short assignment for Vigilance."

"She doesn't go with you?" Marissa asked.

Blake shook his head. "I have an assistant who works for me. Sam hits a couple of stops now and then, when her schedule allows it. So, you in town visiting?"

"No, I moved here about two years ago." The story rolled out smoothly. "I got tired of the rat race in the big city and wanted someplace where the pace of living was slower. And running a gallery is something I always wanted to do."

"Marissa owns Endless Art," Justin added. "The gallery just two blocks down Main Street from here."

"Maybe Sam and I will stop by. We're looking for some things for the townhouse in Tampa."

She curved her lips in her professional smile. "I'll be happy to have you visit. We have some excellent pieces on display."

"Good. Maybe we'll see you later." He started to leave, then turned back. "Oh, in case either of you might be interested, I'm doing an informal thing at Read the Book on Saturday afternoon. Part of the whole holiday weekend thing. Come by if you get a chance."

"I'll do it." Justin nodded. "Thanks."

"He's very nice," Marissa commented after Blake moved away.

"Yeah. Local boy makes good. Really good. Anyway, let's get you some coffee and pastry. What's your pleasure?"

The scent of the rich coffee mingled with the aroma of fresh cinnamon rolls. When Justin placed her mug and plate in front of her, his hand just brushed against her arm. She swore sparks were visible, jumping between them, and wondered if he thought the same thing. When she looked up into his face, she saw the hunger in his eyes, the blazing desire.

And she knew hers had to match his for strength.

Before she realized it, the little alarm on her watch went off, and she wanted to turn back the time.

"Time to get to work?" he asked.

"Yes." She sighed. "This was very nice. Thank you for asking me." She grinned. "Again."

"My pleasure. And I hope we'll do it a lot more." He rose from his chair and gathered up their trash. "Come on. I'll walk you down to the gallery."

He cupped her elbow, steering her toward the entrance, and the heat of his hand seared her skin. She knew tonight when she closed her eyes she'd be dreaming about him again, maybe this time with his clothes off. And from the looks he'd given her across the table, she had an idea he would, too.

"Oh, you don't have to," she protested, even as she wanted to prolong the intimacy.

He held up a hand. "No problem. I'd like to look around, anyway. See what you've got that's new."

She cocked an eyebrow. "I didn't know you were interested in art. You've never been by before."

He winked. "I take a look through those big windows, whenever I walk by."

"Well, come on in, if you've got some time, and take a real look around."

The oversized display windows had made her nervous at first, exposing her to anyone and everyone. But you couldn't drape or shutter windows in a gallery. The original windows, however, had been replaced with bulletproof glass, and the alarm was connected to Vigilance. A few other minor adjustments had been made to keep her as safe as possible.

Even with all that, she kept to either her office or the rear of the main gallery. And she always had her small 9 mm easily accessible. Arrowhead Bay might be a typical Southern tourist town, but she wasn't taking any chances. Ever.

She unlocked the door, and as soon as she was inside, hit the code on the security system to shut off the alarm. She was faithful about always resetting it, even if she was just going down the street for a few minutes. Then she flicked on the lights and dropped her purse in the tiny office.

"Well, this is it." She stood in the middle of the place, arms outstretched. "Welcome to Endless Art."

Justin walked around, looking at the art hanging on the walls and those placed on easels at strategic locations. She noticed he stopped at several and spent a few minutes studying them.

"I see you have a lot of local artists here." He turned back to her. "Is there a good market for them?"

She wiggled her hand back and forth. "Depends. I say for most of them. Are you looking for something for your place?"

She didn't even know where he lived. Did he have a house? A cottage? There were no apartment complexes in Arrowhead Bay. The closest thing was a small community of duplexes at the edge of downtown. *Where*, she wondered, *do all those agents live, anyway?* She'd never thought to ask.

He laughed. "Not hardly. I have one of the suites on the top floor at Vigilance. It's where Avery houses what she calls her homeless agents."

Marissa studied him. "You don't want a place of your own?"

He shrugged. "Not at the moment. I'm usually on one assignment or another, and it works not having to worry about maintenance and upkeep."

"Doesn't that make it a little difficult if you want to, uh, spend time with a woman?"

Oh, for crap's sake. She should shut the hell up.

The look he gave her scorched her body to the soles of her feet. She had a feeling his own body was heating up, and she couldn't help lowering her gaze to his crotch. Her eyes widened in reflex at the significant bulge.

"Yes." He spoke in a soft tone of voice. "Sometimes I do. Like the one in front of me right now."

"Oh." She wet her lips. "Well."

"You have to know I would love to get together with you for more than coffee."

"I do." She tilted her head in a tiny nod.

"But I'll never push. It's all up to you," he told her in a soft voice. "I hope you're reading my signals, Marissa. I think we could have something going here, but it's your call."

Heat crept up her cheeks, but she forced herself to look directly into his eyes. "Justin, I-I mean…"

"Just so you know, Avery has not said a word to me about you, nor have I asked. I won't invade someone's privacy. But I've been in this business long enough to know when someone's in a thorny situation. Whatever it is, tell me or not, I will always keep your confidence and always protect you. That doesn't change the fact that I want you. Want to see where whatever we start can be going."

"I-I know." And she did. God, what should she do? She felt like a dithering idiot.

"In my line of work, we learn to respect people's boundaries. Whatever you're dealing with is none of my business unless you choose to make it so." He shrugged. "We've danced around this, Marissa. Pretended it isn't there. Ignored it. But take it from me, it's not going away. All you have to do is give me the signal, because it's all up to you." He grinned. "And if not, you'll still be my star kickboxing student."

She opened her mouth to say something, but before she could get any words out, the front doorbell tinkled.

"Customers?" he asked.

"I hope." She wet her lips. "Thank you for the coffee and pastry. It was a nice break."

"My pleasure." His smile could have curled her toes. "Don't forget Friday's session."

"I won't. And thanks again."

"And remember. It's all up to you."

Then he was gone.

She turned and smiled at the couple looking at the art hanging on the east wall. She'd have to be very careful with Justin Kelly. More than her safety could be at risk here. She wondered, with a touch of regret, if the day would ever come when she could relax, be completely free of her past, and enjoy a normal life.

Chapter 3

Marissa had forgotten how much fun special events could be, especially those in a small town like Arrowhead Bay. Last year she had managed to avoid participating in the Fourth of July festivities, other than having a special show at the gallery. It boggled her mind that what used to be a three-day celebration in this town now encompassed most of a week. Avery had insisted she join them at some of the events this year and even offered to pick her up.

"I can get there on my own, and I will," Marissa had promised with a laugh. "At least to the biggest deals."

She wasn't quite sure how much she'd participate this year. She'd wait and see how she felt. But it was only Monday, and the town was already jammed with people. Out of curiosity, she took a slight detour past the marina, checking things out. The place was so full there were boats anchored just past the piers, their guests taxied back and forth by the makeshift ferry service the marina had set up. Most of the boats were decorated or in the process of being fancied up for the parade this weekend. The Driftwood Restaurant next to the marina, owned by the same couple, was already wall-to-wall people.

As she drove down Main Street, Marissa noted that, even though it was only Wednesday, the sidewalks were already jammed with both residents and holiday visitors. She was glad she'd decided to open the gallery early. Fourth of July banners hung from the lampposts along the streets and in almost every store window. She congratulated herself on bringing her own coffee and sweet roll. The lines at Fresh from the Oven and next door at Fresh Roasted snaked out both doors and down the sidewalk.

Lord. What would it be like by the time the weekend got there?

She wondered if Justin was teaching classes today, or had Avery sent him off on assignment? She hadn't seen him since coffee two days ago, and she knew he was giving her the space he was sure she needed. He'd left a note on the gallery counter with his email, and she couldn't count the number of times she'd started to enter it in her email program.

But she'd finally decided to talk to Avery first, confide in her. Ask her if she should clue Justin in. Right or wrong, she didn't feel she could move forward with…whatever this was, unless he knew what he was getting into.

Maybe after this weekend, she'd ask Avery to carve out a few minutes for her. She sure didn't want to wait much longer. Her body had turned itself into a constant state of readiness, and she was sure combustion was only moments away.

In a stroke of luck, a car was pulling away from a spot in front of the gallery just as she drove up. She was only mildly surprised to find people waiting in front, looking through the windows, and sipping coffee from their to-go cups. Or maybe it wasn't coffee. They could be drinking mimosas or even straight vodka. She reminded herself to be calm and gracious, and lock up if the visitors got too unruly.

"Oh, you're here." A woman in walking shorts and a hot pink T-shirt smiled at her. "Good. We hoped you would be. My husband and I—we're the Danforths, Laura and Howard—would really like a better look at the seascape in the window."

"That's one of my favorite pieces," Marissa said, unlocking the door. "Come on in and take your time looking at it. I think you have to make friends with art before you decide to take it home."

"Oh," Laura Danforth said. "You are just so right. Howard, come look at this right now."

Marissa hurried to hit the alarm panel then deposited her purse and her breakfast snack in the office. Then she slipped her handgun into her pocket and shrugged on the long vest that covered it. She had no idea what it was that had the hair on her arms standing up, or her neck itching. This was just a tourist couple out shopping. What was wrong with her?

But better safe than sorry was a motto she lived with each day. Brushing imaginary lint from her blouse, she eased back into the gallery, staying to the back so she didn't crowd the couple. The seascape was by a local artist she'd been working to promote. This sale would be a big boost for her, especially if these people passed the word to others.

So, she occupied herself adjusting the other displays and sipping on her coffee.

"Oh, excuse me," the woman called. "Could we ask you a couple of questions?"

Marissa ditched the rest of the coffee and walked over to them, smiling.

"Of course. What would you like to know?"

She went through her usual spiel with them, answering questions about the artist and what location the painting depicted. She considered it a good omen for the weekend when they bought the painting and didn't quibble about the price. Still, she couldn't shake that bad-vibe feeling. She was wrapping the painting in protective paper when she looked up to see Laura Danforth standing in the doorway of the packing room.

"You know, we've been coming here every year for the past ten years, all except for last year. I just told Howard I don't think I remember seeing the gallery before this. Are you new?"

Marissa paused for a moment, her hands stilled in the process of taping. She'd be new to a lot of people. It didn't mean anything.

Or did it?

"Well, new to you, I guess. I moved here two years ago. I think just about a month after the Fourth of July celebration."

"How do you like it?"

She looked up at the woman and smiled "I love it. Arrowhead Bay is a warm and friendly town. I'm on the water. The people are great. This was a very good move for me."

"What brought you down here?" Howard Danforth had joined his wife and stood there with his arm draped around her shoulder.

Marissa studied them for a moment. They looked harmless, relaxed and happy like any other tourist couple here for the celebration and festivities. But she'd learned over and over that appearances deceived, and you should never take anyone at face value. She had their information from the credit card receipt. She'd just ask Avery to run a check.

She lifted the wrapped picture and handed it to Howard.

"Enjoy your painting."

"Oh, we will," Linda Danforth gushed. "Every time I look at it I'll think of being back here at Arrowhead Bay." She looked around as she and her husband headed toward the door. "This is a very nice gallery. You have a great selection, and I always love discovering local talent. I'll be sure to tell our friends about it."

"Thank you so much. Please come back again next year."

The moment they were gone she hurried to her little office, grabbed a bottle of water from her minifridge, and drank half of it down before taking a breath. It disturbed her to see a slight tremor in her hands. What was the matter with her? For three tense years in London, under the very nose of one of the most vicious men in the world, she'd had nerves of steel. Now, despite the safety of her new surroundings, it seemed she was jumping at shadows. She supposed that was what happened with living every day knowing that Stefan Maes had vowed to destroy her.

She capped the water bottle and returned it to the fridge. This was ridiculous. Her old identity was buried under multiple layers. She'd grown out her hair from the short auburn flip she'd worn for three years and let it go back to its natural long honey brown. Just that alone had made a drastic change in her appearance. She'd even gained ten pounds; a fact she wasn't sure she was all that happy about. She had changed her wardrobe, and even trained herself to walk differently. It still amazed her the things the CIA could train a person to do when changing or burying an identity.

So cool it, she told herself. The Howards were just what they seemed, a boating couple here for the weekend. Still, it wouldn't hurt to have Avery check them out.

As busy as the morning turned out to be, she didn't have time to give much thought to the situation, and by noon her nerves had settled, and her sales had exploded. She made a note to bring out items she had stored and to contact the local artists she worked with to see what they had they'd like her to show.

She was just closing down her computer and thinking about lunch when the bell jingled to announce someone. Wearing her best public face, she hurried out of the office and relaxed when she saw it was Justin.

He lifted an eyebrow. "I can't tell if that expression on your face means you're glad to see me or if I should turn around and walk out."

Her laugh had a slight hysterical edge. "Glad to see you. Very glad."

His face sobered. "Trouble?"

For the first time since the CIA had recruited her, she was struck with an urge to unburden herself to someone and have them assure her things were fine. What was up with that? She hadn't needed anyone for a long time. Maybe it was the unsettled feeling she'd been plagued with of late, a feeling that told her she might not be as safe as she thought.

Stop it, she thought. Why was she seeing dragons all of a sudden?

She forced her mouth into a smile. "Oh, no, no trouble. Just very busy. Way more than last year."

"But that's good, right?"

"Yes. It is." She waved her hand around the display area. "I've replaced at least half of the art on display since I opened. I don't remember the crowd being this big last year."

"It keeps growing every year. Avery sent me to fetch you for lunch. She has a table at the Driftwood and she saved space for you."

Lunch? With people she didn't know?

But why was she spooked? Nothing had happened.

"Oh, I don't know…" She twisted her hands together. The Danforths had tickled her Spidey senses and unnerved her. She wasn't sure she was up to facing the crowd at the restaurant.

"It's just lunch, Marissa. With a couple of nice people." Justin smiled, but she caught a questioning look in his eyes. "Come on. You can sit next to me and I'll protect you. Or maybe you can try out some of those kickboxing techniques if someone pisses you off."

She couldn't help the tiny laugh that escaped.

"You must think I'm an idiot. I'm just not a very social person."

"Oh, I think you're very social." He winked. "And sociable. Come on. Lock up and we'll head over there."

"I can't believe she got a table. Is there even a place to park?"

He nodded. "A little thing like a crowd never stops Avery."

Marissa double-checked the alarm when she set it. Her training had taught her to be extra cautious whenever she sensed something might be off. Even though she might be chasing shadows where there were none, she wasn't about to take chances.

Justin helped her into the black Vigilance SUV he'd parked by a fire hydrant.

"Aren't you afraid of getting a ticket?" she teased.

"I didn't think I'd be long. And besides, I have a little pull with the police department." He glanced over at her. "All set?"

She nodded.

"Not my business, but you seem a little uptight today," he commented as he pulled smoothly away from the curb into traffic.

"I've just got a lot on my mind right now. This big weekend. Some other stuff."

"You know, I'm a good listener if you ever want to bounce anything off of me."

What she wanted to bounce off him weren't ideas. Her hormones, so ruthlessly suppressed for so long, had decided to revolt.

"Good to know. And thank you. I'll remember that."

The parking lot at the Driftwood was as jammed as she'd expected, but Justin wheeled the SUV into a slot with a Reserved sign.

"It's good to know the right people," he teased. "Come on. I prescribe a glass of wine with lunch."

Marissa seldom drank anything stronger than iced tea or coffee, but she had to agree that a glass of wine sounded good. And Avery's friendly face at a table out on the covered porch helped her relax, even if it was an infinitesimal amount.

"I'm glad Justin was successful dragging you out of that gallery," she said. "I'm sure you've been busy, but everyone has to eat lunch and I figured you could use a little break."

Justin pulled out a chair for her then sat down in the one next to her. Sheri March sat next to her sister. Blake Morgan and a woman she figured was his wife occupied the other two chairs.

"We meet again," Blake greeted her. "Marissa, this is my wife, Samantha. Sam."

Sam held out her hand. "Blake tells me you own Endless Art. We're going to come by this weekend, if you haven't sold out to the tourists."

"Please stop in." She smiled at Sam. "I love helping people select just the right pieces."

Lunch turned out to be better than she expected, if only she could get rid of this edgy feeling. When she ordered a glass of wine, Avery looked at her and lifted an eyebrow but said nothing. She managed to relax and enjoy the conversation, although she caught Avery sliding looks her way now and then.

"Justin's going to drop me at Vigilance before he takes you back to the gallery," Avery told her. "That okay with you?"

"Oh, sure. It was nice of you to send him to fetch me."

"I wanted to make sure you took a little break."

Marissa said goodbye to Blake and Sam and reminded them to stop by and see her. As they wound their way through the dining room to the exit, she scanned the restaurant, taking note of the crowd, and wondering if any of them had picked up the flyers the Driftwood had been kind enough to put out for her.

She almost stumbled when she spotted the Danforths at a table with two men. It wasn't them, however, as much as the two men they were with who tickled her senses. On the surface they looked like the other tourists in their casual attire. She couldn't define it except to say they reminded her so much of the men she'd dealt with for three years in London.

She wasn't aware she'd stopped walking until Avery bumped into her.

"Oh, I'm so sorry. My mind must just be wandering today." She started walking again but Avery was right in step with her.

"Your mind doesn't wander," Avery said in a low voice. "Not like that. What did you see?"

"What? Nothing. I—Nothing. Really."

Avery gave Justin a silent signal to move on and tugged Marissa off to the side.

"I know that look. I've seen it on enough faces in my line of work. Something spooked you. Who or what did you see that threw you off balance?"

Justin had turned and was looking at her with a quizzical expression on his face. She moved forward again.

"It's nothing. Really." He knew nothing about her situation, so he'd probably think she was an idiot for being spooked by strangers.

Avery, right behind her, touched her shoulder. "It may be, but just in case, let's figure out what spooked you."

Yes, maybe it was nothing, but she didn't want to worry about it all day. Not smart.

"Not here." She lowered her voice even more. "See that older couple with two dark-haired men at a middle table? Just take a quick look, like you're scanning the room."

Avery's mouth turned up in a quick smile. "I think I can do this, Marissa."

Marissa's face flamed. Of course, she could. She was in the business. "I think they're watching us. Let's all go back to Vigilance. I'll tell you what happened today and hope you can assure me I'm jumping at shadows."

"Of course. Come on."

Marissa said little on the ride to Vigilance, digging around in her brain to find whatever it was that had triggered her reaction to the Danforths. She still had no specific answer when she was seated across from Avery in her office, holding a fresh cup of coffee.

"Okay." Avery studied Marissa. "You aren't one to jump at shadows, so let's have it, no matter how insignificant."

Marissa took a sip of her coffee. How to phrase this so she didn't sound nuts? "That couple I showed you," she began. "They came into the gallery this morning. There wasn't anything out of the ordinary about them. They looked like any other holiday couple, tanned, relaxed, casually dressed. They were friendly and raved about the gallery. They even bought that seascape I've had on one of the main easels."

"But?" Avery lifted an eyebrow. "Something set you off."

"The questions they asked weren't any different than I get from so many others, but…" Marissa shrugged. "I don't know. They asked if I was new to the area. Said they'd been here every year but the last one and didn't remember the gallery. When I told them I'd only been here two years, that last year was my first Fourth of July event, they said that must explain it."

Avery nodded. "Sounds like normal chit chat."

"I agree. Even when they kept asking me things like where did I move from and why here, there was nothing I could put my finger on. It just sounded more like an inquisition than casual conversation."

"Was that all?"

Marissa shook her head. "No. Yes. I don't know. When I saw them at the Driftwood, the two men at their table reminded me of the men I met in London who might have you killed for choosing the wrong silverware."

"Well, that doesn't sound good. Brian Gould told me you have good instincts, and I believe he's right."

"If they'd been coming here for several years, wouldn't you have recognized them?"

Avery shrugged. "Maybe, but not necessarily. We get hundreds of people for this weekend every year. Unless I had a reason to cross paths with them they might not have landed on my radar. Do you have their information with you? I can do a quick check."

"Yes. I copied it from their credit card slip." She handed a piece of paper across the desk. "I'd at least like to know if they are who they say they are."

"Okay, let's see what we can find." She picked up her desk phone and pressed a button. "Ginger? Can you come in for a second?"

Marissa knew that Ginger was the go-to person at Vigilance for computer searches. If she couldn't find it, no one could.

There was a light rap on the door, and then Ginger poked her head in. "You rang?"

"I did." Avery handed over the slip of paper. "See what you can find out about these people. And—"

"I know, I know," Ginger interrupted. "You want it five minutes ago. Gotcha."

"If Stefan Maes sent these people, how the hell did he know where I was to begin with?" Marissa raked her fingers through her hair. "The CIA was meticulous about erasing every detail concerning Lauren Masters. And I have not left this place since the first day I set foot in it."

"That's a difficult question to answer," Avery told her. "I—"

Before she could finish her sentence, a cell phone sitting on her desk chimed.

"I need to take this right now." She rose from her chair. "Can you excuse me for just a minute?"

Marissa lifted an eyebrow. "Of course. I'll just step outside. Let me know when you're finished."

She closed the door behind her and leaned against it. Was she making something out of nothing? Letting her imagination run away with her?

Maybe these people were art thieves who scouted galleries and made a purchase to look normal. How on earth would anyone find her here, anyway?

"Avery kick you out?"

Marissa startled as Justin came out of the big electronics room. "What? Oh, no. She got a phone call she had to have privacy for."

"Yeah, she gets a lot of those." He studied her face. "You okay? You look a little shook up. Was it those people you saw at the Driftwood?"

"Um, just some questions I had."

She had a weird feeling Avery's call had to do with her. The same impression that she'd had during her last meeting with Craig Joffrey. She sipped at her cooling drink while she tried to keep herself together. When Avery opened the door and beckoned her back into the office, she had a hard time not yelling for Avery to tell her what it was all about this second. When Avery asked Justin to join them, Marissa knew there was trouble.

"First of all, Marissa," Avery began when they were seated, "I need your permission to fill Justin in on your background."

Marissa clutched the arms of the chair. She was right. Maes had found her. Otherwise why involve Justin? Why tell him her secrets?

"Is it— Do you—"

"Justin knows you. Plus, he would never give up secrets even under torture. And we're going to need him."

She swallowed hard, then nodded. "Yes. All right. If you think it's necessary."

"It's necessary."

"Then go ahead."

Marissa sat there, tense, hands fisted in her lap, while Avery filled Justin in on her CIA stint, the way it had ended, and the fact that Maes had put a price on her head. Justin absorbed it all and when Avery finished he turned to her, his lips curved in a warm, reassuring smile.

"Whatever this is," he told her, "I've got your back. We'll keep you safe."

"Thank you." She looked at Avery. "Okay, let's have it. What was that call about?"

Avery leaned forward. "That was Brian Gould. Talk about a coincidence of timing."

Cold dread landed in Marissa's stomach like a lead fist. She hated that her instincts had been right.

"It's bad, right?"

"I won't lie to you. It's not good. Brian said ever since Stefan Maes learned you were the one who blew the whistle on him, he's had people poking into every corner of the world, looking for you. He's as sneaky as the CIA. Brian assured me they've been keeping an eye on Maes, knowing he has a vendetta against you. This is the first time, however, they've heard one of his people actually sighted you. This couple must have called Maes as soon as they left the gallery."

"So, I was right about them." Cold dread knotted itself in Marissa's stomach. This was no time to fall apart. Besides, she was better than that. Now she needed her training to kick in.

"Yes, you were. The people they were lunching with had to be part of a team in the area in order for them all to connect so quickly."

She did her best to swallow back the sick feeling gripping her. "But how did they know to come here?"

"Sometimes it just happens by accident," Justin told her. "No matter how careful you are. Someone who knew you as Lauren might have come through here and spotted you. You've probably changed your appearance a lot, but it's not impossible. It could be any number of things. Bad luck is a constant companion in this business."

"Adrian McCormack could have spotted you, too," Avery pointed out. "Brian and I thought this would be a great place for you to create a new life, because Vigilance is here, and we can protect you, and Sheri does a great job as police chief. The down side is so many people come through here on their boats it's not as controlled as we'd like."

"Please tell me exactly what Brian said." Marissa was doing her best not to panic. That never helped the situation.

"Word is out now that Stefan Maes is gathering a crew again." Avery shook her head. "He's been doing it so far under the radar that none of Brian's sources got a sniff of it. He learned about that in the same phone call that said you'd been made. He called me right away."

"Maes has enough connections he could put an army together if he works it right." Marissa twisted her hands together to still the sudden tremors. Her trail had been wiped clean. The CIA had wiped her identity from every electronic file. Nothing to do with her current existence was written anywhere and Brian Gould was the only person who knew where she was, or so he'd assured her. But three years in the game had taught her nothing was absolute.

The one thing she couldn't control was chance.

Someone with a sharp eye could see through her current appearance, if they were looking for her. Or maybe Maes had gone to the trouble of having her photo manipulated so, despite any changes, people could spot her.

Just then the message app on Avery's tablet pinged. She read the screen and frowned.

Marissa swallowed back the anxiety that surged. "What?"

"Well, your instincts are still as sharp as ever, and it goes along with what I just heard. There's no record of these people except for credit cards with a post office box for mail. No real estate, no voting records, no navigation information, nothing."

"Color me surprised." She couldn't keep the bitterness out of her voice. "I knew when Adrian McCormack blew the whistle on me I'd have a target on my back for life. Maes is not the type of person to forget. You can bet tracking me down has been high on his list."

"I'm well aware of that." Avery frowned. "Let me think a minute. The first thing we have to do is get you out of his line of sight."

Yes, please. She felt sick to her stomach at the thought that Maes had tracked her here. Killing her would be the most merciful thing he could do if he got his hands on her.

"Maes has had two years to stew over his situation and nurture his hatred for me," Marissa pointed out. "I still don't know why he's not in prison."

"Because he has a team of very expensive, very good attorneys," Avery reminded her. "They have been making the case that everything was done by people who worked for him and that he had no knowledge of any of it. And truly, I think the CIA was just as happy to put him out of business rather than go through a very long, very expensive trial."

"Poor man." Marissa snorted. "He's had to live off his legitimate enterprises, which aren't quite as lucrative."

"He's also had all this time to plot and plan. I'm sure, knowing about him and knowing his type, he's working on some method to fill those coffers again."

"You can bet the farm on that." Marissa shook her head. "I have this weird feeling that he's cooking up some disaster." She stopped breathing for a moment. "I thought he was pretty much neutralized."

"'Pretty much' being the operative words," Avery pointed out. "He's persona non grata in several countries and of course he lost billions when the CIA froze his accounts. It seems none of those banks want to do business with him anymore, even for legitimate reasons. He must be a nasty piece of work. He even had to pull his legitimate accounts from Switzerland and they'll take just about anyone."

"Those accounts are just a drop in the bucket compared to what he made from his illegal activities." She locked her fingers together in her lap. "So where is he getting money to replace what he's lost? He can't exactly fund his revenge from his legal accounts."

Avery nodded. "According to Brian, he's been pulling strings wherever he can, tapping every crooked, evil source to line up some cash. Word is he thinks he can mount some kind of operation to reclaim what he says was stolen from him."

Marissa swallowed back the nausea creeping up in her throat.

"He can do it, too," she told Avery. "He's got all those unstable third world governments beholden to him. If he can gather his core team of monsters he has a good shot. Except…"

"Except what?"

"Except, like I said, he lost billions because of our operation. Many billions. He can't get enough handouts to match the amount. Besides, I know Maes. Revenge will be as strong a need as building a treasury again." She slammed her fist on the arm of the chair. "How does he get away with this? Why can't the CIA or someone just go in and shut him down?"

"You know yourself stealth is his middle name," Avery reminded her. "He knows how to bury his activities until the last moment. After what you did to Maes, there's no way Brian or anyone could get a person into his organization undercover. Because he's been burned, and badly, he's twice as suspicious of everyone and everything." She studied Marissa. "Those people are probably just a small piece of a larger network checking everywhere for you. Maes still has plenty of money to fund an operation like that."

"I know he'll be playing this very close to the vest, like you said." Marissa swallowed back the tendril of fear trying to curl its way through her. "He wouldn't want word to leak out until he's ready to pounce."

"Right," Avery agreed. "He wouldn't risk sending you into hiding someplace else. He didn't count on your instincts still being as good as they are."

Marissa rubbed her face. "I feel like I'm in a bad dream and can't wake up."

"Speaking of hiding," Avery continued, "that's exactly where we're going with this. We need to get you out of here until we can figure out how to neutralize him."

"Good luck with that." Marissa inhaled a deep, steadying breath, trying to think of all the loose threads here. "If I leave so suddenly, just the way I disappeared from London, won't that be sending a signal to him that it's really me? What about the gallery? Won't people think it's weird if all of a sudden, it's closed? And what if that couple comes back again just to check on me for Maes and start asking questions?"

"I'll have someone at the gallery." Avery made notes on her tablet. "If anyone asks, we'll say you were called away on an emergency. We'll cover everything here." She curved her lips in a reassuring smile. "This isn't our first rodeo, Marissa."

"I know, I know. I just feel as if the last two years have been for nothing."

"Not for nothing," Avery assured her. "You've made a life here, friends, and all those things will still be here when we shut down Maes."

"But what can I do? Where can I go?" She wanted to scream and throw things. "This just sucks."

"What *we* can do is get you out of here until this Maes situation can be handled and this whole thing comes to an end."

Marissa raked her fingers through her hair. Didn't she know that shutting down Maes was a near impossible task? "God. Am I going to be running from him for the rest of my life?"

"No. Not gonna happen." Avery took Marissa's hands. "They—we—will stop him, I promise you. But you can't hang around until that happens."

"Where will I go that he can't find me?" *God!* "Montana? It gets very cold there. Or maybe the Yukon Territory. It's even colder."

"I have an idea, but I need a few minutes to take care of the arrangements. Justin will take you to your cottage while I make some calls. Pack only personal items. Write down your clothing and shoe sizes for me, and I'll take care of the rest."

"Sizes?" Marissa frowned. "What for?"

"You've made it a habit to dress down here in Arrowhead Bay. Nothing outstanding in your clothing that would call attention to you. I want you to blend in with the crowd where you're going."

"What crowd? Where? What kind of clothes? No cold weather gear. Please?"

Avery chuckled. "No Yukon Territory, I promise. This is very private resort that's the only thing on a small Caribbean island. I know the owners and they owe me. No one will be able to track you there."

Marissa chewed her bottom lip. "I don't know. Are you sure it's the best place for me?"

"It's perfect. The people who vacation there do it because they are protected from the outside world. They get a lot of very wealthy European businessmen and their wives. Some of them come for private meetings and combine business with pleasure. No reporters. No place where they could be spied on. No commercial transportation to leave a trail. The only access is by boat or water and unexpected arrivals are not permitted. Rosewood has a trained security force to make sure that doesn't happen."

"Europeans?" Marissa froze. "Don't you think—"

"No." Avery shook her head. "I don't. It so happens last year the Morgansterns hired us to vet all their guests, including repeaters in case anything changed. But just to be sure, I'm going to run the current list through the rest of the month past Brian Gould. If it's a problem, we'll look elsewhere. Now get going. I'll take care of your clothes."

"My car," Marissa began.

"No worries. We'll bring your car here and store it in the Vigilance garage. That way people will have to guess whether you drove, or flew and left your car at the airport. Or whatever."

Marissa tried to sort everything through in her mind. I*t's a good thing*, she thought, *that the CIA had trained me in the art of disappearing at a moment's notice.*

"When you get back here I'll have all the details. And Justin will be going with you."

She looked at Justin, who just smiled as if this was an everyday occurrence in his life. But there was something else swirling in his eyes, too. Something that made her nerve endings tingle.

"With me?" Marissa's eyes widened as her body responded. Good lord. She was going into hiding with the man who starred in all her fantasies?

"Of course." Ignoring them, Avery made some notes on her tablet. "You didn't think I'd let you go off without protection, did you? Justin's one of the best I've got. Plus, you know him and will be more comfortable than with a stranger."

"But can he just take off like this? Doesn't he have assignments?"

"Yes." Avery nodded. "This one, right here. Just like any other I might send him on."

"Avery, that's really very nice of you, but I can't afford your prices. Or the cost of wherever you're sending me."

"This one is on the house, my friend. I owe Brian Gould and I like to think we've become close these past couple of years. I couldn't live with myself if I didn't do this and something happened to you that we could have prevented. Now let's get this show on the road."

As she rose from her chair, Marissa thought again about being in a secluded, exclusive resort with Justin. Alone. With the first man in years who had made her body sit up and take notice of what it was missing. Just how was she supposed to deal with these feelings that kept cropping up whenever she saw him or heard his name? Sure, they'd danced around this a little, each testing the other, but in reality, she didn't know how he felt. What if she was misreading his signals and somehow made a fool of herself?

Was she leaving one kind of danger only to walk into another?

Chapter 4

Justin waited while Marissa grabbed the personal items she'd need. She laughed at the look on his face when she took her Glock 23 from a locked case.

"I'm guessing you know how to use that thing?"

She nodded, and checked it with practiced efficiency before putting it away in her bag.

"I spent hours on the CIA gun range. And Avery's been letting me use the range at Vigilance to keep in practice." She grinned at him. "So, you don't have to worry that I'll shoot myself in the foot. Or you."

"Glad to hear it."

"Don't get jealous when you see what a crack shot I am."

"I'll try to contain myself." Then he winked, clearly trying to defuse the tension of the situation.

At Vigilance, Justin went off to gather his things, and Avery had three brand-new suitcases waiting for her.

"Resort wear for all occasions." She grinned.

"I'm not going ask how and where you got it. But, um, thanks."

"Just so you know, Rosewood limits its guests. Sixty is their capacity. Of course, they charge enough that it doesn't matter. They had a cancellation, so they were happy to have you as their guest. The accommodations are just what you need. Vigilance checked every one of their guests six ways from Sunday, including those who've been there before, and we're good to go in that department."

Justin walked into the office and set the two duffels on the floor. "So who are these people?" he prompted.

"Some of them are couples who've been cruising the Caribbean and are spending a few days there. It's a Tuesday, so the resort is only half full right now."

"Who else is on the list and due to arrive?" he asked. "And when will they be there?"

"There are about twenty couples due to arrive Thursday. Marissa, here's the list. Even though Brian and I have both been over it a dozen times, I want to make sure before we send you off that there isn't a name that jumps out at you. Someone you met during your assignment in London. Someone who could blow your cover."

Marissa studied the screen on the tablet.

"There are a few names I'm familiar with, but not in connection with Maes. I've never met any of them or come across them in Maes's accounts. And I never attended any events where they were likely to be. Besides, my appearance is different now and I'm using a different name."

"Speaking of which…" Avery looked from one to the other. "You guys will be Mr. and Mrs. Kelly. Do not address each other by first names and do not socialize with any of the guests. Walt Morganstern is keeping you out of the database. I didn't even want to use the agency name, just in case."

"Good." Marissa blew out a breath.

Avery took the tablet back. "One more thing. Stay out of the main restaurant, Sunset, just to be extra sure. There's a little casual eating bar called the Bistro, or you can take your meals in your villa. They have excellent room service and I recommend using that most of the time."

"Villa?" Marissa frowned. "Isn't that a little elaborate?"

"It's the furthest guest accommodations from the main building and is completely private. The less you mingle with guests, the better."

"And people won't think that's unusual?" Marissa asked.

Avery shook her head. "Much of the clientele there prefers isolation. No red flags here."

"We'll be fine," Justin said. "Avery, you still have that clearance set up, so we won't have any problem with firearms?"

She nodded.

Justin looked at Marissa. "You know under normal circumstances we'd have to land in Nassau, clear customs and go through a big hassle with firearms."

"I wondered about that when you didn't say anything back at my house."

"But thanks to the relationship Vigilance has with various customs services, and the favors they've done for numerous people, we can bypass all that."

"What are you bringing?" Avery asked.

"My favorites. The Heckler & Koch 45 CT, the one the SEALS adopted, plus my personal favorite, the Smith & Wesson M&P .45 cal. It's slightly lighter to carry." He looked at Avery. "Do you know Marissa's got her own firepower?"

"I do. I checked her out on our range when she first got here."

"I thought about bringing my LaRue Tactical OBR but decided it was probably overkill."

"What's an OBR?" Marissa asked.

Avery answered for him. "Optimized Battle Rifle. And yes, you aren't preparing for a massacre, just self-defense."

"Then I guess we're good to go," he told her.

Moments after that they were racing for the new Vigilance Sikorsky helicopter, already warming up in front of the hangar behind the Vigilance office. The pilot shook hands, loaded them and their luggage into the bird, and they were off.

They flew down the west coast of the Florida peninsula, over the Florida Keys, and then a scattering of small islands in the Caribbean. Marissa looked out the cabin window, trying to focus on the gorgeous scenery below them. But Justin was so close to her, reaching around her to point out things they saw, that she had trouble thinking or appreciating anything. His clean, outdoorsy scent was tantalizing her nerve endings and sending her brain into orbit. When he rested his hand on her shoulder, she was sure his fingers left scorch marks. She'd been fighting this for so long, and now, here they were, heading for a tropical paradise where they would be alone and—

Damn!

What was the matter with her, anyway? Stefan Maes, one of the most evil men in the world wanted to punish her for what he saw as betrayal. And his idea of punishment was enough to give her nightmares. She had no idea how long she'd have to stay in hiding, how long it would take for Brian Gould to neutralize the threat or even how he was going to do it. The key to her safety was keeping a low profile at this place they were going to. That needed to be her focus.

"Princessa Key is right below us, guys," the pilot announced through the headphones they wore, his words jarring Marissa out of her thoughts.

"Right there." Justin touched her elbow and pointed.

Marissa looked harder, trying to take in the details. Most of the small island was shielded from view by the thick leaves of the palm and palmetto trees and the exotic bushes that grew almost as tall as small trees themselves.

Somewhere in the center of all that was Rosewood, the ultra-exclusive resort where she and Justin would be staying until it was safe for her to come home. She supposed if it didn't happen quickly, they could create another identity for her. Lord, she had never thought of this when she'd gone willingly into the CIA.

The helicopter made a sudden slight bank to the left, and in a moment, the resort itself came into view. The main building rose two stories, with large wings extending on either side. The walls facing the sea were all windows. To the left of the central core, scattered along paths among the trees, were individual cottages available for those who wanted more privacy than the primary facility afforded.

A carpet of green lawn stretched out, sprinkled with patio tables and chairs and a large curve of white sand at the water's edge. Canoes and pedal boats filled the water, and a couple sailboats tacked into the breeze. Colorful lounges and umbrellas dotted the beach, and some of the guests stood at the edge of the water. No one seemed to be paying much attention to the chopper, though it was one of only two methods of transportation to the island, the other being the large white motor launch just past the beach.

The helo banked again and Justin nudged her arm.

"We're getting ready to land. You all set?"

She nodded and gave him a smile. "I'm used to playing a part."

The chopper hovered then lowered smoothly to the wide helipad at the rear of the resort. Marissa took in a second helicopter off to the left on the apron of a small hangar. A low metal building sat at right angles to the hangar, with two extended golf carts parked next to it. When they finally settled on the macadam, Justin pushed open the cabin door and jumped down, then reached a hand up to help her out. Behind him, next to a third golf cart, stood a man in khaki pants and a white shirt with the Rosewood logo on it.

"Mr. and Mrs. Kelly. Welcome to Princessa Key and Rosewood." He gave them a warm smile and held out his hand. "I am Albert."

The Kellys. Yes. That was them. Her name would not appear anywhere, and no one could make the connection between her and Justin except Vigilance and the Morgansterns. She allowed herself to draw a breath.

She and Justin both shook hands with him. The pilot offloaded their luggage, and Justin had a few final words with him while Albert dealt with their bags. Then they settled in the cart, and were off down a path of crushed seashells toward the main building. On both sides of the path were the trees she had seen from the helo, leaves and fronds waving gently in the soft breeze. The air was rich with the scent of bougainvillea, hibiscus, oleander, and plumbago, and the different hues of the flowers blazed in the sunlight.

When they reached the center of the complex, Albert stopped for a moment.

"Most of the amenities are there," he told them, "except for the spa, which is in a separate small structure. Our guests expect every luxury, so we make sure it is all available. You have only to make your needs known."

"I see only golf carts in the parking area," Marissa commented. "No cars or SUVs?"

Albert chuckled. "Where would they drive them, madam? The island is small and can only be accessed by air or water. We have some small trucks to haul equipment, but they are over by maintenance."

"Of course." She wanted to smack her forehead, she felt like such an idiot.

Albert accelerated again, made a right-hand turn and drove them down another path, through the towering trees, past cottages barely visible from the cart. Finally, he made one more turn and pulled up to the entrance of a villa with the sign Orchid House over the front door.

Albert hopped off the cart. "I have your keys right here. Mr. Morganstern took care of it all after speaking to your employer. As requested your names will not appear in the computer. Everything else you will need is already inside the cottage. Come."

He jogged up the two wide steps, pulled a key card from his pocket, and slid it into the reader. Then he opened the door wide. "Welcome to Orchid House."

Marissa just stood there and stared. "Wow!"

"Nothing but the best for my bride." Justin gave her a casual hug and a peck on the cheek.

"The best on the island," Albert agreed. "The Morgansterns are delighted to accommodate you. We have been instructed to respect your privacy and putting you here at the end of the conclave is one way to do it." He winked.

Marissa look at Justin, who shrugged.

"I guess we're the royal couple." She turned back to Albert. "Please tell Mr. and Mrs. Morganstern we are very grateful for their hospitality."

"You will have a chance to tell them yourself. They have invited you to have dinner with them tonight in their suite. Now. Let me get your things inside."

Albert refused Justin's help, juggling the bags with an expertise borne of long practice. Following behind him, they stepped into a wide foyer with a high, sweeping ceiling. Slate steps led down into the large living room, and beyond that a wall of glass doors opened on to the pool area.

Albert turned to the left, into the bedroom that appeared almost as big as the living room.

One bedroom.

Marissa glanced across the living room for the door to another room, but all she saw was unbroken wall. Well, wasn't that interesting? Apparently, they had a decision to make regarding the sleeping arrangements. Should she bring it up now? Wait for Justin to say something? Just announce she was taking the bed? Too bad they didn't write etiquette books for these situations.

"Jesus!" Justin breathed the word as he stood in the doorway to the only bedroom.

Marissa peeked around him to see what had caught his attention, then slipped around him into the room. Jesus, indeed! A magnificent four-poster dominated the bedroom, its wood gleaming. She ran her hands over it then stroked the finish of the huge carved dresser. The satiny finish of the wood felt warm and smooth beneath her touch.

"Rosewood," she whispered to Justin.

"Of course," he whispered back, and grinned.

The wall facing outside was again all glass sliding doors, and right now the afternoon sun cast its rays inside, bathing everything in a warm glow.

For a moment she forgot Albert was still in the villa with them, until she heard his voice in the doorway.

"There is a full kitchen off the living room," Albert told them after setting their luggage down. "Although hardly anyone ever cooks. Let me show you a couple of additional things."

They followed him into the living room where he pressed a switch next to a painting on the wall. The wall slid open to reveal a fully stocked bar.

"If you prefer something not there, you have only to press One on the house phone and tell them what you'd like. The kitchen also delivers full meals. Press Two if you would like a cart to fetch you up to the main building. The portfolio on the counter will give you any information you need about the resort itself. It also includes a map, which a lot of guests find helpful."

He closed the sliding wall. "One more thing, if you will please follow me?"

He opened the glass doors and led them through the pool area into the yard bordering it. Then he pointed to a narrow path between two very large bougainvillea.

"This will take you down to a private section of beach. You of course are free to enjoy the resort beach but many of our guests prefer privacy."

"I'll bet they do," Justin murmured. The look he slid at Marissa sent a flash of heat over her body.

"Excuse me?" Albert looked at him. "Did you need something?"

"No, we're fine. Thanks. And thank you for all your kindnesses." He reached into his pocket and slid some folded bills into Albert's hand with an almost-invisible motion.

"Thank you so much." Albert handed two key cards to Justin. "And the Morgansterns dinner invitation for this evening? Does seven thirty work for you?"

"Of course." Marissa wanted to say anything worked for them, but she was still dazzled by everything. "And please thank them for us very much."

She waited until Albert had left and the door was closed before allowing herself to give in to a tiny flush of pleasure and spin in a circle, arms wide.

"Ohmigod, Justin. Just look at this place. I mean, look at it. Is it so wrong to be excited about this when the reason we're here has nothing to do with fun and pleasure?"

Justin laughed. "You mean to tell me on your European sojourn you never saw places like this?"

"I saw opulent homes but none that I took any pleasure in. Not like this." She stood at the glass doors facing the pool. "God! If I have to hide away, can you imagine a better place?"

"No. I can't."

She sobered and turned back into the room. "For a moment—a very brief moment—I forgot about Stefan Maes and the target he has painted on my back."

"A target I'm going to keep covered up," he assured her, coming up to stand behind her. "Trust me on that."

"I have to believe he can't get to me here." She searched his face. "Right?"

"That's the plan. And by the way, no, it's not wrong to appreciate our surroundings. Better than a sand hut with no air conditioning. Besides, it's nice to see you smile."

They were standing so close together she could feel the light fan of his breath on her face. They stood that way for what seemed an endless moment, his gaze locked with hers, his eyes filled with a mixture of hunger and heat. This is it, she thought. If she hadn't misread things, he'd reach for her, testing the waters. Otherwise he'd take a step back and she'd deal with her embarrassment. When he pulled her closer, so their bodies were touching, she went willingly, holding her breath, mesmerized, waiting. He threaded his long fingers in her hair and cupped her head, holding it in place, and in the next moment his mouth descended on hers.

His lips were soft against hers, and warm, a mere touching of skin, until the tip of his tongue came out and traced the line of the seam. Fire streaked through her as if he'd put a torch to her body. Even as she gripped his upper arms to hold herself steady, the pulse between her legs throbbed with an insistent beat and moisture drenched her panties.

She opened wider to accept his tongue that swept inside and licked every inch of her mouth. Everything except the feel and touch of this man disappeared from her mind. She closed her eyes and let the sensations grab her, felt the hard wall of his chest against her breasts, and the thick ridge of his cock against her sex.

She had never responded to another man this way, had wondered often if she just chose badly or there was something wrong with her. For the past five years she hadn't had to worry about it. That part of her life had been shut down out of necessity, only now Justin had found the right switch, just as she'd known he could.

It seemed forever until they ran out of breath and he lifted his head. She stared at him through fogged vision, finally taking a deep breath. He studied her face as if trying to read her thoughts.

"Marissa." His voice was low, thrumming through her body. "Two things before this goes any further."

She held her breath, waiting for him to go on, encouraged by the fact his arms were still around her, pressing her to his body.

"I have one assignment here and that's to protect you. I promise you whatever happens between us is not going to interfere with my ability to do that. Nothing will distract me from keeping you safe." One corner of his mouth kicked up in a smile. "I'm that good."

She caught the intense look in his eyes and smiled back at him. "I believe you. I do. I feel safe with you."

And that was no lie. She knew he was one of the top agents at Vigilance.

He slid his hands up to cradle her face. "I've been trying to convince myself since the first time we met that you were off limits. Too bad neither my mind nor my body seem to be listening. Tell me you've been feeling the same pull I have all these weeks."

"Yes." She whispered the word, although she really wanted to shout it. She was scared and exhilarated at the same time.

"Things don't always happen on a convenient timeline," he told her. "I've always made it a rule to never mix business with pleasure. The problem with you, from the beginning, is it's a lot more than just pleasure. Or could be. I've never wanted to grab on to something as much as I do this thing, whatever it is, that's happening between us. Do you want this as much as I do?"

She nodded. She wanted this. Oh, yes, she absolutely did.

"Say it." His mouth hovered just over hers.

"I want this." She whispered the words. "But I have to be honest with you, before…things happen." She took a deep breath. "I mean, between us. I, um, have to let you know I've never responded well to men. Physically." She gave a tiny laugh. "And no, I don't swing the other way. I just think there's something wrong with me."

"I don't agree. Not after that kiss." He was still cradling her face. "We have an unexpected gift here, an opportunity to see where this goes and if it means something. I want to take that chance." When she didn't answer he cupped her chin. "Marissa?"

She let out a slow breath. "Yes. I want to see where this goes, too."

"Good, because this is more than casual for me." His smile reached into every one of her dark corners. "Now. I say let's get unpacked and do a little exploring. And later…" He let his voice trail off.

"Yes." She let out a slow breath and nodded her head. "Later."

"Good. Come on. I want to know about every nook and cranny of this entire place. Avery would not have sent us here if she expected trouble, but I always do, and I like being prepared." He brushed his lips against hers in a soft caress. "We need to check this place out."

"Albert said there's a map in the packet on the kitchen counter," she reminded him.

"See?" He ran the tip of one finger along her cheek before stepping away. "That's why you get the big bucks."

She snorted. "Yeah, right."

"Let's put our stuff away, and then go exploring."

They unpacked efficiently, trying not to be too obvious about ignoring the big bed that dominated the bedroom. Instead she focused on putting away the contents of the suitcases. She had no idea where Avery had gotten this wardrobe, but every piece was more gorgeous than the last, and every one in the correct size. Including some very naughty lingerie.

Had Avery been expecting this? Was she doing a little matchmaking?

"Got it." Justin walked back into the bedroom unfolding an overlarge sheet of paper. "I thought we'd take a little walking tour, so I can get the layout fixed in my mind."

Marissa looked at him and frowned. "You don't think we're in any danger here, do you? We're really off the grid and Avery wouldn't have sent us if there was the least chance—"

"I don't expect trouble, but I've learned if I don't prepare for it, it's sure to show up. In the SEALs, we learned never to take anything for

granted and always have an escape plan. Same when I joined Vigilance."
He winked. "Can't lose my precious cargo."

She sighed but then nodded. "Yes, you're right. Let me just get a couple
of things from my purse and I'm ready."

She shoved a lipstick and small comb in the pocket of her slacks, pulled
her hair into a ponytail, and she was ready. For a brief moment, she thought
about taking her gun but decided she wouldn't need it.

"All set," she told Justin. "Let's see what the rest of this place is like."

As they followed the path toward the center of the resort, Marissa caught
glimpses through the trees and thick brushes of more cottages nestled away
for privacy. Avery had explained to her that only the world's richest and
most elite came here to vacation, with others of their wealth and social
standing. Sometimes they came here for business meetings that needed
to be out of the public eye and privacy was crucial.

"I can't imagine having so much money that paying to stay at a place like
this is nothing." Marissa shook her head. "I just find it so hard to believe."

"Yeah?" Justin turned his head to look at her. "I thought you rubbed
elbows with people like that in London."

"I did," she agreed. "And that boggled my mind, too. You know, it's
funny. When I dealt with accounts it was all just so much paperwork to me.
Not real. It's the conspicuous consumption that makes me shake my head."

"Think you can handle this for a week or two?" he joked.

She laughed. "I'll force myself. And it's not that I'm complaining, but
I hope that's all it takes to find Maes."

"However long it takes, you'll be safe with me."

As if it was the most natural thing in the world, he reached for her hand
and threaded his fingers through hers as they continued their walk. A tang
of salt drifted in on the breeze from the water.

At the end of that path they realized there were four more branching
off in different directions, and directly in front of them was the massive
structure that housed most of Rosewood. Beyond the entrance she could
see a patio surrounded by iron fencing and more foliage, where the rich
and beautiful were laughing and chatting over drinks.

"Let's scope that out," Justin said. "I want to see if it's the only entrance
through the hotel. Then we'll check out the beach and the rest of the
waterfront. Let's just smile, go for a casual stroll, and see what's what."

Marissa forced herself to relax but it wasn't all that easy. She knew she
was in a protected environment, but she also knew Stefan Maes would
stop at nothing to get to her. He had people everywhere. If he had been

gathering his merry band for the last couple of years, there was no telling who was feeding him information.

"Justin."

He stopped and looked at her. "Problem?"

"What if one or more of the guests here are friends with Maes and report to him that this is where I am?"

He reached for her other hand, so he was holding both of them in his warm grasp.

"Two things. One, remember Avery said the Morgansterns have Vigilance investigate every single guest who comes here, even the ones they know personally. When reservations are made, first-time guests are also required to submit headshots to make sure someone isn't using another person's name. And when the guests check in, they are compared to those photos. They do not want people like Maes staying at Rosewood, and believe me, he would not get past their research into his identity. I can promise you that."

"And the second thing?" she asked.

"And the second thing is the first thing. There is no way Maes or his people can get on this island, not without people knowing. Unauthorized aircraft and watercraft are not permitted. And no way would people known to be friends of Maes be accepted here. So back to the research and vetting again. We're just giving ourselves that extra edge, in case."

It was the *in case* that worried her. But Justin was right. They were in an isolated situation that was nearly impossible to breach, and she had Justin as her personal secret weapon.

"Thank you."

He dropped one hand and cupped her chin, rubbing his thumb against the line of her jaw. "You are safe here, Marissa."

The touch of his hand on her skin was like an electric shock. Every nerve popped to life as if a switch had been flipped in her body. Her pulse beat with a heavy throb and she realized with astonishment that her panties were damp. She was seized with an urge to strip off her clothes and beg this man to take her, right now.

Get your act together, for the love of heaven, she told herself.

Nevertheless, she didn't pull her hand away as he tugged her toward the main entrance so they could scope out the primary building.

She had to admit the place was exquisite. The sand on the wide beach felt as soft as talcum, and the water of the Caribbean where it lapped the shore or rolled in soft waves to the long pier was a mixture of emerald green and sapphire blue. There were a few young couples at the shoreline, standing ankle deep in the water, oiled with protective sunscreen, and chatting and laughing. Older couples relaxed on the loungers, either in the sun or beneath one of the colorful umbrellas. Two waiters in black Bermuda shorts and white beach shirts moved back and forth between the beach and the patio bar, serving the guests.

The dock stretched out from the far end of the beach. Two sailboats and half a dozen small runabouts were tied up there. Marissa was sure the runabouts were used to transport people back and forth to the large white boat anchored in deeper water. Since it had the logo of Rosewood painted on the side, she assumed it ferried passengers back and forth to the mainland.

But there were four other large yachts at anchor, too.

"Belonging to guests," Justin confirmed. "According to all the info Avery gave me, they can call ahead if they have a reservation, so someone is ready to pick them up when they arrive."

"If you own a yacht that size," Marissa mused, "why would you want to leave it to stay someplace ashore?"

Justin shrugged. "Change of scenery? Meet friends? Any number of things. The people who come here have so much money they can do just about anything they want."

She had to agree. Many of Heath Financial's clients had been just like that.

They walked out onto the dock, so Justin could check the runabouts.

"They've got enough horsepower to run people back and forth," he told her after checking the motors. "And to take a little trip out of the inlet if someone is so inclined." He frowned.

"What's the matter?"

"All the boats have the keys in the ignition. I wonder why they leave them there?"

Marissa laughed. "Who is going to steal them? Not the employees. How far could they get before the owners called the Coast Guard? And certainly not the guests."

"Yeah, I guess you're right. It's just a little anomaly that makes my neck itch." He looked at the map, then up at a big tree close to the dock. "There's a camera up there. Anyway. I guess they'd know if someone was trying to make off with a boat."

"See? All is good."

"Just being the efficient bodyguard," he teased. He looked at the map again.

"What's wrong?"

"Nothing, really. They just don't seem to have many security cameras. Look." He pointed. "Besides the one here, there's one at the back of the main building, one overlooking the beach, one at the hangar, and one halfway down the path where the villas are."

Marissa looked over his shoulder. "My guess? These are just to see if any guests are in trouble and need help."

"Yeah, you're probably right. Okay, I found out what I need to know. Let's head back."

The people they passed as they walked appeared engrossed in their activities. They paid little attention to Justin and Marissa, focusing only on their own particular group.

"I'm glad they're ignoring us," she murmured as they strolled along.

"Me, too, but it doesn't matter. We won't be socializing with anyone." He squeezed her hand. "Remember, we're better off sticking close to the villa and keeping a low profile."

"I hear you." She sighed. "It's a shame to stay in a luxurious place like this and not take advantage of all the amenities, but you're right. The less visible I am, the better. Just in case the unthinkable happens."

When they'd finished their casual tour of the resort, Justin ordered drinks for them at the outdoor bar. They carried them to the end of the beach and sat down on an oversized lounger. They sat side by side, and Justin spread out the map on his lap.

"I've got a good picture of the place fixed in my mind now. Look here."

Marissa sipped her drink, pretending to give the map a casual glance, but in reality, following Justin's finger as he pointed to crucial spots.

"When we get back to Orchid House I want to go over it with you again," he told her, folding up the map. "Just want to make sure I haven't missed anything. We can do this again in a couple of days, just to refresh our minds where everything is."

Of course, Marissa knew Justin already had everything firmly marked in his brain.

"It's so strange to sit in this beautiful place," she told him, "and think about the ugliness I'm hiding from. I know we won't be doing any socializing but what if someone says hello while we're out and about? What do we tell them if they ask us about ourselves? We never did get to discuss that in detail."

"If we end up needing a story? We're a couple taking a break from life to have a few weeks to ourselves. A romantic break." He reached for her hand and squeezed it. "Think that might work for us?"

She smiled at him. "Let's just say it's not off the table."

His gaze raked over her, his eyes devouring her even as she sensed him exercising his ruthless self-control. "I'll take that. Now I think we'd better get back to our villa and get ready for dinner. I'm anxious to meet the people who created a place like this."

Chapter 5

Stefan Maes sat at his desk in the study of his eight-bedroom, multibillion-dollar house in the elite section of London known as Chelsea, staring at the screen on his tablet. This one had a triple security code on it so no one, not even Val, could access it. Next time the shit hit the fan—although if he had his say there would never be a next time—he'd be better prepared.

He thought about the years he'd fought his way up from the streets of Zagreb, killing those who got in his way, as bit by bit he built the image of an international, polished, urbane businessman. Most of the time he looked every inch the part. Despite pushing sixty now, he had a body that surpassed many others his age and younger. He was a tall man, over six feet, with broad shoulders, a square jaw, and piercing eyes a strange color of grey. His custom-tailored clothing and expensive haircut enhanced the appearance he presented to the world. Because Maes knew appearance was everything.

He kept himself in shape with a rigorous exercise schedule. Years ago, when he was just dipping his toe into dangerous waters, he'd discovered working out relieved a lot of stress and kept the mind clear. When he bought this house in Chelsea he had a gym constructed, and since then he spent the first hour of every day going through a routine. When so much of his world fell apart, he had been more than grateful for a place to work off his burning anger.

By choice he remained single. He preferred variety in his life, and marriage had never appealed to him. He would not have tolerated some woman sticking her nose in his business. As it turned out, that was a fortunate decision on his part. A woman would only have muddied up the mess he found himself in even more.

No, he preferred to focus on business and choose from a variety of females when he needed arm candy for an event or someone to satisfy his still very strong sexual urge. He never lacked for female companionship. At the moment, however, he didn't look like his usual impeccable self. His tie was off, his shirtsleeves rolled up, and sweat made his collar damp. Sweat! He never sweated. That was what he caused his enemies to do.

He'd never expected his life to shatter and go completely to hell the way it had. Everything had crashed, the fucking CIA grabbing the enormous wealth he reaped from his vast network of illegal activities, bringing them all to a crashing halt. Access to those bank accounts was locked and the assets seized, his computer records breached, and his entire network of dark operations destroyed. Even his legal business accounts and activities had come under such scrutiny that at times doing any kind of business was damn near impossible. Not that he was poor now, by any means, but the bulk of his money had come from those activities.

If not for a team of the most expensive lawyers in the world, he'd probably be rotting away right now in some godforsaken prison. It galled him that years of work to reach the position he'd attained were wasted. Gone, with the snap of a finger.

As if that had not been bad enough, when the shit hit the fan, so did his contacts. People who had been more than happy to suck his dick all of a sudden wouldn't wipe their shoes on him. He knew they were worried about guilt by association, the fuckers. They had no appreciation of the fact that their names never appeared anywhere in any of his records. He had set things up that way in the beginning to protect himself, just in case any of them went south. In the end it came back to bite him in the ass.

Then the banks in Switzerland, who took everyone as clients including the Nazis in World War II, had politely told him they'd prefer he move his business elsewhere. Notoriety affected the other clients and was bad for business. He'd wanted to reach through the phone, grab the assholes by the throat, and squeeze the life out of them.

Just like the others, they wanted no dirt from tainted money to fall on them. *Supaks!*

Assholes.

He was consumed with a desire for vengeance he could barely control, an emotion that had been his constant companion for two years now. It began with the betrayal that cost him almost everything, and continued to grow each day after that. He sometimes wondered if he was angrier at what had been taken from him or the treachery itself.

Fuck! Just damn fuck.

Every time he looked at the list of names and the headshots on the tablet, he fought to control the anger that had become his constant companion. His muscles knotted and the headache he'd been fighting pounded in his skull. These were people he once did business with. People who were thrilled to be part of his inner circle. People he'd helped achieve untold wealth. People who had formed some kind of unofficial cabal and proceeded to shut him out as if he carried the plague. And then picked over the bones of his shattered empire.

Today a new emotion was added. Anticipation. The knowledge that before this week was over, he would exact his revenge and punish those who took part in his downfall and cut him out of their lives.

Well, most of them. All but one person. Someone he would like nothing better than to torture, and then dismember. For two years he'd had people searching for Lauren Masters, the bitch who'd done it all. As soon as he got his hands on the traitor, *then* perhaps he could get on with his life.

It was all her fault. Miss Cool as Ice Masters. Miss Financial Wizard.

That little bitch.

He swiped the tablet screen until he reached the photo that had been emailed to him, and there she was. Oh, she'd changed her appearance somewhat, and she no longer looked like the financial expert she'd portrayed, but it was her. No question about it. And who was the man with her, sitting next to her at the restaurant table? No one he'd ever seen, but he had a proprietary look about him, as if he was protecting her from the world.

You can't shield her from me, jackass, he thought. He'd hunt both of them down, and then she'd be sorry for everything she did.

If he had his hands on her right now he'd—

He hauled in a deep breath to calm himself, sure he'd have a fucking heart attack if he wasn't careful. This disaster was all he'd been able to think about for two years, the way he'd been taken in by her.

It didn't ease things to know Val Desmet had also been fooled, and that was a real anomaly. A bitter taste surged into his mouth as he thought about that yet again. Desmet was his shield to the outside world, the person who vetted everything for him. The person he'd depended on. The person he'd been positive could not be conned. But Lauren Masters, the tight-assed bitch, had been damned good, fooling both of them. If not for Adrian McCormack giving him a heads up, he'd have lost everything, even his legitimate businesses. The fucking CIA would have wiped him clean.

He couldn't seem to get Lauren Masters out of his head. Of medium height, she appeared taller because of the very high heels she wore. Her auburn hair, pulled back in a ruthless twist, accented her high cheekbones and slender neck. How many times had he stifled the urge to yank the pins from her hair and run his fingers through it? To tear off those severe tailored suits she always wore and see the woman beneath all that fine material.

He'd always thought she'd be a hell of a fuck.

He would never, of course, have followed through on it. He never mixed business and pleasure, and she had done too good a job with his accounts to screw that up. Of course, now he knew what she'd really been doing. He'd made a promise to himself. If he ever got his hands on her he'd fuck her brains out before giving her a slow, painful death.

The damn CIA had done a good job of hiding her away. One minute she was here, just as he was about to get his hands on her. The next she was gone without any trace at all. He'd tapped into the few contacts he could still use, hungry enough for cash they didn't care what mess he was involved in. He gave them all her picture and told them the person who found her would be one million dollars richer.

And then, God damn it, scant hours after someone found her, she'd just disappeared again. How in the fuck had she known she'd been made? Now he had two people screaming that they wanted their money and threatening all kinds of things if they did not get paid. Too bad. They'd lost the prize. He never reacted well to pressure, especially when they'd let her slip through their fingers. Now, again, he had no idea where the fuck she was.

She had to have help, and not the fucking CIA. They couldn't have made her disappear in a matter of hours. Just his damn luck they'd relocated her to that jerkwater little town where that damned agency was based.

Vigilance!

The name was a dirty word to him. He knew of their reputation, and the jobs they'd taken that had cost several of his friends dearly.

He looked at the picture again and had to grit his teeth. They'd be sorry they tangled with him. He didn't care what their reputation was. He played dirtier than they did, and they'd find that out before long. After he took care of the immediate, pressing business.

He scrolled through the pictures again, anger surging as he studied each person. He and Val Desmet had done their painstaking research and put all this information together. Men and women he'd done business with on a legitimate basis, powerful people, who had pulled back from him because they didn't want to dirty their skirts. Information could be bought, and he'd paid dearly to learn the people he sought were vacationing *this very week* at a private resort.

First, he would destroy them. Show them no mercy Then he would hunt down Lauren Masters, or whatever the hell she was calling herself now. And he would enjoy every vicious, violent moment of her pain. No one would ever fuck with Stefan Maes again.

He pressed a button on the desk phone.

"Val. Where are you?"

The house was so damn big. Most of the eight bedrooms and five sitting rooms went unused except when he entertained or had special guests. Val lived with him, in a suite at the opposite end of the house, where he also worked when Maes didn't need him right at hand.

"In the kitchen getting coffee," came the answer. "Althea is fixing a tray for you. Would you like me to join you?"

"Yes. Right away."

He fiddled with the gold pen on his desk, flipping it back and forth over his fingers until the door to the room opened and Althea, his longtime housekeeper, walked in carrying a tray with coffee for two and a plate of pastries. He always liked to indulge himself late in the afternoon. The sugar somehow assuaged the fury eating at him with such a vicious punch these days.

Althea set the tray on the little table between two club chairs, backed out of the room, and closed the door. She had learned early on what he expected of her, and she was well paid to meet those expectations.

Desmet joined him, and they each fixed their coffee. Maes picked up a pastry, took a small bite, and savored the taste before he spoke.

"Are all the arrangements made?" he asked Desmet at last.

The man nodded. "Just as you requested."

He'd had to move quickly to take advantage of the information, but everything was now in place. The key element to his plan was gaining access to Princessa Key and Rosewood, where the traitors were on vacation. An unexpected helicopter landing there would alert everyone before he was ready for that, so he needed a logical, acceptable way in. Then, as if fate decided he needed a break, one of the group of traitors, Henri Joubert, backed out of the trip to the resort due to illness.

Truthfully, Maes didn't give a fuck if the man was on his deathbed. He just had to live long enough for them to make the trip, get them through the arrangements at the private airport, and confirm his identity over any radio communications. Joubert lived just outside of London, which made him convenient and accessible. A threat to his family would make him compliant, and Maes had put that threat into place almost at once.

"How is Joubert holding up?"

"Better than you could have hoped." Desmet's lips curved in a cruel smile. "Thoroughly acquiescent. He was stunned to see me when I showed up at his house. I was surprised he let me in so easily." He gave a dry chuckle. "Your phone call while I was there put the fear of hell into him, along with the two men you had show up before I left."

"I needed eyes on him at all times, and a threat to make sure he was, shall we say, accommodating?"

"Their daily reports say the plan is working."

"And his call to Rosewood to tell them he's coming after all?"

"No problem, especially with the threat to his family hanging over his head."

"Good, good." Maes rubbed his hands together.

"The men know they will remain with his wife and daughter until we no longer need him."

"We need to be careful with this one, Stefan," Desmet cautioned. "Joubert has more tentacles than an octopus, and his wife comes from a very well-connected family. Just stick to the plan. Afterward you'll be so insulated it won't matter who tries to come after you."

Maes glared at him. "Are you questioning my decision?"

Desmet threw up his hands. "Not at all. Just trying to be the voice of caution here."

Maes slammed his hand on the arm of the chair, then pushed to his feet and began pacing. He was losing the self-control he'd spent years learning, and it pissed him off.

"I was cautious all those years and where did it get me? Almost destroyed. Now is not the time for caution. Now is the time for action. I'm going to show those bastards they can't fuck with me. And when I've drained them dry and my network is operating again, I'm going to go after your Miss Lauren Masters and make her sorry she ever heard my name."

"Fine. Just be sure you follow the plan."

"You confirmed that they are all at the resort this weekend?"

Desmet cocked an eyebrow. "Would I be wrong about something that important?"

"Forgive me." Maes waved a hand in the air. "My only excuse is the anticipation of revenge now at hand. After all, it's quite a stroke of luck that they will all be in one place at the same time."

Desmet pulled out his phone and scrolled to Notes. "They arrive at the resort two days from now. They will stay through the weekend. There is a business meeting somewhere in there. Then Saturday night they will all be at Sunset, the restaurant, having dinner."

"I hope they enjoy their dinner," Maes ground out. "It may be the last one they ever eat. The men are all in place and ready?"

Desmet nodded. "Just waiting for your call."

"The plane? The helicopter? What about Joubert's pilot?"

Val's smile was anything but pleasant. "Taking an unexpected vacation until this is over. We have our own man in place. Everything is arranged."

"Good. Then let's get moving."

* * * *

Justin opened the door of Orchid House and waited for Marissa to precede him inside.

"Dinner was very nice." She smiled at him. "For a little while I could almost forget why we were here."

"A little relaxation was nice, but—"

"I know, I know." She held up a hand. "Never forget even for a minute and all that."

He reached for her hand and tugged her around, so she faced him. "Your safety is my number one priority. And I take that very seriously."

"I know. I don't mean to be flippant." She looked up at him. "And I'm very grateful you're on top of things."

He stroked two fingers gently down her cheek. "Situations like this can throw a person off balance." He blew out a breath. "It's been a long day and we don't know what tomorrow will bring. You should get some rest."

"I guess." She stood there, again nibbling on that lip.

Just watching her made him hard as a rock.

Down, boy.

He wanted to run his tongue over the surface of that lip, soothe the tiny teeth marks. Jesus! He hadn't felt this way about a woman in, well, maybe forever. When he was with the SEALs, he hadn't wanted a relationship that would distract him from his commitment to his team and their missions. When he joined Vigilance, his complete focus was on his assignments. And truth to tell, he hadn't met a woman in all that time with whom he wanted anything more than casual sex.

But Marissa was different from the moment Avery introduced them. The kickboxing lessons were a special kind of torture for him, watching that toned body with the curved hips and nicely rounded breasts execute maneuvers without grabbing her and hauling her in for a kiss.

Shit! Avery would castrate him if he let his dick screw this up. Although two of her agents had recently married their charges. Avery had begun joking people would think Vigilance was a dating agency instead of a security agency.

Meanwhile, Marissa was still standing in the foyer with him, looking around for—what?

"Justin, there's only one bedroom in this place and it does not have two beds in it. How do we handle this?"

He allowed himself a tiny grin. "There are a lot of ways to answer that question but…how about you take the bed and I'll sack out on the couch? It's huge and looks comfortable enough."

She frowned, a tiny vertical line creasing her forehead as she drew her brows together. "I hate to make you do that."

He shrugged. "I've slept in a lot worse places."

Indecision swept across her face. "I'm sure. But I'll feel guilty about it."

He shrugged. "Do you have a better suggestion?"

He waited, holding his breath. It had to come from her. He'd opened the door earlier. Now it was up to her. If nothing happened, he could rein in his libido and still do his job better than a hundred other men. But shit, he'd wanted her from the first moment he saw her.

He had a job to do. Could he protect her if they got involved?

His answer was yes. Maybe even more so. There was something so different about his feelings toward her than what he'd ever felt for another woman. They'd smacked him like a blow to his body the first time he met her. And they had only grown stronger with each meeting. Her safety was his first priority, now. If they allowed this *thing* between them to grow, to be tested, he knew he'd have an even stronger motive to protect her. For the first time he could apply all his years of training to a person who was more to him than just an assignment.

He watched as a hundred emotions played out across her face, hardly daring to breathe. *Please say yes*, he thought. Then, at last, she nodded.

"Did you mean what you said earlier? About seeing where this could go?"

"I never say anything I don't mean."

"Neither do I."

He reached out and pulled her into his arms, felt the press of her breasts against his chest, and the round softness of her belly where his aching cock pressed into it. The heat of her body against his. Thrusting his fingers into her hair, he held her head firm in his grip while he licked her full lips then teased the seam of her mouth until she opened for him. She was hot and liquid, the inside soft as he swept his tongue over every inch of it.

When she reached her arms up and wrapped them around him, pulling him even closer, he sent up a silent prayer of thanks before deepening the kiss even more. When he finally lifted his head, they were both breathing hard. From somewhere he dredged up the remnants of his sanity.

"Will I sound idiotic if I say I don't make a habit of this?"

He touched a fingertip to her chin and tilted her head up, so he could look into her eyes. "I want you to be absolutely sure of this, Marissa."

Her lips curved in a tremulous smile. "As sure as I can be. And sure that if we don't do this I might regret it for the rest of my natural life. But…"

"But?" he urged when she stopped.

"You may be disappointed in me. This hasn't been in my life since the CIA recruited me."

He shook his head. "Never. Not even a chance of that."

"Are you sure? You can still change your mind."

"Hell to the no. Just wait right here. Don't move. Do. Not. Move."

He made sure the deadbolt and chain were in place on the front door before he lifted her and carried her into the bedroom. He stood her on her feet beside the bed and touched his mouth to hers for a brief moment.

"I'll be right back."

Although he rushed through his routine he was thorough. Double check the front door. Make sure the lock on the back gate was in place. Lock the sliding doors. And finally set the alarm. The code had been included in the packet of information. He didn't want to think about the kind of people who came here for vacations or meetings who needed security alarms in their individual villas in addition to what the resort provided.

Then he was back, standing in front of her, drinking in the sight of her. She was like a feast just waiting for him, and he didn't know quite where to begin. Her hair was loose around her shoulders, framing a face that needed little makeup. The dress she wore flowed around her body to her ankles, leaving her neck and shoulders bare and gently outlining her breasts. His palms itched to cover those tempting breasts, squeeze them gently, and slide his tongue across the nipples.

He'd had many women during the past several years, but they were little more than encounters where the only thing each of them looked for was gratification and some fun. From the moment he laid eyes on Marissa Hayes he knew she was going to be someone special in his life.

But he also knew his track record didn't make him a good candidate for a relationship. He'd never dared hope they would connect on this level or have the opportunity to see if it worked. Now his palms were sweating and his nerves jumping because he didn't want to make a mistake.

Marissa looked at him with a mixture of heat and expectancy in her eyes, and that was all it took. He reached out a hand, tugged her closer, and slid his other hand around her neck and into the silk of her hair. Her lips when he touched them had the same satiny feel he remembered from before. He couldn't resist running his tongue over the surface, then edging just the tip into the seam.

Without hesitation she opened for him, and he slipped his tongue inside. The heat of her mouth surged through him, her delicate tongue dancing with his. Every nerve in his body danced with anticipation and his cock was so hard he worried it would break through his fly. He pulled her tighter to his body, and she responded by putting her arms around him and pressing herself against him from shoulders to feet. He could feel those wonderful breasts against the wall of his chest and the heat of her body through the layers of their clothing.

With an effort, he dragged his mouth from hers and trailed his lips along the line of her jaw. She tilted her head back, giving him access to the slender column of her neck, which he peppered with small kisses before sucking on the hollow of her throat where her pulse beat a frantic tattoo.

"We have too many clothes on," he murmured.

He slid his hands down to her hips, bunched the fabric of her dress, and dragged the garment up and over her head. His own pulse accelerated at the sight of her silk and lace bra and the tiny scrap of bikini panties that barely covered her sex. The skin on either side of the tiny triangle looked smooth as glass, tempting him. He watched her face as he ran his thumbs along the edges just to be sure, sucking in his breath at the possibility of a Brazilian wax job.

Jesus Christ!

He wasn't in favor of barbering a woman's mound so severely that every bit of skin was exposed. But Brazilian wax jobs that left a tiny strip of curls on either side of a wet slit, the outlined swollen lips? Shit! He could come in his pants just thinking about it, and he was a man who prided himself on his self-control.

"Damn." He'd better go slow or the party would be over before it started.

Marissa drew in a deep breath, resting her hands on his shoulders to hold herself steady. When he dipped his head to capture one taut nipple in his mouth, bra and all, she pressed her fingers into his shoulders and her breathing hitched.

He took his time, not wanting to hurry tonight even a little. From the moment he met her he'd known sex with her would be cataclysmic, and he wanted to take his time and savor every minute. He paid equal attention to the other nipple, all the while stroking his thumbs along the crease where hip and thigh were joined.

"Exquisite," he murmured, sliding his hands back up and around to unclasp her bra.

He stared with hunger at her exposed breasts and the dark rosy nipples, flicking his tongue over each one in turn. They were hard now, and he couldn't resist closing his teeth just for a moment over each one. When he did, a soft moan drifted from her mouth.

Hungry for the sight of her bare sex, he hooked his thumbs in the tiny lace bands at her hips and dragged the fabric down to her ankles. In seconds, he had her seated on the bed, the bikini panties tossed to the side. Placing his palms on her inner thighs, he pressed her legs apart and drank in the sight of her gorgeous sex. Sure enough, two narrow strips of hair the same warm brown as the hair on her head framed her very tempting slit.

Overcome with lust, Justin knelt between her legs, lowered his head, and took a long lick of her pink flesh. Her sexy little moan speared through him and made his cock jump against the restraint of his clothing. Pressing his face to her body, he inhaled her scent before treating himself to another swipe of his tongue.

Jesus, she was wet. Deliciously so.

He glanced up at her and saw she was leaning back, bracing herself on her hands, her eyes half-closed, a rosy flush suffusing her face.

"More," she whispered.

He bent to his task again, licking the glistening pink flesh with long slow lashes of his tongue, getting drunk on the taste of her. Her sexy little cry when he closed his teeth over her clit made him bite down harder. He held her open with his thumbs while he lapped and sucked and nibbled and ate at her like a starving man.

When he thrust his tongue deep inside her she hitched her hips toward him. Oh, yeah. He set up a rhythm. Thrusting his tongue in and out while with thumb and forefinger he tormented her now very swollen clit, pinching and tugging. The more he worked her, the more she thrust at him.

Finally, he lifted her legs and draped them over his shoulders, tipping her back on the bed and giving him greater access to her body. And then he began in earnest, fucking her with his tongue while his fingers played with her swollen flesh. Her cries were one steady stream of sound now, as arousing to him as touching any part of her body.

He knew she was getting close, so he stepped up his rhythm even more, his tongue moving harder and faster.

And then she exploded, tightening her legs around his neck and pressing his face to her body. Her liquid poured into his mouth, the sweetest nectar he'd ever tasted, and he swallowed every bit of it while spasms shook her body.

At last the shudders slowed, and then subsided. Justin gave one last lick to every bit of her sex before easing her legs from his shoulders. He rose from his knees and bent over her, resting on his forearms. Heat still blazed in her eyes, but satisfaction showed on her face. And something else. Surprise? Had she not expected it would be good? Shit, he'd known from the moment he first set eyes on her they'd set the sheets on fire if he ever had the chance.

What he hadn't expected was the sudden pinch of emotion that resonated through him. Oh, yeah, he'd known it would be different with her. For the first time, more than his dick was involved. That meant it was doubly important for him to keep her safe, so they could see where this thing could go.

He pressed his mouth to hers, sharing her taste with her, sliding his tongue inside and licking everywhere. When he drew back her lips curved in a slow smile.

"That was..." She blinked. "I don't think I can find the right words."

He sprinkled kisses across her cheek, and then along her jawline. "And we're just getting started."

She brushed her fingertips through his hair. "If that's so, you'll just have to take off your clothes. Why are you still dressed, anyway?"

He pressed a kiss to the hollow of her throat again. "Because if I had gotten naked already I would have embarrassed myself like a sixteen-year-old boy."

Marissa slid her hands beneath his shirt, running her palms up and down his back. Just her touch against his skin was enough to make his balls ache. He pushed himself off the bed and stripped off his clothes with a long-ingrained efficiency. He watched her eyes widen as his thick, swollen cock popped free. When she ran the tip of her tongue over her lips he felt as if someone had thrust a hot poker through his body.

Pausing only long enough to grab a string of three condoms from his shaving kit, he stretched out on the bed with her, shifting her so they were touching everywhere. He stroked her shoulders and her arms, the curve of her hip, and her very fine ass. When he let his fingers trail in that hot, dark crevice she sucked in a breath and pressed harder against him.

Jesus!

He closed his eyes for a moment, imagining the feel of his cock sliding between those two firm cheeks, into that cleft and pressing against the dark opening, and it was all he could do not to come right then and there.

Burying his face in her neck, he inhaled a deep breath, drunk on her scent, a mixture of wildflowers and woman. With her head cradled in his palms, he treated himself to another deep, drugging kiss. Her juices still thick on his tongue, he was overcome with a desire and a need to taste her everywhere at once. Moving slowly so he did not miss a spot, he proceeded to do just that.

She moved beneath him as his mouth found that hollow of her throat again, her breasts, her tempting nipples, her tummy, her hips, and her thighs. She not only smelled incredible, her skin was like fine satin, smooth and soft. Like an animal in heat, he wanted to rub himself all over her. He was like a starving man at a banquet, not knowing which delicacy to enjoy first. He wanted to taste every single inch of her.

But his cock was sending him an urgent message that he could no longer ignore. He sheathed himself with one of the condoms and positioned himself between her legs. She bent her knees, widening to open herself to him, and planted her feet on either side of him. He nudged her opening with the head of his shaft then pushed slowly into her hot, wet sheath.

Jesus!

He sucked in a breath, and willed himself to maintain control enough to get them both to the finish line. It was going to be damned hard, though. She felt so good, her inner walls gripping him like a heated vise. He clenched his jaw and began to move, slow, dragging strokes in and out, making sure to hit her sweet spot each time. He never took his eyes from hers, watching the hunger in them, seeing them flare with each thrust forward.

God! It was like going to heaven and being immersed in every sensual pleasure he could imagine. In, out, back, forth. His cock throbbed with need, and every muscle in his body strained as he fought to maintain control. At the moment he felt the muscles of his back tighten. He could not remember sex ever being this intense, this all-consuming. His mind was engaged as much as his body. Nothing existed outside, this room, this bed, except the two of them.

Marissa wrapped her legs around him to pull him tighter into her body. Wrapped together, her heels digging into the base of his spine, he rode her to completion. His shaft pulsed as he emptied himself inside the thin latex, her very tight sex milking him and squeezing him.

At last he collapsed forward, his body pressed to hers, his weight carried by his forearms. If sex could be a religious experience, he had just had one. His heart beat so hard it echoed in his ears, and he struggled to draw in a full breath. He looked down at Marissa's face and saw the same things mirrored there. And something else. Uncertainty? From a woman who really had her shit together?

Had she thought...

"Marissa." He managed to speak despite his choppy breathing.

"Mmmm?" She looked at him with that question still in her eyes.

"I—"

She touched the tips of her fingers to his lips. "Ssh. You don't have to say anything."

"But I do." He brushed a kiss over her lips. "I have rules, and I never break them. One of them is no sex with a client."

She gave a short nod and tried to hide the sudden pain that flashed in her eyes. "I know—"

"Nothing. Not at all what I'm going to say." He treated himself to another kiss. "First, although you are a client, this is much more personal than just a business arrangement. Second, I wanted this from the minute I set eyes on you. Scratch that. I wanted *you*." He shifted his weight a little. "But it was easy to see you weren't interested in or ready for anything like this. Avery never shared your story with me until today, but I've been in this business a long time. I can tell when someone is hiding out from danger."

She frowned. "Was it that obvious?"

He shook his head. "Not to most people, but then again, I'm not most people. This is a touchy situation we're in. Despite all the precautions, I've learned things can go south in a hot minute. So just keep this in mind. I want you, and not for just one roll in the hay or a short interlude. I'm never letting my guard down, but I'm not going to pass up this chance, either, to let you know how I feel and hope you feel the same way."

She waited so long to answer, studying his eyes as if trying to read inside his head, that he began to wonder if he'd even like what she said.

"I haven't had a relationship of any kind in five years," she began. "I was undercover for the CIA all that time and couldn't risk it. Same thing when I landed in Arrowhead Bay."

He was afraid she was about to tell him this could never work, his punishment for all the times he'd used that line. He searched for the right words to say to her.

"But," she went on, "I'm not stupid. There's something going on here besides sex. But...what if it just lasts while we're tucked away here in this vacation from reality?"

"Don't you want to find out? I know I do."

"I just don't want to screw it up." She closed her eyes for a moment. "Or end up putting either of us at risk because of it."

He brushed a few strands of hair back from her damp cheek. "That's not going to happen. You know why? Because we're both smart people. Let's just give this a chance, okay?"

For a long moment he was afraid she'd say no. Then she nodded. "Yes. I want to."

"Good." He let out the breath he'd been holding and eased himself from her body, being careful to hold the condom in place. "Don't move. We're just getting started here."

He couldn't believe the huge sense of relief he felt. He'd protect her with his life, and somehow, in all of this, make sure she knew they could have something real. The last thing he wanted was for her to get scared and walk away when this was all over.

He took the time to double-check the alarm system and the locks on all the doors. He wished the villa had external cameras. Tomorrow he'd figure out how to set his own booby traps. But tonight? That belonged to him and to Marissa.

And one thing he knew for sure. Their relationship had changed, and he didn't plan to let it change back.

Chapter 6

Stefan Maes hiked the sleeve of his custom tailored Brioni shirt and checked the time on his Patek Philippe Nautilus watch. The labels were important to him, emblems of his wealth and status, even if those had diminished for the moment.

"Val?" Where was that man? "Valentin?"

"I'm here." The man in question entered the study. "You need to relax, or you'll have a stroke before we even get to Rosewood."

"I have an important dinner meeting this evening, as you know. I cannot be late."

"Are you ever?" Desmet lifted an eyebrow. "The car has been ordered. You will arrive at the restaurant in plenty of time."

Tonight was a key part of his plan, as was the rest of the week. He had to appear to be conducting business as usual. But lately he'd had the feeling someone was watching him, something more than the usual eyes on him. He couldn't pinpoint anything specific. It was just an uncomfortable feeling. It had just begun this week, and he had to convince himself it had nothing to do with his quickly put together plans. How could it? No one outside his immediate circle knew about them and they all knew they were dead if they leaked anything.

Nevertheless, he wasn't taking any chances. He would not deviate from his routine one single bit. Not do anything to put anyone on alert. And Saturday he had made arrangements to camouflage everything when they went to the airport. This close to the culmination of his plan, he was not going to let anything, or anyone stop him.

"Any word from Joubert's house?" he asked.

Desmet nodded. "Everything is in place. The men will remain until you give the word."

"And Raca?"

"As I said, just waiting for your signal. He has the men and equipment all set." Dag Raca was the lead man in the group of twelve who did his dirty work and wet work for him. They had all grown up on the streets of Zagreb together, learning how effective the worst atrocities could be in protecting themselves and getting their way. They had been his support and his enforcers, the bedrock on which he'd built his empire. They had stuck with him when it all went to hell and were richly rewarded for their loyalty.

"And you cleared everything for the plane and the helicopter?"

Maes had demanded the use of Joubert's equipment., a Gulfstream 650 that could fly seven thousand miles nonstop, and a Sikorsky S-92 helicopter that had great maneuverability. In his ever-growing vanity, Joubert had painted the name of his conglomerate on the fuselage of each so there was no question about the ownership.

"Joubert made arrangements for both."

"Excellent." Maes rubbed his hands together then checked his watch again. "Drive time to the airport is roughly an hour. We should be wheels up at eight o'clock Saturday morning."

Desmet nodded. "Flight time from London to Nassau is about ten hours. Add another at the Nassau airport and the short trip to Princessa Key. Dinner begins at seven and we arrive at seven thirty."

"Perfect." Maes nodded. "Allow them time for their predinner drinks and their appetizers, time to relax and look forward to the evening."

"Stefan, you will give yourself a coronary if you don't ease up. You won't even be alive to enjoy the fruits of your labor."

"You don't worry about me," Maes snapped. "I will be plenty alive to enjoy every single moment of misery I inflict on those bastards. Every. Single. Minute."

They could have helped him when the shit hit the fan. Instead they'd turned on him, those animals. Buried their connections with the *Grupa*. Acted as if he was diseased. Rolled up their carpets and ran like scared children, afraid they would lose their own fortunes and operations as the CIA and Interpol systematically destroyed his *Grupa Industrijska—* Industrial Group.

He knew the disaster with the Swiss banks was due to pressure they applied. He'd even had to move all the accounts for his legitimate business. But now. Now! He would have his revenge and in a most spectacular way.

"Stefan?"

He looked up at the sound of Val's voice.

"Yes?"

"How about a drink to start the evening?"

"Good idea. I think that single-malt scotch you like so much. Let's drink a toast to our success."

Val filled two crystal tumblers with ice from the small refrigerator set beneath the bar against one wall. Then he selected the bottle of Dalmore and poured a precise two fingers into each glass. He handed one to Maes, then touched his glass to the other man's in a toast.

"To Saturday," he said.

"To success," Maes corrected.

As they each sipped the aged liquor, Maes hoped they would be truly celebrating come Saturday night.

* * * *

Marissa floated in the water, the warm breeze blowing bubbles in the water on her skin, the scent of hibiscus and plumeria thick in the air. They were surrounded on all sides, a strong metal fence extending out from the house and concealed by the thick shrubbery but there nevertheless. In addition, Justin had set the alarm system and double-checked the entire area around the house.

Safe.

She could relax.

And lazing in the pool was one of the best ways to do it.

For the most part, she and Justin had basically stayed within the grounds of Orchid House. Once a day they took a stroll along the main beach, but most of the time they kept to themselves. At least once a day they heard the sound of a helicopter arriving, either bringing new guests or ferrying others away. And one day they saw two of the runabouts taking people out to one of the yachts at anchor.

Still, she was glad for Justin's obsession with security.

"I know this place is secure," Justin told her over and over, "and we have no reason to believe Maes knows where you are, but let's not take unnecessary chances."

"Just keep in mind that man can find a flea at the ends of the earth. I'm not sure any place is really safe where he's concerned."

He tugged her toward him and wound his arms around her. "With me. That's the safest place for you."

"I believe you."

And she did, even if every once in a while, a shiver raced down her spine. These people did not now Maes like she did. She had a deep down feeling she'd only be safe if he was dead.

Meanwhile she was more than happy to spend the time alone with Justin. It wasn't the private island or the secluded villa. It was the man himself. If she could feel secure with anyone, it was Justin Kelly. She'd closed herself off emotionally for five years. With Maes's price still on her head, she hadn't been sure she'd ever be able to relate to a man again. Not to mention the fact that sex had been the last thing on her mind in what seemed forever.

Until Justin.

Here she was, all her senses awakened along with emotions she'd kept in mothballs. It was way more than the stupendous off-the-charts sex. It was the way they connected on every other level. In odd moments she wondered what would happen when they returned to Arrowhead Bay. If she could ever get out from under this cloud over her...

This morning they'd lingered over a very late breakfast, delivered in perfect condition by a very efficient room service waiter. Now they were in the heated pool in their very private yard, enjoying the sun and the water. She was in the shallow end, leaning against the wall of the pool, head tilted back, eyes closed.

"You look like some heavy thoughts are chasing around in your brain."

Her eyes popped open when she felt hands sliding along her arms and a very aroused male body pressing against her.

"Somebody likes being in the water," she teased. And who would have thought she'd be in a teasing, playful mood ever again?

"No kidding."

He moved his hands around to her back, nimble fingers untying her bikini top and tossing it up on the tiles. In the next second he cupped her breasts in his palms, thumbs brushing softly over her nipples. Back and forth, just the barest of touches but enough to wake up every nerve ending. At once heat streaked to her sex, a flutter set up in the muscles of her inner walls, and just that quick she wanted him.

He lowered his head, touching his mouth to hers with a light brush before tracing the outline of her lips with the tip of his tongue. His thumbs and forefingers were busy squeezing and abrading her sensitive nipples. Her entire body felt as if electricity sizzled through it. She wanted to tell him to pinch the taut buds, to scrape them with his nails, the way he'd done before, setting off a waterfall of sensations in her body. But then he gave his attention to her mouth, drugging her senses.

She clutched his arms to steady herself and opened her mouth to welcome his intrusion. He invaded her, that was the only word for it, licking every inner surface, sliding his tongue over hers, coaxing her to do the same. When he scraped the surface with his teeth she had to squeeze her thighs together to contain the intense throbbing.

"Mmmm." She hardly realized she was moaning until she heard Justin's low, rough laugh vibrating against her flesh.

"I think I created a monster here." His voice was husky with need.

In a way she had to agree with him. After that first night it seemed they couldn't get enough of each other. For Marissa it was like a feast after a long period of starvation. Only the offering was so much better than anything in her life before this.

In the days when sex had been a part of her life—and wasn't that just a long time ago—for whatever reason she had never been an adventurous lover. But with Justin, she wanted to explore everything, try everything. Feel everything. She scraped her teeth along his tongue again and sucked hard on it. He groaned and tightened his fingers around her breasts, gave them a gentle squeeze. Desire streaked through her body.

The magic of his hands and his tongue sent delicious sensations cascading through her. Eyes closed, she gave herself over to them, until it wasn't enough. She wanted to touch him, feel him, curl her fingers around the thickness of his shaft.

Wriggling her hand through the water, she reached into his bathing shorts and wrapped her fingers around his cock. It pulsed in her hand, and her inner walls clenched in an answering spasm. She squeezed her thighs together as she stroked up and down the thick shaft in her hand.

"Jesus!" Justin sucked in a hard breath, and his fingers tightened on her breasts even more.

"Should I stop?" she teased, already breathless with need.

"Fuck, no."

He moved his hands around to her back and slipped them down inside her bikini bottoms until he was gripping the cheeks of her ass. He flexed his fingers around her flesh in the same rhythm as her strokes. When his fingers eased into the tight cleft between the cheeks of her buttocks she clenched around them and increased the speed of her strokes.

"Okay, stop." Justin wrapped his fingers around her wrist to keep her hand form moving.

"Stop?" She looked at him, puzzled. "But—"

"We have to get out of the water, so we can do this properly."

He hoisted himself up on the deck, then reached down and lifted her up, too. He shucked his bathing shorts and tossed them aside, then divested her of her bikini bottoms. Kneeling in front of her, he nudged her thighs apart and spread the lips of her sex.

"Fuck, Marissa. I could feast on this all day, every day."

His words and the knowledge of what he was about to do made her legs so shaky she had to balance herself with her hands on his shoulders. He had such an educated tongue, knowing exactly where to lick and swipe, when to tease her with broad, flat strokes, and when to nibble on her clit. When to trace lines with his tongue and when to take little bites. She dug her fingers into the hard muscles of his shoulders as need rocketed through her, making her body shake. When she tried to squeeze her thighs together to contain the heavy pulse beating in her inner walls, Justin deliberately forced them apart, so he could continue to stroke her sex with his tongue and fingers.

He looked up at her, his mouth wet with her juices and blazing heat in his eyes. "You are so fucking sweet," he rasped, "I could eat you all day and all night."

Oh, God!

The moment his mouth touched her again, her orgasm hit, rocketing through her and shaking her entire body. Justin slid two, then three fingers inside her, her muscles tightening on them as she rocked back and forth, riding out the spasms. When the last tremor subsided, Justin rose to his feet and carried her to the double-wide lounger under the overhang.

"Now it's my turn," he teased.

"More than you know." Even though she was still shaking from her release, Marissa pushed him onto his back next to her, rose to her knees and took his cock in her hand. "Much more."

She had to stretch her lips to take him all in, but his taste was so intoxicating she didn't care. With her lips tight against the crown, she swirled her tongue around the velvety head, working hard to find room to allow the movement. She slipped her free hand between his hard-muscled thighs and cupped the sac that held his balls, grasping gently, and working them in concert with the rhythm of her tongue and mouth.

"Fuck!" Justin groaned and lifted his hips to her. "Take it easy. I want to be inside you when I come."

Marissa slid her mouth from his cock, gave the velvety head a gentle lap, and grinned at him. "Only if you promise to let me make you come with my mouth later on."

Was this her? She'd never been so aggressive in sex. But then, she'd never been with a man who touched her so deep inside and made her want *everything* with him.

"I'll promise you anything if you'll let me be inside you right now."

Easing her hand from between his thighs, she turned and stretched out on her back. Justin lifted a condom from the little table beside the lounger and rolled it on. She was pleased to see his hand was shaking as much as hers.

He knelt between her thighs, spreading them wide, and paused to take a long look at her.

"Keep this in mind. When we can finally get you home? This"—he pointed at her, and then himself—"is not over. Not even a little."

His words sent a tiny buzz of excitement tumbling through her. She looked hard into his eyes, and what she saw there thrilled her. Could she believe that was possible? She hadn't dared let herself believe this could go on, and she wanted to hang on to his words. To hug them close to her.

Then there was no more time for thinking. With one swift thrust he slid all the way inside her, his passage eased by the liquid from her orgasm. But he filled every inch of her, making her entire body tremble. And then he began the slow, steady in-and-out movement that set every nerve in her body on fire.

She wrapped her legs around his waist and locked her ankles at the base of his spine. His body was solid muscle everywhere, the skin smooth except for the soft hair on his chest that rubbed deliciously against her breasts. In an instant she was ready again, her body so receptive to his it almost scared her.

"Look at me." His voice had a gravelly sound. "Look at me, Marissa."

She opened her eyes to see him looking into them as if he could see clear inside to her soul. The brown of his irises was almost as dark as rich chocolate, and now she could see little golden flecks like amber.

"Don't close your eyes," he demanded.

If she'd been able to speak, she'd have told him that would be impossible. Their gazes were still locked when her orgasm exploded from deep inside her, the walls of her sex milking the thick shaft inside her. Her eruption triggered his, and in seconds he was pulsing inside her. At the height of their shared release he took her mouth in a soul-searing kiss, tongue thrust deep inside, while he held her so close to him they were almost one person.

She didn't know which heartbeat was shaking her body, his or her own, or whose breath was rasping in the air. And she didn't care. At last their breathing settled and he caught his weight on his forearms, smiling down at her as he brushed the damp hair from her face.

"Never before," he told her.

"Never before what?" She wanted him to say it.

"Never like this with anyone else."

She smiled and hugged him close. She had never, ever, felt so at one with another person. She hoped he meant what he said about a future when this was all over. But if not? She would hold every memory of this time together deep inside her heart.

Chapter 7

Anyone watching Stefan Maes's house Saturday morning would not have seen anything out of the ordinary. He and Desmet left the house early. They had a stop to make before they could even pick up Joubert. The car was waiting for him out front, as arranged.

"The men have all the usual firearms to take with them?"

"Of course." Desmet nodded. "Assault rifle, machine guns, handguns and more than sufficient ammo for all of them. His lips quirked in the trace of a grin. "A little overkill here?"

"It's not that I expect the visitors at Princessa Key to be armed to the teeth if at all, or whatever guards they have to use more than basic artillery. But it's nice to know we control the firepower." He leaned back in the seat. "And the arrangements have been made to transport them, including transferring to the helicopter at the Nassau airport?"

He knew they were but that weird feeling still prickled at the nape of his neck, so he wasn't leaving anything to chance.

"Yes, as I've assured you every day since we set this in motion, everything is set."

"And you have gone over the logistics with everyone again?"

Desmet chuckled. "So many times, they can recite it to me in their sleep."

"That's what I want. There is no room for even the tiniest error. Once the helicopter touches down we follow everything with precision. I must have success."

"And you will," the other man assured him. "Stefan, after this weekend there will be no question you are back in full force."

"As soon as the luggage is loaded we will head to Joubert's place. All is still good there?"

"Yes. His concern for his family overrides his illness and his fright."

"Excellent. We only need him to be compliant until takeoff."

Again, not taking chances that they were being watched, Stefan told the driver to take them to a building at Canary Wharf. They entered a restaurant famous for the breakfast pastries he loved, and that he was in the habit of frequenting. Thirty minutes later, disguised, they left the restaurant and got into a cab.

No one would be following the cab. They'd be watching for the limo that Maes favored, and that had dropped him off there. At last they hooked up with their driver and headed for Joubert's home.

The man was definitely nervous when they arrived. He kept looking from Maes to his wife and child standing in the foyer with him to the two "bodyguards" Maes had sent to keep the family in line.

"You will recall your men when we have arrived at Princessa Key, right?" he asked.

"Of course," Maes answered in a smooth tone of voice. "These men are only here to keep your family safe should anyone find out about this trip. Once we reach our destination no one will bother them."

He was glad the man didn't ask him what about after this weekend.

Joubert hugged his daughter and kissed her, then gave his wife a hug and kiss as if he'd never see her again, which, after all, wasn't so far from the truth. At last they were on their way to London City Airport, in the heart of the city. Joubert had called and given the proper instructions to have the plane ready.

He could not afford one slipup here. If the timing was off, if someone asked the wrong question, if… There were a million ifs. He could say he needed a little luck, but he believed you made your own luck.

In a little more than an hour they arrived at the Jet Centre at the airport, where someone waited to wave them through to the tarmac. One of the Jet Centre managers walked out to the plane to meet them. He shook hands with Joubert.

"Just wanted to wish you a pleasant flight, Monsieur Joubert," he said.

"Thank you." Joubert was sweating and looked a little shaky.

The manager frowned at him. "Are you sure you're well enough to travel?"

"Yes, yes." Joubert pasted on a smile. "Business, you know."

He stood there, looking at Maes and Desmet, obviously waiting for an introduction. Henri, however, at Maes's direction, kept his mouth shut. *Smart man*, Maes thought.

"I understand," the manager said at last. "Sorry your regular pilots got sick and you had to get substitutes."

Maes watched Henri carefully as he answered. "They must have the same thing I've been fighting. I was lucky these men were available."

The manager looked from Henri to Val to Stefan then back to Henri. Then he dipped his head in a slow nod. "Well, be sure to take care of yourself. And let us know if there is anything we can do to facilitate things for you." At the sound of car engines, he looked across the tarmac. "Well, I see the rest of your party has arrived."

Maes looked up to see two limos heading their way across the tarmac.

"Yes, yes." Joubert forced a smile. "We'll be leaving shortly."

"All right," the manager said at last. "I'll leave you all to get settled in the plane."

Joubert looked so shaky that Maes directed Val to help him up into the plane while his crew took care of business.

"He's all set," Val told him, jogging back down the stairs.

Maes greeted the men exiting the limousines, all dressed in their signature black. He knew that beneath the loose shirts they wore full body armor to protect them in a firefight.

Dag Raca, first out of the limo, approached him and shook his hand.

"We are ready, my friend."

"The weapons are packed as requested?"

"Yes. The insulation shields are in place. Once we leave Nassau, we'll be able to retrieve the guns and be ready to go as soon as we land."

"Excellent." Maes nodded. "Let's board, then. Shall we?"

The men climbed the stairway, each carrying black high-impact resin cases that were, in fact, gun cases designed to masquerade as luggage. And each had been fitted with special, illegal shields to make the contents invisible to scanners. No way were those pieces going in the plane's luggage compartment.

Maes shook hands with the co-pilot standing by the stairway.

"We'll love flying this baby," he told Maes. "Thank you."

"No thanks necessary. Just do your part."

Then he also entered the cabin, followed by Val, who carried a messenger case. Poking his head into the cockpit, Maes greeted the other pilot and thanked him for making himself and his co-pilot available.

"It's always a pleasure flying for you, Mr. Maes. We just wondered why you aren't using your own plane."

"We want to surprise some people," he explained.

The pilot shrugged. He didn't care. He had flown for Maes for more than five years and seen and done things most pilots didn't even think of. For what they were paid ,the two men put their morals and scruples in the closet.

Raca stood in the middle of the aisle, chatting with their sniper, Jablan Babic. He turned as Maes entered the cabin, and the two shook hands.

"We are ready," he confirmed. "All the weapons have been field tested and everyone has their orders."

"Excellent. And the layout of Princessa Key?"

"Everyone has memorized it."

Again, Maes nodded. He did not insult the man by asking him if he was sure. These men had been his solid team of mercenaries for fifteen years. Without them, he would never have been able to accomplish half the things he had. Now he was depending on them to help him recapture what he had lost.

Henri Joubert had been strapped into a seat halfway back in the plane. Maes stopped beside him.

"This will all be over soon," he assured the man.

"I don't know why you needed me along," Joubert said. "Surely you could get permission to land at Princessa Key without me."

"Tsk, tsk, tsk." Maes sighed. "Now, Henri, you know they would insist on speaking with you personally. I am not on their list of approved guests, so you have a very important role to play."

"And the use of my plane and my helicopter? So, you'd have aircraft with my name and logo on them?"

"Very smart of you."

"And once we land and they verify that I am with you, I am free to walk away from you? Call my wife? Whatever?"

"Of course." *Not.*

"I want you to know," Joubert told him in an unsteady voice, "that I was against what the others did. I did not want to pull away from *Grupa Industrijska*." He wet his lips. "You made a lot of money for me, Stefan. I appreciated it." He held out his hands, palms up. "But I was helpless, a lone voice in the wilderness. Many times, I've started to pick up the phone and call you. Tell you we needed to reconnect."

Liar.

"I appreciate that, Henri."

"Perhaps when we get back from this little trip, you can settle things with the others and we can pick up where we left off."

The man was so pale he looked ready to pass out.

Maes smiled. "Perhaps." He patted the man's arm. "Why don't you close your eyes and rest? I'll be back here after a while."

The fear was a living thing in the man's eyes before he closed them and leaned his head back. An expression of resignation crept over his face, as if he sensed what might be coming.

Maes walked toward the rear of the plane, where Val awaited him in the small conversation area. He settled himself in one of the plush chairs.

"It's a beautiful day," he said, and smiled. "A good day to go to a party. Don't you think?"

* * * *

The sound of an incoming text woke Avery out of a semi-sound sleep. She blinked and looked at her watch. Three a.m. What the hell? She tapped the phone.

"This is probably a stupid question, but you do have a secure video conference-call setup, right?"

Uh-oh. Something was drastically wrong. She scrubbed her face to be sure she was awake and texted back.

"Yes. Can I have my tech people contact you to set it up?"

In seconds the reply came back.

"Call this number for instructions."

"Hold on. I'll be right with you."

Jesus, Mary, and Joseph. If Brian Gould wanted a secure video connection at three in the morning, a big pile of shit was hitting the fan. She thought at once of Justin and Marissa, and a knot formed in her stomach.

Avery lived in a large suite at the back end of the Vigilance building, accessible only through her office. She pulled on a pair of sweat pants and an oversized T-shirt, stuffed her feet into scuffed flats, and unlocked the door into Vigilance proper. The offices never closed. Vigilance was a twenty-four/seven operation, with agents in place all over the world. If she shut down, people were left hanging in dangerous situations.

The building was quiet, all except for the low hum of voices coming from the big tech room near the front. She knocked twice then opened the door. All sixteen computer screens against the far wall were live, monitoring situations her agents were involved in. Only the big video conferencing screen was blank. Johnny Braswell, her nighttime tech crew chief, sat in his specially made leather chair, eyes constantly moving from one screen to another while he sipped on what had to be his tenth soft drink of the shift.

Two other people worked away, heads bent to what they were doing. Hildy Coyle was busy at the massive computer setup, running information, trolling for anything that had to do with whatever cases were in progress. And off to the side, Noel Gardner monitored the security system set up for various clients. On a corkboard facing him were numbers to call if one of those alarms went off.

Vigilance never slept. Hence the name of the agency.

"What's up?" Johnny asked, setting his drink down on his desk.

"Do you have eyes in the back of your head?" she teased.

"Nope. Just extra-good hearing. Besides, no one else would be coming in here at three in the morning. Otherwise every alarm in the place would have gone off. What can we do for you?"

She mounted the one step to the platform where he sat and held out her phone.

"Call the number on my screen. Someone's going to give you instructions to set up a secure video conference for me."

Johnny shook his head. "I don't need to call anyone. We do it all the time."

"This is different." She ground her teeth. "Just do me a favor and make the call."

He shrugged but called the number, setting things up according to instructions.

"Done," he told her in less than two minutes. He positioned her at the screen and flicked on the camera eye. "We'll be up in three, two, one."

The screen came to life, and Brian Gould's face filled it.

"We've got a big problem," he said.

"Yeah, so I gathered. What's up?"

"Since our call the other day, we've had people monitoring every move Stefan Maes has made. We tried tapping his phone calls, but all his cells are encrypted and what he discusses on landlines is pure bullcrap."

"Get to the point, Brian." Avery's nerves were doing a jitterbug on her skin. She smelled disaster as if it was right here in her office.

"Up until today it's been business as usual. Then, this morning, he went to a place in Canary Wharf where he often has breakfast. But he never came out. He just…disappeared."

Avery stared at the screen. "Disappeared?"

"When my men finally went in to check it out, they were long gone."

"Disguise, right?" She wanted to scream at the sloppiness and stupidity.

Brian nodded. "Wherever he went, he and that sidekick of his, Val Desmet, are long gone."

"And when did all this happen?" she asked.

Brian's features twisted in a grimace of distress. "Four hours ago."

"Four hours—" Avery stopped, ground her teeth, and made an effort to pull herself together. "And you're just now hearing about it?"

"They were sure they could find him. He's been very visible. They went to every one of his regular spots that he hits during the day. They even went to his house with a phony warrant. He's in the wind and so are the regular driver and Desmet." He sighed. "Avery, I don't even know what to say."

"How about you're hiring new help."

"Yeah." He scratched his head. "No kidding."

"Well fuck. Just…fuck."

Avery wanted to say things even worse than that. She wanted to rail and rage at the stupidity of the situation. She wanted to put her fist through the video screen, or take out her gun and shoot it. But she was a professional and she had to address the most important thing here.

"Is our couple compromised? Do you think he's headed to Princessa Key?"

Brian took a moment to answer while Avery tried not to fidget. But shit! If this whole thing had blown up in their faces, after trying to cover all bases, she might have to go on a rampage herself.

"Well?" she prompted.

"I'm trying to think of the best way to answer this. There is no evidence that Maes knows where Marissa disappeared to. And we left no paper trail anywhere. But with Maes, nothing is absolute. You know that. However, I can't imagine why he'd be going there."

"So, you woke me up to, what, tell me you've lost the target and you have no idea who's in danger and who isn't?"

She was as angry as she'd ever been, but she could not let it get to her. She was above all else a professional. Besides, she had to figure out what to do about Marissa and Justin.

"I woke you to give you a heads-up that Maes is in the wind and we don't know where he'll show up next. He could even be heading for Arrowhead Bay, since that was the last place Marissa was spotted. I thought you might like to know he could show up in your neighborhood. If he can't find her, he'll start tearing up the countryside, go after anyone he thinks might give him information. That's how he operates."

"Fine. If he shows up here, we'll be ready for him. And I'm going to warn Justin and Marissa. I might even pull them out of there."

"And go where? If we don't know where Maes is headed, is anyplace safe?"

Avery wanted to put her fist through the screen, but she didn't have the luxury of anger.

"You're right. But I will put them on alert.

"Good. It's always better to be prepared." He heaved a sigh. "I don't know where to begin apologizing, Avery. My people dropped the ball on this and I can tell you, they won't be happy with what comes next. But that's another game."

"So, we just wait to see where he shows up?" God. She wanted to shoot those people herself. They were supposed to be professionals.

"No way. I have my own handpicked people casting a net for them. And I will make sure every piece of information, good and bad, gets forwarded to you."

"Okay." She shook her head. "I'll get my own people ready."

"I'm damn sorry, Avery. You know this isn't the way I operate."

"Yeah. Later."

She signaled Johnny to cut the connection.

"What next, boss?" He wasn't one to mince words.

"Wake up Mike Perez and tell him we need available firepower just in case." She slapped her hand against her forehead. "And this would have to happen during Fourth of July week when this place is loaded with every kind of stranger. Today is Saturday, so there probably isn't two square inches of free space anywhere. What better way to slip into town?"

Johnny scrolled down on the screen that listed their agents and where each one was at any given moment.

"We've got ten bodies not currently assigned. I'll send the list to Mike and tell him you said to get his ass out of bed and put them on standby."

Avery snorted a laugh. "I'm sure he'll love that. Hildy?"

The girl looked up from her keyboards. "Yes, boss?"

"Get me every single thing you can on Stefan Maes, his associates, even his maid. Go back two years and find out who his associates were when the CIA and Interpol took him down, and where they are now."

"On it, boss."

"And all of you? I want updates the minute you get even the tiniest piece of information."

In her office, she turned on the desk lamp and brewed herself coffee in her single-serving coffeemaker. The moment it was ready, she carried the mug to her desk and treated herself to a swallow of the rich, hot brew. Then she sat at her desk, woke up her tablet, and turned on her computer.

She hated to wake Justin and Marissa at this ungodly hour, especially when there was no clear indication Maes was headed their way. But better safe than sorry, she told herself, as she punched Justin's number into a burner phone.

As she waited for him to answer she wondered if things could possibly be any more fucked-up.

Chapter 8

Maes had made sure Joubert ordered the pantry on the plane fully stocked for the long, transatlantic flight, although he deliberately had not brought a steward on this trip. His regular man was doing another errand for him, and he was unwilling to add one more strange face to the mix. Instead, one of Raca's men served coffee and pastries to them once they were airborne, and would handle lunch.

Maes took his and moved to the seat beside Joubert. The other man was pale, and his hand shook as he lifted the coffee mug to his lips.

"You know, Henri," he said in a mild voice, "none of this would be necessary if you fucking bastards hadn't all turned your backs on me."

Joubert wrapped his thin fingers around his mug. "We had no choice, Stefan. The authorities were all over everything. We would have been left with nothing if they knew of the connection."

"So instead," Maes went on, still in that deceptively mild voice, "it is I who lost it all. Even the Swiss banks kicked me out because of the pressure brought to bear."

"We had no choice," the other man mumbled, and took another sip of his coffee.

"Well, no matter now." Maes tamped down his anger. "This will all be over soon. I want to thank you for your cooperation."

"I'm only doing this because of my family, you bastard," Joubert snapped. "I have no idea what you're planning to do at Rosewood, but it is my fervent prayer someone will put a bullet in you."

"I wouldn't say that," Maes said. "Remember, someone has to give the orders to the men, um, staying with your wife and child."

Joubert's face paled. "You'd better not hurt a hair on their heads," he said. He might have been more effective if his voice hadn't trembled.

Maes just smiled. Not saying a word.

"I want to speak to my wife."

Maes saw the fear in the man's eyes but also determination. He could accommodate this. As long as Joubert thought his family was safe, he'd do whatever they wanted.

"We can do that." He pulled his phone from his pocket and dialed Joubert's house. When one of the men he had stationed there answered, he said, "Put the wife on."

Joubert's hand was shaking when he took the phone. "Nathalie? Sweetheart? Are you and the little one okay? Is everything good?" He listened for a moment. "I am going to do exactly what they want. No worries. And then they will let you go." He paused. "*Je t'aime.*"

Maes grabbed the phone back and disconnected the call. "Satisfied?" he asked the man.

"As much as I can be."

"Just do your part and all will be well."

The men had unpacked their weapons and were checking them. "You aren't going to kill all those people, are you?" Henri took out a handkerchief and mopped his face."

"Now, Henri," Maes soothed, "this is just a little extra insurance to convince people we mean business. Just close your eyes and rest until we land. Your part is over for the moment, and you played it well."

Retreating to his seat in the back, Maes set the alarm on his watch.

"Keep checking on Joubert," he told Val. "I don't want him to stroke out before we're finished with him. We need him to be alert and give nothing away until we're finally on the helicopter and he has radioed to Rosewood."

"No problem."

Val had opened his laptop and would be checking activity in Maes's businesses and emailing to people where necessary. Raca would have the men checking and rechecking their weapons once more before packing them again in the rigid cases.

Maes leaned his head back and closed his eyes. Now he could take the time to rest during the long flight ahead of them.

* * * *

After three tours as a SEAL and a career with Vigilance, Justin had perfected the art of waking instantly. The moment the phone in his nightstand pinged, his eyes opened, and his years of training had him instantly alert.

He looked at the screen. Avery.

This couldn't be good.

"What's up? You wouldn't call at this hour just to see how we are."

"Just listen to me," Avery told him. "Don't say anything until I give you the whole picture."

"Understood."

He listened while Avery relayed all the data she'd received from Brian Gould.

"Is there any indication Maes knows where she is?"

"No," Avery told him. "but keep your sat phone with you at all times, and report in regularly."

"You think we should get ready for an invasion? Really? Should I have brought my LaRue anyway?"

"No." She sighed. "I just want you guys safe."

"Also at the top of our list," he assured her.

"I explained the situation to Walt. And don't worry," she said before Justin could object. "I can share information with him. Walt's almost more closemouthed than I am. But he does deserve to know why she's there just in case the unexpected happens."

"Understood and agreed."

"I have Hildy digging for anything that would give us even the slightest hint where Maes is heading, and why," she told him. "Ginger will take over when she gets here after eight. That's it for the moment. I just wish I didn't have the feeling we're missing something here. Brief Marissa without scaring the pants off her, and check in regularly."

"Ten four."

He disconnected the call and placed the phone back on the nightstand, right next to the Smith & Wesson he was never without. Even in the most intimate situations, it was always within immediate reach.

"That has to be the most cryptic phone conversation I have ever eavesdropped on," Marissa said. "And believe me, I've listened in on plenty. So, let's have it. Has Maes been spotted?"

Justin leaned back against the pillows and drew Marissa's body against his, keeping his arm around her. He took her right hand in his and played with her fingers as he tried to figure out how to phrase what he'd learned without scaring the shit out of her.

"Justin?" She looked up at him. "I appreciate that you want to choose your words carefully, but I am not a hothouse flower. I know you were a big bad SEAL and want to take care of me, but keep this in mind. I spent three years running a dangerous op for the CIA. Whatever it is, I can take it. Just spit it out."

"Okay, then. Here it is. Stefan Maes has up and disappeared."

"What?" She pushed herself to sit up straight. "He's disappeared? Are you kidding me?"

"I wish. Brian Gould just called Avery. Since the chatter popped up and you spotted that couple and their friends, he's had people keeping an eye on Maes. Apparently not very well."

He repeated everything Avery had told him.

"But that's—that's—unbelievable." She shook her head. "What kind of people did he have on the lookout?"

"Not his usual, it seems."

She frowned. "Do they think he'll come here? We covered our tracks very well. There's no way he can track us to Princessa Key. I mean, I am so far off the grid here I practically don't exist."

"Agreed. But since our motto is never to leave anything to chance, she wanted us to have a heads-up."

She started to get up, but Justin pulled her back. "Where are you going?" he asked.

"We need to make sure our guns are loaded and ready."

He pulled her back against his body and wrapped his arms around her.

"They've been loaded and ready since we got here, honey. I don't think we'll need them, but if we do, we're ready. Now." He turned her to face him. "Since we're wide awake and sunrise is a long time away, whatever shall we do with our time?"

She laughed, that warm throaty laugh that made his cock stand up and sent heat surging through his body. No other woman had ever affected him this way. There was something very special about her that woke up emotions he had deliberately locked away. Despite the fact that two Vigilance agents had recently married, he'd never felt a relationship was good for someone in this business. Then Marissa moved to Arrowhead Bay and the first time he saw her he thought, *Run as fast as you can. She can mess up your life.*

But it seemed impossible for him to do that. When she signed up for the kickboxing lessons with him, he'd thought to refuse her. Then he was glad he didn't. He'd had plans to take it slow. Very slow. And maybe that's the way it would have gone except for Stefan Maes and the price on her head.

But now here they were, thrust into this situation, sharing a villa—sharing a bedroom!—and with every passing hour she became more important to him. They hadn't really discussed what would happen when this thing with Maes was resolved, but he wanted to figure out how to keep her in his life. He hoped she wanted the same thing.

Later they'd talk, he reminded himself. *After.*

He tugged her sleep shirt over her head and eased her down to her back. Her skin was warm from sleep, and smelled of the scented cream she liked to use on it. Flowers of some kind. He wished he could identify them. Whatever it was, it made him want her more than ever.

He lowered his head and took her mouth in a kiss, at first gentle, but more intense by the moment as hunger grabbed him. He thrust his tongue inside, tasting the liquid silk while he coasted a hand slowly down her body. When he brushed his fingers over a breast he discovered the nipple already taut and beaded, and laughed, a low sound.

"Aren't you the woman who told me she had a hard time responding to men?"

She pressed a soft kiss to his neck. "Apparently you've put that worry to bed."

He trailed tiny kisses along her jaw and down the column of her neck, pressing his tongue into the hollow of her throat to feel the heavy beating of her pulse.

"Mmmm." She hummed in satisfaction. "Despite the phone call, what a great way to wake up."

After a while, they fell back asleep, awaking to the bright sunshine of a classic tropical day. As he'd been doing every day since they arrived, Justin ordered breakfast from room service then did his usual tour to make sure the house was secure. But this morning he added something to his routine. He lifted his Smith & Wesson M&P .45 from the nightstand, checked the load, and tucked it against the small of his back. The slightly larger Heckler & Koch he brought out to the patio, leaving it on the table where they'd eat breakfast.

Marissa cocked an eyebrow when she spotted it. "You think we'll be attacked by the pool?"

He smoothed his hands along the soft skin of her upper arms. "I don't think we'll be attacked anywhere, but I'd rather have them and not need them than the other way around."

"Okay. I should probably keep mine with me, too. Right?"

He nodded. "Not a bad idea." Then he grinned. "In case we have to defend ourselves against tropical bugs."

She laughed, which was what he'd been hoping for, but then she went to get her Baby Glock and put it on the table next to his H&K.

"We'd better not let the room service waiter see it," she reminded him, "or he'll think we're planning to attack the place."

"You never know what things he's seen here." But he took one of the towels and placed it over the guns. Then he pulled on a T-shirt that effectively disguised the S&W.

They were lingering over coffee when the doorbell sounded. Justin checked the video screen on the security monitor, thankful their hosts installed such high-tech protection for their guests.

"It's Walt Morganstern," he told Marissa.

"Sorry to bother you." Morganstern followed Justin out to the patio. "I just wanted to touch base."

"Thanks. And no bother. As I said the other night, we're very grateful to you for the hospitality."

"Morning, Walt." Marissa smiled at him. "Sit down and have a cup of coffee."

Justin looked around to see where she'd hidden their armory and spotted a pile of towels on the foot of a lounger. *Smart girl*, he thought. He was pretty sure Walt would understand the necessity of them. But he also didn't want the man to think they were getting ready for the next world war.

"I'll sit, but I think I've had my limit of coffee for the morning. I just wanted to make sure Avery had reached you."

Justin nodded. "But we both agreed that it's highly unlikely Stefan Maes will show up here. Among other things, there is no way he could know Marissa is here."

Morganstern nodded. "I agree. Although I'm sure we'd all breathe easier if we knew where he'd disappeared to."

"No doubt."

"I'm sure he's been working very hard plotting revenge against the people he believes set out to destroy him. We knew from the beginning he wasn't in this alone, but the one thing I could never find, no matter how deep I looked, were the names of who else was involved in his criminal activities."

"Maybe there was no one," Justin suggested. "I'd guess Maes likes to be the kingpin and not share the glory."

Marissa shook her head. "There were too many indicators otherwise, but I'll give the bastard this. He was a master at hiding the identities of others. And he can't have been too happy at being hung out to dry by them. I know the CIA watched carefully to see who picked up his activities and funneled money back to him." She shook her head. "Nada."

"Well, whoever they are, I hope they're heavily armed and well fortified. Anyway, I wanted you to know I did alert my security guards to let me know if anything unusual happened." He rose from his chair. "I know you're keeping a low profile here, but you might think about having dinner at the Sunset tonight. We've got a five-star chef whose menu is out of this world." He grinned. "Of course, so is his salary."

Justin looked at Marissa, who shook her head. "Thanks for asking, but we'll pass."

"Yeah, I figured, but I thought I'd ask anyway. If you don't want to chance the crowd at Sunset, we keep the Bistro open until eight. Just in case you want a change."

"We'll think about it. Thanks."

"At least you won't be bothered much today with the sound of helicopters flying in and out."

"How so?"

"No one is leaving until tomorrow and we only have one arrival. Henri Joubert wasn't well enough to arrive with his friends, but he's coming in at dinner time tonight."

"Yeah?" A nasty little tingle was working its way up Justin's spine. "He a regular?"

Morganstern nodded. "Sort of. Last year he came with the other people in that group that arrived Wednesday. He heads an electronics empire in Europe and is one of the nicest people you ever want to meet."

"It's nice that he could join his friends," Marissa commented.

"I thought so." He chuckled. "Actually, his delay was your good fortune. He was booked into Orchid House, so I didn't have to evict anyone to accommodate you two."

"So where is he staying now?" she asked.

"I put them up in the large suite we keep on hold in the main building. Well, let us know if you need anything. We're delighted to be able to do this for Avery. Without her our family would have been destroyed."

He shook hands with both Justin and Marissa, and Justin walked him to the door, locking up after him.

"Would you like to try what Walt suggested?" he asked Marissa. "The Bistro, I mean? He said it's quiet and we could eat out in the covered porch in case we got an itch to leave in a hurry."

Marissa frowned. "You think we'd have to? Leave in a hurry, I mean?"

"No. But I always like to keep my options open."

"Well, maybe. We can think about it." She smiled at him. God, her smile just did it for him. "We don't have to get dressed up for it. In fact, we don't even have to go inside the main building to get to it. There's an entrance from the outside."

Justin nodded. "One of the reason I suggested it. We can eat on the porch and not be bothered by anyone. Meanwhile I'm calling Avery to make sure she has the late arrival on her radar and the agency has him vetted."

"Good." Marissa nodded. "I'll feel better, too. Trusting my instincts kept me alive until they could smuggle me out of London."

"Well, I could be seeing gremlins where there aren't any. But the coincidence of a late arrival on the same day Maes disappears makes my nerves jangle." He sat down at the table and pulled her into his lap then hit the speed dial on his cell.

Avery answered at once.

"Problem? There's no update on Maes, if that's why you're calling."

"No, I figured you'd let us know if there was. I just have something I need you to check out."

He told her about Henri Joubert and what Walt Morganstern had said.

"I'm sure it's nothing," he added. "I'd just feel a lot better if Vigilance pulled up his file and made sure there are no changes."

"Can do. I'll get on it right away and I'll email a copy to you."

"He's due here around seven or so."

"On it."

He disconnected the call and looked at Marissa. "You heard what I told Avery, right?"

She nodded. "Walt didn't seem to be bothered about it. But like we both said, anything that's the least bit hinky makes my nerves do a jive dance."

He leaned back and pulled her body up against his, wrapping his arm around her shoulders. "Let's see what Avery has to say before we panic too much about it. But we need to be sure all our weapons are loaded and with us every minute, just in case. Even at the beach."

"You're right. Damn." She rubbed her forehead. "Sometimes I wish I'd never heard of the CIA."

"You did a damn good job for them, Marissa. I'm proud of the work you did."

"Thanks." She frowned. "Too bad it has to blow up in my face."

"For the moment, I prescribe a little more sleep followed by some sunshine and maybe a relaxing swim?"

But even as he said the words, he didn't think either of them would do much relaxing today. Even if Joubert turned out to be a false alarm, he'd be extra alert until someone discovered where Maes was hiding. Nothing was going to happen to Marissa. He'd make damn sure of it. "Can we take a walk on the beach later?" she asked. "Just a little change of scenery?"

"Sure, as long as we stick to our private section."

Justin handed the H&K to her. "Put this in your little beach tote along with your Glock, and some extra ammo."

She lifted her eyebrows. "You think we'll be attacked on the beach?"

"I think the possibility exists that if Maes finds out where you are, no place is really safe. Do I think he's waiting to nail us on the sand? No. But I told you. Whatever else happens between us, protecting you is my first priority." He pulled her next to his body and gave her a hug, then brushed his lips over her forehead. "Now I have even more reason for that. Come on. Let's take a walk."

Chapter 9

Early afternoon, Desmet woke Maes to let him know lunch was being served.

Maes left his seat and walked down the aisle to where Henri sat. The man had been so nervous earlier Val had finally given him a sedative and he'd slept. Now Maes woke him and insisted he eat.

"You need your strength, Henri. After all, you're just getting over an illness."

Joubert looked at him with a volatile mixture of despair, hopelessness, and rage.

"I'll be getting over it a lot better when I am home with my family," he snapped.

The words would have had more punch if Joubert didn't look so much like he was about to expire. But Maes simply shrugged.

"Nevertheless, be sure to eat something."

Maes moved toward the front. Where Raca was once again polishing his Tavor assault rifle. The others were all outfitted with Colt M4 carbines, easy to obtain, easy to use, and precise and accurate.

"You treat that thing better than a baby," he told the man.

Raca looked up at him, his face devoid of expression. "There's no baby that can do what this can."

Maes just nodded. "I want you and your men to eat. You must be one hundred percent when we land."

"We always are," Raca assured him and gave him what Val called his dead fish stare.

Maes returned to his seat, where Val brought him his meal, which he ate sparingly. He never went into battle on a full stomach, and he had no illusions that this was most definitely a battle they were facing. Even if all the firepower would be on one side.

He spent the balance of the trip with his own laptop, checking and rechecking information on the businesses he was about to destroy. When he left Princessa Key he would be back in command again. No one would dare come after him then. He'd destroy anyone who tried, civilian or government.

He had just closed his computer when the co-pilot came into the cabin to announce they were almost on the final approach to the Nassau airport. He rose and walked to where Joubert sat, dozing lightly again from the mild sedative.

"Time to wake up, Henri." He nudged the man's shoulder. "We're almost in Nassau and your role in this game is nearly at an end."

The look of relief that came over the man's face almost made him sad, knowing what was ahead for him. Almost. But Stefan Maes did not feel sorry for anyone. He'd lost that ability before the age of ten, on the streets of Zagreb.

"And my family?" the man asked, fear etched on his face?

"They are being taken care of," he reassured him.

Only not the way he expected.

Maes looked him over again and decided he'd do for what they needed.

Raca and his men still had their weapons out, checking and rechecking. Maes knew they had probably done that the entire trip. Those weapons were like an extension of them, their tools of the trade. Like him, they'd learned before puberty the best way to kill efficiently was to make sure your artillery was ready to use. Now they repacked everything and buckled in for the landing.

"Is Henri going to make it?" Val asked, when Maes took his seat again.

"We'll make sure he does. We don't need him that much longer."

The landing was smooth as glass, and the plane taxied over to the private hangar area. As soon as the door was open and the stairway lowered, Maes tugged Joubert up from his seat.

"Remember your lines," he whispered in the man's ear.

Then he nudged him down the stairway and onto the tarmac. A man in dark slacks and a spotless white shirt with a dark tie walked out to greet them.

"Welcome to Nassau," he said in a lilting accent. "Monsieur Joubert, your helicopter is ready and waiting for you and your guests."

"Thank you." Joubert worked hard to keep his voice steady. "You always take very good care of me."

"Our pleasure." The man gave a slight bow.

He nodded and led them across the tarmac to where Joubert's helicopter waited. On paper, this man was dong the mandatory customs check of anything they loaded on the bird. In reality, the fat payment Joubert always transferred to an account for him in the same way Maes and others did had him looking the other way.

"I see you have a different pilot this time," the man said in a conversational tone. "Is your regular man ill?"

"Yes, yes," Joubert answered him in a nervous voice. "He recommended someone for me."

"I see."

They were at the chopper now, where a pilot Maes used for his own helo waited for them. Maes was holding Joubert's arm and gave it a hard squeeze.

"Thank you for coming on such short notice," Joubert recited the words Maes had fed him. "I appreciate it."

"I'm happy I was able to do it," the man answered, careful to avoid looking directly at Maes.

Raca and his men had disembarked from the plane carrying their black rigid cases and filed one by one into the body of the large Sikorsky S-92. The pilot greeted them with a smile.

"Good evening, gentlemen. The preflight is complete. As soon as your party is all on board we are cleared for takeoff."

Again, boarding was accomplished with great efficiency. Maes urged Joubert into the chopper, seating him in the cockpit with the pilot so he would have access to the radio. Raca and the others took their seats in the cabin, with Raca himself sitting close to Maes. They all fit nicely into the helicopter, and in minutes they were airborne.

Maes relaxed his shoulders a fraction. It had all gone well. At Maes instructions, Joubert gave the pilot the information to radio ahead to Rosewood that they were on their way and gave them their approximate ETA. Then he moved Joubert back to a seat by the cabin door. The man had served his purpose well, but it was time to get rid of him.

"I want to speak to my wife again," Joubert insisted.

Maes had anticipated this, and handed the man the sat phone. He waited with controlled impatience until the call was finished. Then he took out his phone and tapped a message to one of the men at Joubert's house. *Do it now.* He pushed Send, then strapped himself in and waited for the next task to be completed.

The flight to Princessa Key was scarcely ten minutes long. When they were about five minutes from the mainland and in clear airspace, Raca slid open the cabin door. Henri Joubert's screams echoed in their ears as

Raca and another man pitched him out of the chopper. They watched him splash into the waters of the Caribbean, and then slid the door closed.

"Nicely done," Maes told him. "Now we get ready for the main event."

When the helo touched down at Princessa Key, they were ready. Raca and his men held their assault rifles plus belts of additional ammo. Additionally, each carried their handguns now locked and loaded and fitted, for the moment, with suppressors. If they had to fire any bullets, it was important no one heard the shots and gave warning. Added to all that were small packets of Semtex, a general-purpose plastic explosive.

After double checking each of the weapons and equipment himself, Raca slid the cabin door open and jumped out, his men following him.

A man wearing what Maes assumed was the uniform of the place stood by an extended golf cart. As soon as they hit the tarmac he walked forward, a puzzled look on his face.

"Excuse me, I was told—"

That was as far as he got. At Raca's nod, one of the men stepped forward and pumped six bullets into the man from his suppressed Walther PPK. The man collapsed in front of the golf cart. Raca kicked the body to the side and motioned everyone forward.

"You have your gizmo?" Maes asked Desmet.

Val held out his hand, palm open to show him the little item that looked like a harmless flash drive. In reality, it was an electronic jammer that would disrupt the feed of the security long enough for them to reach Rosewood.

"I wish I knew how many cameras they had," Desmet commented. "None of the maps of the place I pulled up on the internet showed them."

"Probably don't want to advertise their locations, although I don't know why. In any event, it doesn't matter. We're not taking any chances."

They were soon on the move, Maes and Desmet riding in the seat just behind the driver. Those who did not have a seat walked behind the cart with long-legged strides.

They had just made the first turn in the crushed shell path when two guards appeared, possibly checking on why the cameras were out. The oversized golf cart and a bunch of men with assault rifles certainly were not what they expected to find.

"Hey," one of the guards said, stepping in front of the cart. "What the hell is going on here? What—"

Before he got another word out, one of the men, using a handgun with a suppressor, had stitched bullets through both of them.

"Take their radios," Maes ordered. "If someone calls them to check in during the next few minutes, we can fake it. Besides, you never know when they'll come in handy."

After tossing the bodies into the bushes, they continued along the path. Maes swept his eyes left and right as they moved, checking for anyone else who might be outside. Apparently, everyone was at the dinner, and whatever staff wasn't working the event was off for the night. The map of the island had pinpointed employee quarters about a quarter of a mile from the center of the resort, a fact Maes reminded Raca of now.

"When we get to where the restaurant is," he told the man, "send two of your people over to make sure no one leaves that building. There must be a central room to gather them all into. Tell them to shoot anyone who gives them trouble."

Raca nodded.

They encountered two more security guards along the path. This time there was no wait for orders. Double bursts from two guns, and the guards were dead on the path. Again, they just shoved the bodies out of the way in the bushes. Closer to the main building, a grounds maintenance crew was doing a little early evening cleanup. Startled by the group of large men dressed all in black, one of them grabbed a radio from his belt. But before any of them could say more than a word or two, the suppressed .45 spoke again, and three more bodies were added to the total.

"There will be more guards," Desmet reminded Maes. "A place like this will have a full complement of them."

"I don't know what for." Maes shrugged. "It's not as if they have to worry about keeping people out."

He laughed at his own joke. The feeling of anticipation that had been growing in him all day now threatened to bubble over, and he had to take a deep breath to steady himself.

"We'll handle them," Desmet assured him.

Even as he spoke, the radio on one of the dead guards crackled to life.

"Halsey? What's up with the cameras? Come in."

Maes looked at Raca. "Leave one of your men here. Tell him to take out anyone who shows up. Val, let's get moving again." He brushed imaginary lint from his jacket. "Tonight we will show them who is really top dog, right, Valentin?"

Desmet nodded, his mouth stretched in a tight smile.

* * * *

For Marissa and Justin, even though they were both on edge, the day had passed quietly. Just being together gave them a feeling of satisfaction. Something was blossoming between them at a rapid rate. Something they were afraid to put a name to. Something that was so strong they could not ignore it.

They walked the small private beach that was part of Orchid House and even played in the surf for a little while. Kissed standing in the gentle surf until they were both so aroused they had to race to get inside. Bathing suits were flung to the floor, covers jerked back on the bed. Their lovemaking was intense and frantic, as if driven by an urge to take it all. Now.

Avery called about the middle of the afternoon. By then they were sitting in the shade by the pool sipping on cool drinks, hands linked. Every time their glances collided it was *there*.

"I'm sending you what we've got on Joubert. It took a little longer because we're looking for a connection to Maes, if one exists."

"And?" he prompted.

"So far, nada. On the surface Henri Joubert looks like exactly what Walt said," she told him. "A billionaire with a nice family and a semi-lavish lifestyle. Brian is still digging, but I'm also keeping Ginger on it. It's just too much of a coincidence for me not to do that. If there's a connection to Maes, we'll find it."

"Hopefully before Joubert arrives this evening."

"Planning on it."

Justin used his tablet to pull up the file and they stared at the picture of Joubert.

"Look familiar?" he asked Marissa.

She shook her head. "Not even a little. Of course, I never got to meet a lot of the people he did business with. That wasn't part of my instructions or goal. My orders were to be in a position to steal his accounts from whoever was handling them, give him great advice to grow his finances and at the same time be able to dig into all of his accounts to find where he was hiding his blood money."

"From what I understand, you did it very well."

She gave a very unladylike snort. "So well, I have a price on my head." When he started to say something, she held up her hand. "I would not have done anything differently. Innocent people were being killed because of his businesses. I was happy to help put an end to them. And now, enough of Stefan Maes. I think I'd like a short dip in the pool."

At five o'clock, pleasantly relaxed—or as much as possible under the circumstances—by the sun and sand and pool, they decided to take showers.

Or should I say a *shower*, Marissa thought.

Just the image of the two of them naked in the shower sent shivers sliding over her skin and every pulse point throbbing. This *thing* with Justin, whatever it was, had come at her out of the blue. She hadn't expected it, hadn't planned for it, but now, worst of all, didn't want to let go of it. She could no more stop this emotional rollercoaster than she could a runaway train. Nor did she think she wanted to.

If only her future weren't so uncertain. Thank you, Stephen Maes. Was it terrible of her to hope somebody managed to kill him so she could have some peace and get on with her life?

In the bedroom they stripped off their clothes and stepped into the massive shower together. Marissa's body throbbed with need, just as it always did when she was this intimate with Justin. Her sex was so wet she smelled the scent of her own musk even in the shower.

Justin's nostrils flared.

"Jesus, Marissa." He looked down at his fully erect cock. "It seems all you have to do is take off your clothes and I'm ready for you."

"Same here," she whispered.

He cupped her face and nipped her bottom lip. "I just want to make sure I'm not taking advantage of you in a vulnerable situation."

She smiled. "I may not be the most experienced lover you've ever had, but I'm no weak wallflower, either. You said it was my choice, and I chose this. This thing between you and me? It's what's keeping me going right now, and I don't want to lose it."

He nipped her lower lip. "Good, because neither do I. And after this is over—"

"If it ever is." Her shoulders slumped. "What if no one can locate Maes? What if I'm running from him for the rest of my life?"

"Hush." He touched the tip of one finger to her lips. "Don't even go there." He grinned. "On the other hand, it means I have a lifetime job."

"Guarding me?" She didn't want to read too much into his words. "I'm sure you have other things to do with your life."

This thing between them grew more intense with every passing moment. She hoped it wasn't just the danger ramping everything up. Accelerating their emotions. She knew danger could do that, and she wondered if that's what it was with Justin.

All the humor left his face, replaced by a serious expression. "I can't think of a better way to spend it. And when this really is all over, that's what we're going to discuss."

"Can something like this happen so fast?"

"Just because it's quick, doesn't mean it's not right." He touched his mouth to hers. "It blindsided me. I wasn't looking for any kind of connection to anyone. For a lot of reasons, it wasn't on my to-do list. But that doesn't mean it's not special."

He was silent, but just for a moment.

"When Logan Malik, another Vigilance agent, got married a while ago, he told me something very profound."

"And what's that?"

"He pointed out that at Vigilance we work in a dangerous environment. When you find the right person, you don't want to waste a moment."

"And do you think you've found the right person?"

He tightened his arm around her. "I do. And I hope you feel the same way."

The sudden flood of emotions swamped her so intensely she couldn't speak, so she just nodded.

"Is that a yes?" he persisted. "I'd like to hear the word."

"Yes," she whispered.

He took her mouth in a kiss so intense she felt it in every inch of her body.

"So, when this is over," he said when he broke the kiss, "I want to give us a real chance, okay?"

"Okay," she whispered.

"I think we should seal this deal." His laugh was hot and dirty. "Just close your eyes, sweetheart. Let me make you feel good."

She noticed he'd placed his cell on the vanity by the shower, along with his M&P and a condom.

"Multitasking?" She grinned.

"You know it. Something I'm an expert at."

He cradled her head with the palm of one hand, while the other slid between her thighs. When she opened her mouth to say something he slammed his lips against hers and thrust his tongue deep inside. At the same time, he played with the lips of her sex, rubbing her slit with his fingers.

She moaned into his mouth as his nimble fingers worked her flesh. Hands shaking, she grabbed his shoulders to steady herself and gave herself over to the sensations cascading through her. Beneath the taut skin of his back, slippery from the shower, she felt the flex of firm muscles. His fingers were doing magical things to her body, so tantalizing she rocked on them, trying to impale herself on them.

She attempted to slide her hand between their bodies, needing to find and grasp the thick length of his cock now pressing into the soft flesh of her tummy, but Justin brushed it away.

"Not yet, not yet." Another sexy, dirty laugh. "Let me lead this dance, okay?"

She nodded and squeezed her thighs hard against his hand, continuing to move her hips back and forth. Her entire body had ramped up from wanting and needy to ravenous and desperate in scant seconds. She had never been this ready so fast in her life.

Justin shifted to slide open the shower door, reached for the condom, and rolled it on with expert speed. She didn't want to know how many times he'd done just this in order to be so quick about it. This was about them, about right now, and that was all she wanted to think about. With the condom efficiently rolled on his very hard shaft, he lifted her enough to slide into her, filling every inch of her.

"Wrap your arms around me." His voice was raw with need.

She did as he asked, and with her legs, locking her ankles at the small of his back. Pressing her back against the shower wall, he thrust in and out of her with hard, fast strokes. Marissa hung on for dear life as her body raced to completion. And then, there it was. An explosion so intense it shook both of them.

He cupped the cheeks of her ass with his palms and held her steady as his breath seesawed out of his lungs. Marissa wasn't doing much better herself, gasping to breathe steadily, her heart beating like a trip hammer. At last her inner walls, clamping down on him like a wet vise, stopped pulsating and her heart rate slowed, until she could unwind her legs from his body and make herself stand there steadily.

Justin looked at her with so much emotion in his eyes it nearly brought her to her knees.

"It may have been fast, but it was better than the best. But later? When I have more time? You better believe I'll be taking a slow tour of your body."

His words threatened to set off more tiny explosions inside her, so she took a step away from him.

"We'd better get dressed or we might never leave the villa."

"If I wasn't so curious about the late-arriving guest I'd vote for that." He took a step backward. "Let's just check out what all is going on, and then we can come back here."

"We've actually got enough stashed in the fridge here to make a meal," she pointed out. "I wouldn't mind eating here by the pool."

"That actually sounds pretty good."

While they were dressing they heard the drone of a helicopter overhead. Justin look upward. "That must be the missing guest."

"Probably. What time is it?"

He checked his watch. "Seven thirty. I didn't realize it had gotten that late."

"Time flies when you're having fun," she teased.

"Let's see what's going on. If everything checks out, we can head back here and shut out the world."

Chapter 10

Marissa slipped on her shoes and looked up from the big walk-in closet where she was standing to see Justin with their guns laid out on the bed.

"Checking everything over again?" she asked.

"A habit I'll probably never break."

"That's good, because it's one of those habits that saves lives. Are you finished?"

He nodded and handed her the Glock, the H&K, and extra ammo for both. "Get that purse you took to the beach and put all of this in it. I'll be ecstatic if we don't need them."

"Me, too." She put everything in the cloth bag and put the strap over her shoulder. "I learned in London it's always best to be suspicious."

"Right. Besides, Avery hasn't called back yet with info on Maes's whereabouts or anything else on Joubert, and I don't like the way my neck itches. I think we need to suspect everyone and everything right now. I should have insisted she send the chopper back for us earlier today."

"And if Joubert turns out to be just what he looks like, a millionaire who recovered enough to join his friends?" She shook her head. "I could end up being shuttled off to another place where Maes might find me. We don't know where to go, Justin, because we don't know where he is. At least here we are in a controlled situation."

He nodded. "Okay, let's go."

He shoved the M&P in the waistband of his slacks at the small of his back, and stuck what he called his utility tool—a jackknife with other attachments that he swore were magic—into his pocket. After one last look around, he set the alarm and locked the door behind them. Then they set off on the long, twisting path to the main building.

"It seems really quiet." Marissa glanced at Justin as they walked. "Don't you think so? Although I suppose no one is walking around because they're all at the dinner, but still..."

"Yeah." He stopped and looked around. "You'd think at least some of the staff would be out and about."

Marissa shivered, but not from any cold. "My nerve endings are sending me messages. Are yours?"

"Somewhat. Let's just be careful on our way to the building. And if everything looks okay, I'd like to check in with Walt before we eat. Is that okay with you? We can see if the new guest has joined everyone for dinner."

"Assuming he's changed this fast. The brochure indicated people dress more formally for Saturday night dinner."

Justin nodded. "If he isn't in the restaurant yet, let's hang around and check him out when he comes down in the elevator. I'm not one of those people who thinks the unexpected should be ignored."

She grimaced. "Tell me about it."

They had reached the big area in front of the main building. Marissa stood next to Justin, cloaked by all the foliage at the end of the path, and looked around, puzzled.

"Where is everyone? Justin, something's wrong. Every resort has people wandering around in the evening."

Justin scanned the area. "How likely is it that no one—not one single guest or employee—is visible and moving?"

"There should at least be one of the security guards patrolling." Marissa looked at Justin. "Right?"

"Right." He frowned. "The brochure says there are four on duty at all times. We haven't seen one. And I know Walt has his guards doing a walk-around every evening, just in case one of the guests gets into a hassle or a strange boat tries to dock here."

A chill slithered along her spine. "Let's check at the front desk. And I know I don't need to tell you to be very careful."

The lobby of Rosewood was a high-ceilinged rotunda, with short hallways branching off to elevators, various resort amenities, and the elaborate restaurant Sunset. They started toward the building entrance, toward the big glass doors, but Justin stopped and held out a hand to stop Marissa from going any farther. He stepped behind some thick plants and tugged her with him.

"What's the matter?"

"Stay here. Something's wrong. There's no one in the lobby, not even behind the registration desk, and there's always someone there. The spa and shop are closed, right?"

Marissa nodded. "The spa closes at six, the shop at seven.

"I think those employees are going to consider themselves lucky." Justin shook his head. "I don't like this. Something doesn't smell right."

She had to agree with him. The same trickle of fear that had raced up and down her back that last week in London was teasing at her again. Her stomach knotted, and she had to ease out a breath to relax it.

"Come on. There has to be a side door. Let's find it."

Before they could move forward, however, they heard a sharp sound that was familiar to both of them.

"That's a gun shot," she whispered.

"It fucking damn sure is. I knew there was a reason for my itchy feeling."

"Mine, too."

"Come on." He took her hand. "Let's find that side entrance. Everyone is in Sunset, or almost everyone. They can't see us if we approach from the other side of the building."

Justin pulled out his S&W and Marissa took her Glock out of her drawstring purse. They both checked their guns one last time to make sure a bullet was chambered. Then they moved around to the far side of the building and the entrance from the outdoor bar and the Bistro.

"Well, at least there are no dead bodies here," Justin said as they cleared the covered porch and the Bistro itself. "I don't see any servers."

"God." Marissa blew out a breath. "I hope no one decided to go investigate what that noise was."

"I don't think it came from the lobby. It didn't sound that close."

"The restaurant? You think it came from there?"

He nodded. "That's my guess."

"That could mean that—"

"Joubert is not the harmless person everyone thinks he is. Come on."

They made their way quietly through the Bistro, eased into the empty lobby area and moved toward the registration desk. The first hallway they passed was clear and the other was on the far side of the rotunda and led to the restaurant. Faint sounds drifted out to them but no more shots.

Marissa touched his arm, and then her ear.

"*Voices*," she mouthed, and pointed toward the hallway to the restaurant.

Justin listened, then nodded and peered over the counter at Registration.

"Shit." He growled the word in a low, tight voice. "Double shit."

"What?" Marissa stood on tiptoe to see what he was looking at. "Shit is right," she echoed in a soft voice. "God, Justin."

Whoever had been handling guests wouldn't be doing it any more. She lay on the floor at an awkward angle, her hair falling loose from its braid, a large circle of blood staining her pink uniform shirt and pooling beneath her.

Justin grabbed Marissa's arm and pushed her back the way they'd come. They stopped outside the building, out of sight of anyone on the other side. Still, he moved them into a tight, thick grouping of tall shrubbery where they'd be impossible for anyone to spot.

"Whoever this Henri Joubert is," he said in a low voice, "he's not here for relaxation. I can't believe Avery is missing something about him. This can't be the first time he's done this."

"We don't even know what he's done yet," Marissa reminded him. "Or even if it's him."

"Only one helicopter landed today," he pointed out. "So, either he's here on monkey business, or…" He let his words trail off.

"Or something is way out of whack."

"We have to get a look in that restaurant," Marissa told him. "Something's going down in there."

"Not *we*, sweetheart. Me. I am not going to put you at risk in what is obviously a dangerous situation." He gave her a tight grin. "If I thought I could get away with it, I'd lock you in Orchid House until this was all over."

She glared at him. "Fat chance."

"I figured you'd say that."

She curled her hands into tight fists to gather in her control.

"Listen to me. I'll only say this once. I spent three years undercover to get the goods on one of the world's most dangerous men. I know stealth, I score ninety-eight percent on the target range, and I can understand enough of five different languages to know what people are saying. I'm aware you've been hired to protect me, but I am not hiding in the closet. And I can be of help to you. So do *not* think you are tucking the little lady in a corner for this."

Despite the seriousness of their situation, he managed to crack a smile.

"Duly noted. And by the way, I'm more than the bodyguard hired to protect you. I thought we settled that before."

She wasn't sure whether to smack him or hug him. "You are. Much more. And we did." She swallowed. "Now. Where's that map you've been marking up? I saw you shove it in your pocket back at the villa."

He pulled it out and unfolded it. "Okay. Here's Sunset." He pointed. "Right here where the windows begin is a place we can get a peek without being seen. At least we can assess the situation. We need to go back outside and around the building."

"Okay. Let's do it."

They moved around behind the building, past the loading area where supplies were received, past the employee entrance, to the other side of the building. Two walls were all windows, so they moved until they could just see inside Sunset at an angle. What she saw made Marissa's entire body turn cold and nausea rumble up into her throat. A tall man dressed in an expensively tailored suit stood addressing everyone in the room. Behind him was another man holding what she knew was an assault rifle, and deployed around the restaurant itself were several more, all dressed in black, all holding the same type of weapons. Some had handguns stuck in the waistband of their slacks.

The guests in the restaurant, at least the ones they could see, were gaping at the men with a mixture of horror, anger, and fear.

Marissa sucked in a breath and stared at the man, fear invading every part of her. These people had good reason to be afraid.

"Oh, my God." She whispered the words, nausea gripping her at the shock of what she was seeing. "Justin? T-That's Stefan Maes. And the man at the doorway is Valentin Desmet. Oh, my God." She grabbed Justin's arm, digging her fingers into the hard muscles, trying to stabilize herself. She was trembling and had to reach for every bit of self-control. How was he here? *Why* was he here? If he had found her, was her absence from the crowd what was setting him off? Dear Lord.

"Jesus." Justin let out a breath. Then he turned and took a moment to pull her hard against his body.

She swallowed, pushing down the fear that wouldn't let go. "God, I hope he's here for something else. He has to be. If he had discovered I was here, Avery would have called. Right?"

"Yes," he assured her. "Besides, we know she covered our tracks very well, and our names aren't in the registration program. It has to be something else. A coincidence. A very nasty one."

"One arranged by the devil." How had this happened?

He cupped her cheek. "But whatever it is, we'll get Avery to find out."

"I just can't imagine what it could it be." She drew in a shuddering breath, then dug for every bit of control she had. "I feel sorry for whoever his target is. That man's cruelty knows no boundaries."

He stopped and took both her hands in his. "Listen to me. You're tough. You can do this. We can do this together. And I am not going to let Maes get his hands on you. That's a promise."

She blew out a breath. "Okay."

With a supreme effort, she pulled herself together, swallowing back the nausea that threatened to erupt as she imagined herself the man's prisoner. She had heard too many stories about Maes's cruelty not to be afraid. She needed Lauren Masters the CIA operative now, not Marissa Hayes, target in hiding. Justin did not need her to fall apart on him.

"You know Henri Joubert's late arrival is part of this." Justin rubbed his neck. "Maybe he and Maes are friends and he's doing him a favor."

"Then the CIA should take lessons in secrecy from him," Marissa said, "because there's no trace of a connection between them anywhere."

"Whatever it is, though, this doesn't look much like a fun dinner party. Wonder which one of the men in there is him?"

"I can't tell you because I've never seen him. Can you bring up the link Avery sent you earlier? Oh, wait a sec. I can find it."

She pulled her cell phone from her purse. Thanks to Princessa Key's satellite setup she could access the internet with no problem. She typed in Henri Joubert's name and when the picture loaded, she showed it to Justin.

"I don't see him in the room," she said. "But some of the men have their backs to us."

He shook his head. "I have a feeling good old Henri isn't here. I don't know where he is, but I'd say it's not good. Maes probably used him to gain access to Princessa Key."

"But for what purpose?"

"If we can get inside and listen, we can find out."

"Look." One of the men was standing not too far from Maes in an open area, holding a garbage bag. "What do you—"

"Cell phones and any other electronics," he interrupted. "And watches. One of the others is wanding each one after they dump their stuff. Checking for watches that can be used as cells. Anything that they could use to get a signal out. And crap. They've got the waitstaff in there, too. If anything happens they'll get caught in the crossfire."

"You're right," she agreed. "Maes would not hesitate to execute anyone, no matter how helpless or uninvolved."

"Let's check the path from here to the hangar. It won't take long, and I'd like to know where the guards are. And I need to call Avery."

"We need to remember to stay away from the security cameras you marked the other day," Marissa reminded him. The last thing she wanted was for either of them, her especially, to show up on the cameras in case Maes had someone monitoring them.

"There are only a few," he reminded her.

"I know. I just want to fix them in my mind."

Justin opened the map again to see where he'd put the little checkmarks, just as a last-minute review. He'd already gone over it several times.

"Got it?" he asked her.

Marissa studied it, then nodded. "I'm good."

"I'm calling Avery before we do anything else."

They moved to the rear of the building, out of line of anyone's sight and far enough away that he couldn't be heard. Then Justin hit speed dial for Avery.

"Trouble," he said the moment she answered, and gave her a terse summary.

"I'll call Mike," she told him. "The team will be wheels up in thirty."

"I'll text you the best place for them to land. There are only a few security cameras, but they'll want to avoid them. I'm sure Maes has someone tapping into them."

Avery was silent for a moment.

"You're right. I'll have them do a HAHO jump. That way the chopper will be high enough that little if any sound will be heard in the restaurant. Nothing to alert them."

Justin had done high-altitude, high-opening jumps before. The team would be virtually undetectable at night on regular cameras, and he doubted Maes had brought anything infrared with him.

"Tell them to deploy on the two sides of the building that are all glass. I'll see about killing the outside lights. Can you find out why Maes is here?"

"I'll call Brian. Listen. Flight time from here is a little over an hour, so you're probably looking at close to ninety minutes before reinforcements get there. Can you handle the situation until then?"

Justin barked a humorless laugh. "It's not like I have a choice, Avery."

"Take care of yourself," Avery ordered. "And your precious cargo."

Precious Cargo was a term adopted by many elite groups to signify the person for whose safety they were responsible. For Justin the phrase now had a double meaning.

"Will do. Back atcha soon." He disconnected the call and shoved the phone in his pocket. "Okay. Let's find the guards."

The first bodies they discovered in their search weren't the guards but those of the grounds crew. Someone had executed them and just kicked them to the side.

"Holy mother," Marissa whispered, icy fear creeping up her spine again. She'd heard many stories about Maes's careless disregard for human life, but this was the first time she'd seen it up close and personal.

"No shit," Justin said.

A few steps farther they discovered two of the guards, shot and pushed aside the same way. Marissa liked to think her three years as a CIA covert operative had toughened her, but the one thing she'd not had to deal with during that time was dead bodies. Now she was doing her best not to fall apart at the sight of the carnage.

"My God." Marissa stared at them, sadness washing over her. "I'll bet the bellman that showed up with the cart is history, too."

"And probably the rest of the guards. So. Time to see if there's a way in there so we can find out what the hell is going on. And figure out how to stop it."

She gripped his arm, nails digging into his skin. "We have to be very careful."

He nodded. "Careful is my middle name."

* * * *

When Maes and his men entered the rotunda, the registration clerk stared at them with wide, frightened eyes. She picked up the phone to call someone, but he shook his head.

"You don't want to do that, do you?"

She looked at Raca standing beside him, gun at the ready, and shook her head."

"Which way is the restaurant?"

She pointed to a short hallway on the left. "T-That way."

"Excellent. Thank you." He turned to Raca. "Shoot her."

Her mouth was still open to scream when the bullet hit her.

Entering the restaurant, he assessed the situation at once. People were busy enjoying their dinner, not paying attention to who walked in.

"Get their attention," he told Raca.

The man obediently fired his assault rifle into the ceiling. Maes always thought that was an outstanding way to get everyone's attention. People screamed, some just sat open-mouthed. But it caught everyone's attention. One moment they were eating and drinking and talking. The next moment the peace of their evening had been shattered.

He looked around the room. "Good evening, everyone. Forgive me for disturbing your dinner this way, but I have a little business to conduct with some of you. Once that's finished, I'll be on my way. Some of you may be a little poorer, but if you all behave, at least you will be alive."

"I see several waitstaff here in the main room. All of you, sit on the floor over there." He pointed to one wall. "Raca, get out the flex cuffs and have someone secure their hands behind their back."

"Done."

He nudged Goren and pointed toward the entrance to the kitchen.

"There will be more staff in the kitchen. The chef. His assistants. Maybe a dishwasher. Bring them out and secure them, also."

Goren nodded, took one of the men with him and headed toward the double doors. Maes knew they would not hesitate to shoot anyone who objected. The rest of the men automatically deployed around the restaurant.

Then Maes walked to the corner opposite the entrance, a place where he could see everything, and no one could get behind him. True, the walls were all windows but there was no one out there to do him any damage. Not the dead guards. Not anyone. He looked around the elegant restaurant, at the people dressed in evening regalia. They all stared at him, stunned, their expressions a mixture of disbelief and fear.

"Some of you may not know who I am," he began. "So let me introduce myself. I am Stefan Maes, head of the *Grupa Industrijska*, formerly a multibillion-dollar business until men I made rich conspired to sweep my empire out from under me. These men are the reason I am here tonight. It is unfortunate for the rest of you that you are caught up in a situation created by those men."

His gaze swept the room again. He saw them, all of them except of course for Joubert. With eyes full of rage, they watched him, but none of them made a move. Were they stupid enough to think he wouldn't recognize them? That they could blend into this crowd? Why did they not show any fear? Apparently, they were willing to sacrifice everyone here just as they had sacrificed him.

A man seated at a table to his left rose. "Excuse me. I'm Walter Morganstern. My wife and I own Rosewood. If there is something we can help you with, please, just ask us."

Maes smiled at the man. Such a foolish person. He was in no position to satisfy him. And he would not be cheated out of his revenge.

"Can you give me back all the money eleven men in this room cheated me out of? If not, you would do well to sit down and be quiet." He paused. "There was one other man but unfortunately he met with an accident on the trip here."

For a moment the man looked as if he had something else to say. Then a woman, probably his wife, tugged on his sleeve and he sat back down. Maes looked around the room again. "You would all do well to sit quietly until I have gotten what I came for. If you all behave, perhaps I will let you live."

A woman at the table closest to him smothered a scream and looked as if she was about to faint.

"Madam, compose yourself," he ordered. "You do not want to make me upset."

Maes nodded to one of Raca's men, Franjo Pavic, who promptly slapped her across the face so hard her head jerked. Her husband started to protest, but the same gunman rested the barrel of his gun against the man's temple.

"I wouldn't upset him," Maes said in a mild voice. "He has an itchy trigger finger on that gun. An M60 can blow quite a hole in your head."

He was gratified to see the man turn pale, while his wife almost passed out. Her husband handed her a glass of water then just sat quietly, holding her hand.

"Anyone else?" Maes looked around the room. "Good. Very good. If you all listen to my instructions and follow them, we will be gone before you know it and you can proceed with your dinner."

Not fucking likely, he thought.

He spotted one of the waitresses, frozen in place, holding two glasses of water.

"Put those down," he ordered. "Now. And go stand against that wall. Over there. The rest of you, also. Valentin, you know what to do now."

Desmet walked over to a table near where Maes stood.

"I need your chair," he told the man sitting closest to him. "And your wife's."

"But—"

Desmet took out his small handgun and smacked the man's face. The woman next to him emitted a small scream, while the man pressed his napkin to his wound. But the two of them got up.

"Sit on the floor with the staff," Val said. "And don't make a sound."

He took a laptop out of the messenger bag he'd brought with him and opened it, booting it up. The computer was loaded with every kind of hacking program they could get on it. In seconds he looked up at Maes and nodded.

"I'm in."

He had pulled up the few security cameras scattered around the resort, and would monitor outside activity while Maes's men maintained control inside. Just in case.

"Ladies and gentlemen." Maes's gaze swept the room. "I am not playing a game here. It is important for you to understand that. I will not hesitate to kill anyone who tries to get in my way. Keep that in mind."

He paused, waiting for someone to say something, but for the moment they all seemed struck dumb. Assault rifles stuck in their faces had a tendency to do that.

All right, then.

"Now to the business at hand. The men who caused my fortunes to drop, who turned banks and businesses against me, who caused me to lose most of my money, are now going to reimburse me. You will know who they are once we are ready to begin the real business of the evening."

"These men"—Maes pointed to Raca's crew—"as you can see, are armed and ready. If anyone makes one wrong move or a misstep, they have orders to shoot. I hope for the sake of all of you it does not come to that."

He heard a *swish* as the doors to the kitchen opened. Three men dressed in the typical white coats worn by chefs and one woman in waitress garb were marched into the room ahead of Goren and his Colt M4.

Maes gave them a tight smile. "Thank you for joining us, gentlemen and lady. Please move to where your fellow staff members are standing. If you are very quiet and do not cause any trouble you may be able to leave here alive."

The waitress turned so pale Maes wondered if she would faint. Still she obeyed with the rest of them. Then he watched while Goren pulled a bunch of zip ties from his pocket. Soon the entire service staff was seated on the floor, backs to the wall, hands behind them.

"I will leave your legs free for the moment," he told them, "but if anyone tries something foolish, I will shoot that person and finish incapacitating the rest of you."

A man in a white dinner jacket at the table close to him rose from his chair. In an instant one of Raca's men was there, the barrel of his assault weapon pressed against the man's cheek.

"If you have something to say," Maes told him in a deceptively mild voice, "then spit it out. Let's get it out of the way. But sit down. If you try to get up again, it could be the last thing you do."

"Why don't you just tell us who these men are you obviously have a grudge against," the man said. "You can let the rest of us go. You don't have any quarrel with us."

Maes stared at the man until his face paled. "Nobody is leaving. Don't ask again. Now." He stretched his lips into a fake smile. "It would be a huge problem if any of you tried to call out from here, thinking someone could come and rescue you. I'm sure you can understand that. Since this is an island, it's not as if you can just call the police. However, I think it best to remove temptation, so we will be collecting all of your electronics. And I warn you, do not try to hide any of them."

One of Raca's men shook open a large garbage bag, while another stood at his side with a three-foot metal pole.

"You will come forward one at a time and deposit any and all electronic devices in this bag. Then you will be wanded to make sure you have nothing hidden on your person. We shall begin with"—he scanned the room—"this table here, to my right. Goren, please escort each person up here. If anyone gives you a hard time, shoot them."

Maes was pleased that no one screamed or tried to object. He wasn't ready to start shooting people. Not just yet.

He stood silently as, one by one, the guests made their way to his henchman holding the garbage bag open, and stopped while the wand was run over their bodies. He wasn't paying much attention to the tables in the far corner of the restaurant at the moment. Instead he was watching the faces of the eleven men he'd come to exact retribution from. He was caught off guard, therefore, when he heard a scream from that area, and looked over there to see Miko dragging a woman from her seat by her hair.

"What's the problem?"

"She's trying to sneak a call before giving up her phone." Miko wrapped her hair more tightly around his fingers and tugged her even harder until she was standing upright.

"Leave my wife alone." The man next to her stood and attempted to free his wife.

Miko slammed the barrel of his gun into the man's head, dropping him back into his chair.

Maes looked at the woman, and then recognized the man. A tiny smile played at the corners of his mouth. The husband was one of the men on his hit list. A man who would pay for what he'd done. Stojan Van Baer had owned a successful but small shipping company in Belgium before Maes had shown him how to expand his horizons. Along with the electronics and other goods *Grupa Industrijska* shipped to third world countries, his ships began to carry arms of all kinds to revolutionary armies and terrorist organizations. Those shipments brought enormous sums because of their nature, and Van Baer's wealth had grown exponentially. When the CIA investigated, that ungrateful swine had denied any knowledge of anything. Now it was his turn to pay the piper.

"Well, Van Baer. I see your wife isn't any smarter than you are. Didn't you tell her it's foolish to do anything that displeases me?" He nodded at Miko. "Release her, Miko."

His henchman frowned at him but dropped the woman back into her chair. "Now shoot her."

Miko pulled a .45 mm handgun from his belt and shot the woman twice in the head. Her body jerked as the bullets hit. Then her lifeless body fell forward, her head resting on her dinner plate. The sound of the bullets was magnified in the room, and people screamed.

"Shut up, all of you." Maes had to raise his voice to be heard. "Just shut up."

Van Baer lifted his head and stared at Maes. "Murderer!" he shouted. "Murdering swine."

"It takes one to know one," Maes retorted in a mild voice. "Sit down, Stojan. I cannot order the same for you because I have need of you this evening. But I'd be perfectly happy for my man to take care of the others at your table."

The room became unnaturally silent as everyone stared, shock plain on their faces. The people closest to the woman scrambled to help her husband. Several of the men rose from their seats.

Were these people just stupid?

He shook his head then looked around. "*Tsk. Tsk.* Did we not warn you about this?"

Maes gave Miko a nod, and the man fired his rifle into the ceiling, the rapid-fire sound of the bullets stunning everyone into silence again.

"Does that get your attention? Stay seated. That is an order. I am in charge. I told you what would happen if someone tried something. Perhaps now you will believe me." He shook his head again. "Too bad someone had to die to prove it. Franjo, get her out of my sight."

Van Baer shifted from his chair, but Raca pressed the barrel of his gun to the man's head. Then Franjo hoisted the body and carried it to the kitchen. With the swinging doors open, they could see him dump it on the floor.

As far as Maes was concerned, it couldn't have been a better example of his intentions. He was doubly pleased that it was the wife of one of the men on his list. It satisfied him, as he looked around the room again, to see genuine fear stamped on the faces of the guests.

He looked around. "If there is no one else foolish enough to defy me, we can move on to the rest of the evening."

He looked around the room, taking note of the strained looks underscored with fear. "No? All right, then. We shall proceed." He turned to Desmet. "Anything showing up on the security cams?"

"No." Desmet shook his head. "But their setup is very basic and doesn't really cover everywhere. I'm sure they never thought in this secluded paradise they'd need anything more."

"This will teach them not to take things for granted."

He glanced at people still dumping their electronics. It was a slow process, but he did not expect to be interrupted, and he wanted to be thorough. The men on his list, for whatever reason, were seated at the tables furthest away from him. It took a while for them and their wives to move to the place to dump their electronics.

Karl Eickner, another of the men on his list, was the first to move into the area. As he approached, Maes noted that rather than being frightened, the look in his eyes was one of extreme anger. And hate. If looks could kill, Maes would be a smoldering heap on the floor now.

His lips turned up in the hint of a smile.

"Good evening, Karl." He took a step closer to the man. "I have a very special evening planned for you and your lovely wife."

Eickner's wife was pale, her face almost as grey as her hair. As she stepped forward she opened her mouth as if to speak, then looked at Maes's face again and seemed to think better of it.

"You're dead after this, you know." Eickner delivered the words in a low, harsh tone.

"Big words from a man who is not in control."

"But we will be," Eickner warned. "What goes around comes around."

Maes actually smiled at that. "Exactly what this evening is all about."

He was pleased to note Eickner's face paled, although nothing diluted the anger.

"Step lively," he told the man. "Others are waiting behind you."

Eickner slammed his phone and watch into the bag, then took his wife's and did the same. Then he took one step closer to Maes.

"Fuck you, you fucking bastard. You think you're so fucking smart? We'll see."

He took his wife's hand to lead her back to their table.

Maes kept the smile pasted on his face, but inside his gut was churning. He could hardly wait for the main event to begin.

"Van Baer?" He looked at the man staring at him with agony and sorrow etched on his face. "I think we'll begin with you."

Chapter 11

"We need to get into the kitchen," Justin said as they made their way around to the back of the building again. "I want to see if maybe there's one person that Maes didn't sweep up. Someone who can answer some questions about how this went down. Something. Anything. Whatever I can use to slow this disaster down. Let's see if the employee entrance is unlocked. If not, I've got my trustee do-everything knife with me."

"What about the camera back there? If they're monitoring the system they'll see you."

"I'll check to see which way it's pointed. If we're lucky, it will be toward any paths, just to keep track of guests who might get lost."

Justin was right about the camera. It was pointed away from the building. He tested the knob on the rear door and smiled when it turned in his hand. Opening it, he motioned for her to follow him, touching a finger to his lips to remind her to be silent.

As if she didn't know.

But she had to keep reminding herself he didn't know exactly what her skills were, and his first priority was to keep her safe.

The door opened into a short hallway. On the left was a door they discovered led into a small storage room. On the right was the kitchen. Normally at this time of day, it would be filled with busy noises, as meals were being prepared, plated, and served. Right now, it was more silent than a cemetery, and not a person was in sight.

At the far end of the kitchen were the swinging double doors that led into the restaurant proper. They looked heavy enough to block most sound. It would be important to keep the kitchen racket from the people enjoying their very expensive meals. But now it also served as a heavy filter for what was going on in Sunset.

"They've cleared everyone out of here," Justin whispered as they slowly toured the kitchen. "Damn. I was hoping for one person."

"Maes and his people pay attention to every little detail. It's how he's destroyed so many people over the years."

Food in various stages of preparation sat on the counter at the workstations or in pots and pans on the huge stove, burners turned off. Everywhere there were signs of the routine of feeding dozens of people, but there was no one to push the process forward. The place looked as if a giant vacuum had come down and sucked up every human being.

Marissa scanned the kitchen, not knowing exactly what she was looking for. She stopped when her gaze landed on what looked like someone's laundry.

"Look, Justin." She moved closer and had to swallow a scream when she saw what it was. "Oh, my God. It's a body."

Justin crouched and rolled the body, so he could get a better look. It was a woman, at least in her sixties, in a pink chiffon dress. The front of it was heavily stained with blood.

"Jesus," Justin whispered. "Let's at least move her out of the way."

"What if one of them looks in here and sees she's been moved?"

"My guess?" He shook his head. "They just tossed her in here without looking to see where she landed."

"I told you Maes was ruthless and insane."

"No argument there. Let's see if we can catch what anyone's saying."

They moved to the doors, positioning themselves so they could peek in without being seen.

"You stole my money. I'm taking it back. With interest." The soulless, icy tone told him this had to be Maes.

"Over my dead body."

"If you insist."

A series of gunshots punctuated the air.

"*Not an assault rifle,*" Justin mouthed to Marissa. "It's obvious they've got a variety of weapons in there. I'm going to see if I can get a better look."

"Be careful," she said.

He managed a grin. "It's my middle name."

He held up a hand for quiet as he moved to get a better look through the opening. Marissa saw his body tense even more than it was as he put his ear close to the tiny window to hear better, before taking a look through it. When he turned back she could see his face had hardened into a mask of rage. He grabbed her hand and led her to the far end of the kitchen.

"I didn't want to talk down there," he whispered. "Sound carries, although I don't think he'd pay much attention to me at this point."

"What is it? What's wrong?"

He hauled in a deep breath and let it out slowly.

"The man you pointed out as Desmet is monitoring a computer by the entrance to the restaurant."

"My guess is he's tapped into the security-system cameras."

"Yes. And that will work in our favor. But they're covering all bases, just in case they left someone alive by mistake." He blew out a breath. Just at that moment, the sat phone vibrated against his hip.

"I have to step outside to take this," he whispered. "Come with me. I won't leave you alone in here."

Once outside, he pressed the button for Callback.

"Yeah, Avery, what have you got?"

Marissa watched as the muscles in his face tightened. Whatever Avery was telling him was as bad as everything else.

"Spill," she told him when he disconnected.

"Long story short, some of the men in that restaurant made a lot of money from his illegal activities. He kept them covered up and when the CIA put him out of business they walked away from him to keep their skirts clean. I think he wants revenge."

She swallowed. Hard. She knew what kind of revenge Maes could take. She'd heard enough about it, and Brian Gould had shown her pictures before letting her agree to take the job. "Like what?"

"Like getting his money back and maybe killing all of them afterward. We've got to find a way to slow this down until a Vigilance team gets here."

"Is the kitchen staff in there?" she asked. "Could you see?"

"Yeah. I just got a glimpse. He's got them herded together against one wall. He's too smart to leave people unattended. Let's get back inside and see what's happening." Once inside he started back toward the doors to the dining room but suddenly stopped, and cocked his head, as if listening.

"What is it?" Marissa whispered. "What do you hear?"

He cocked his head, frowning. "There. Did you hear that? Maybe there's someone here after all."

Marissa strained to listen. *Yes. He was right.* There was a tiny sound coming from one of the bottom cabinets. Careful not to make noise as he walked, he moved over to it, grasped the handle and yanked.

"Oh!"

A tiny little squeak startled both of them, but not half as much as the young girl who had curled herself into a ball to fit into it.

She looked as if someone had folded her into place. She was white with fear, and her eyes were like those of a trapped animal.

"Please don't kill me," she whispered, trying to make herself even smaller. Tears ran down her cheeks. "Please, please, please."

I've got this, Marissa mouthed to Justin and crouched beside the terrified girl.

"It's okay," she whispered. "We're not with the others. We're not going to hurt you."

The girl just wet her lips and stared at Marissa, her entire body shaking.

"I swear," Marissa went on. "Come on. We're here to get rid of the bad people. Please let me help you out of there before you can't unbend yourself." She held out her hand. "It's okay."

With very slow movements the girl managed to work herself around until she had her feet out, then little by little the rest of her body. Marissa helped her stand and had to stop herself from pulling the frightened girl in for a hug.

Justin, who had been keeping an eye on the doors to the restaurant, nudged them toward the exit.

"Let's take this out of the kitchen." He had his voice so low it was almost indistinguishable. "I just took a peek in the restaurant again. That big garbage bag is off to the side, so it looks like they've got everyone's electronics gathered. I don't know what's next, but I don't want to be in here in case they decide to check out the kitchen again. Let's move into that storage closet across the way. And everyone quiet. Not a sound."

For a moment the girl resisted, then allowed Marissa to lead her out of the kitchen, even though she was still trembling. She was barely over five feet and didn't look like she weighed much over a hundred pounds. Probably why she'd been able to fit in the cabinet. Her long brown hair was worn in a braid and her face was absent of any makeup. She looked barely twenty years old.

"Okay," Justin said as soon as they were in the storage closet. "Sweetheart, can you tell us your name?"

"D-Dani." She swallowed. "Danielle."

"Okay, Dani. I'm Justin and this is Marissa. We're not going to hurt you." He looked directly into the girl's eyes. "We're the good guys. Understand?"

She hesitated, then nodded.

"How long have you worked here?"

"Two years. They pay well, and I am saving money to go to college."

"Can you tell us what happened?" Marissa asked.

The girl began shaking again, so Marissa put her arm around her. "It's okay. We're here to help."

"No one can help," she blurted out. "Big men with guns came in and shot everywhere in the restaurant. They killed a woman." She swallowed hard. "T-The man who came in the kitchen, he had a big gun. Like you see in the movies." She described it for them.

Justin looked at Marissa. "All these assault rifles seem like overkill to me, if you'll pardon the pun. Does he really need so many for this crowd?"

"That's who Maes is," she told him. "He creates fear and terror in his prey then pounces."

"When they started to come into the kitchen, I hid."

"That was smart." Justin took her hands in his and gave them a gentle squeeze. "I promise you, we're going to try and fix what's happening in the restaurant."

"Are they going to kill everyone?" Dani whispered.

She was still so pale Marissa was afraid she might pass out. She curved her lips in what she hoped was a reassuring smile. "Not if we can help it."

"Wh-Who are they?" Panic flashed again in her eyes.

"Some very bad people. We're going to stop them, but we need your help."

"Me?" Her voice squeaked. "What can I do?"

"Question for you. Where are the rest of the employees? The service staff, the spa and shop attendants? We didn't see anyone except the staff associated with Sunset."

"There is a staff building farther along the path behind this building."

Justin nodded. "I noticed it on the map."

"We all have to live on the island, because it's at least a half hour by boat to and from the nearest town." A nervous laughed popped out of her mouth. "They don't send the helicopter to take us back and forth." The smile disappeared. "Anyway, when the Morgansterns built this place they added a very nice little building for all of us to live in."

Justin closed his eyes for a moment, frowning.

"Okay, I have some ideas. Dani, the electrical plant for the resort is down that same path that leads to staff quarters, right? At least according to the map."

"The what?" She scrunched up her forehead.

"The place that all the power comes from. The building that houses it."

"Oh." She looked up. "Yes. The physical plant. Everything including the computer system is monitored from there."

"Very convenient," Justin noted. "Does that include the air conditioning?"

She shrugged. "I guess. I don't know anything about all that."

He looked at Marissa. "We need to hustle over there. I have some ideas. Do you know the name of the guy in charge?"

"Luis Bernal." She rubbed her forehead.

Marissa looked over his shoulder. "What are you thinking?"

"That Vigilance won't be here for at more than an hour. I have to do something to slow things down until the team gets here. I can't exactly run in there and say, 'Hands up or I'll shoot!'"

"Be nice if we could," Marissa muttered. "So, what do you have in mind?"

"We need to interrupt their flow. Unnerve them. Make them think they aren't really in command. When dealing with the enemy there's a three-word game plan: deny, delay, contain. I'm going to see what we can do about putting that in play."

"Maes will go nuts if you monkey with anything," she warned him.

"Good. Maybe it will put him off his game. He's not going to kill anyone else until he gets his money. He's made his point. So, we have some wiggle room. I also need to find a way to eliminate some of their hired guns. I don't like the odds right now but maybe I can kill two birds with one stone."

Marissa frowned. "Just how do you plan to do that?

"I'd like to shut off the AC but I'm afraid if I do that right away they'll realize someone's on the grounds they don't know about. But if I can monkey with the main electrical, maybe flicker the lights on and off, stuff like that; he'll think there's something wrong with the main power plant. That way when the AC goes out they'll think it's the system's problem. They won't think someone is actually playing with it."

Marissa nodded. "They'll send men out to check on it."

"Yes. They'll want it fixed right away. I'm guessing not more than two at a time and that's manageable. It will help us even the odds." He turned back to Dani. "Where can I find Luis?"

"In the building where the physical plant is. He has an office there with big screens that show him how everything is doing."

"Would he be in his office right now?"

She nodded. "Yes. Tonight is a big event, so he has to make sure nothing goes wrong."

"Good. We need to get over there."

"He won't just let you in," Dani told them. She had calmed down somewhat. "He's a nut about letting anyone into that building."

"I'm sure he's just being careful with all that equipment," Justin soothed her.

"Yes, well, there's a call box next to the door. You have to hit the button."

"Will he let you in?" Marissa smiled at her.

"Yes, ma'am. He knows me. I bring his lunch sometimes."

"Okay, then, Dani. You're a lucky find for us. Maybe you'll even be our lucky charm. You've helped, but you need to get out of the danger zone. Justin, maybe we should stash her in the employee building before we do anything. Get her out of harm's way."

"No, no, no." Dani's words edged with hysteria. "Please. I heard them say they have men there who will shoot anyone who tries to leave the building."

Marissa looked at Justin. "I don't think Maes would have more than a couple of men handling that. I know him. He'll dismiss the employees as useless and nonthreatening. He'll want the bulk of his people in the restaurant with him, keeping the sixty-plus people in line."

"You're right." He looked around. "First we have to get out of this building. Then we go find Luis at control central."

"I'll take you," Dani whispered.

"What about the camera?"

"It's pointed the opposite of the way we'll take to get there. We can avoid it. I know how."

They slipped out through the back entrance, being careful to ease the door shut.

"Follow me," Dani whispered. "I will show you the best way."

* * * *

Things were tense in the restaurant. Maes could feel it as he surveyed all the tables, assessing each individual. Good. That's what he wanted. Tense and afraid. That way they'd be more likely to do his bidding without any more problems.

The shooting of Van Baer's wife was a little radical, perhaps, but he had needed to teach these people a lesson. The others seated at the table kept stealing glances at them, then immediately looking away, doing their best to conceal the terror stamped on their faces. Maes wanted people to see it, to be afraid. Fear was the best control. He had used the woman as an example to anyone else who might have a bright idea.

He'd learned a very long time ago that unless others knew you meant business, you would do exactly what you said if they didn't do your bidding, you lost any advantage. He wasn't bloodthirsty, as so many had said. Just practical. He knew how to bend people to his will.

Desmet was sitting in one of the chairs he'd commandeered, the other being used by each of the men whose money he was extracting. Desmet had taken a second laptop from his messenger bag, the first one being used to monitor the cameras. Between the two on the table was his tablet, which he used to pull up each man's financial information and bank accounts. Maes truly believed there was nothing Desmet could not find.

Except that fucking Lauren Masters.

As each man came up to the table, Desmet called up their financial information A list of their bank accounts and how much was in each one. Now it was Karl Eickner's turn. He headed toward the table, nudged by one of Raca's men.

He glared at Maes. "I'm not doing this. You can go to hell before I transfer one penny to you."

Maes tsked and shook his head. "Will people never learn? Raca, another lesson if you please."

Once again Raca stitched a line of bullets along one wall, just above the seated guests, far enough to avoid hitting anyone but close enough so the bullets rained down on the tables. It had proven in many other situations to be a useful method of control. People put their hands over their heads to avoid the hot lead. Some of the women screamed.

Eickner raised his head to look at Maes. "You bastard. You killed Van Baer's wife and hauled her out of here like trash. Now you've come close again to killing others. Have you no feeling for anyone?"

"For the people who turned away from me? Not even a little." He looked at Raca. "I believe Mr. Eickner requires a little more persuading."

Raca pulled his handgun from its holster, walked to the table and shot Eickner in the leg. The man's scream bounced off the walls.

"Are you done protesting, Kurt?"

He was pleased to note the man's face was almost as white as the tablecloth, and pain lined his face. One of the other men at the table took a napkin and tied it around his leg just above where the bullet entered. He whispered in Eickner's ear then helped the man over to where the laptop was.

"What did you say to him?" Maes demanded.

"I told him it's nothing but money. To just give it up. We'll help him make more."

"Wise words."

But it irritated him that Eickner had people who would help him whereas Maes had none. No one had stepped forward to assist him in rebuilding his empire. Instead, they had all turned on him.

"What do you want me to do?" The pain in Eickner's voice was evident.

"Have you not been paying attention? I want you to transfer all but one dollar out of each of your accounts into the numbered account my associate will give you."

"Y-You want *all* of it?" The man was sweating more heavily, and his voice was strained.

"Every penny," Maes confirmed. "Except one dollar."

"B-But what will I do for money? What will the rest of us do?"

Maes laughed, but there was no humor in it. "You will all help each other. Now stop wasting time. Do you want a bullet in the other leg?"

Eickner said nothing, just turned to the laptop, and with fingers not quite steady, began to type.

Maes let his gaze roam the room. Desmet would monitor Eickner and make sure he didn't do anything screwy. Maes wanted to gauge the reaction to all this. Making an example of Eickner, he believed, set the stage for everyone else's cooperation.

"Done," Val called from his seat. "Accomplished with no problem."

"You're sure he emptied every one of his accounts?"

"Yes. All except one dollar in each."

"Excellent. Raca, have one of the men escort Mr. Eickner back to his seat."

One of the men dragged Eickner out of the chair and pushed him roughly back to his table, forcing him to put pressure on his injured leg. His cries of agony echoed around the room, giving Maes even more satisfaction.

Maes looked around the room, deciding who to choose next. He was enjoying this even more than he had expected.

Chapter 12

The path to the building housing the physical plant wound its way through thick fig leaf trees, the limbs so heavy with leaves it was impossible to see around them or beyond them. They were barely seconds from the main building when they heard the unmistakable staccato sound of an assault weapon.

Dani stopped where she was, dropped down into a crouch, and put her hands over her ears.

"They're killing everyone," she moaned.

"No, no." Marissa squatted down beside her and tugged her hands free. Then she cupped the girl's chin and tilted her face up. "Look at me, Dani. They're a long way from everyone being dead. But if we want to fix that, you have to help us. Right? So, we need to get moving." She looked up at Justin. "Right?"

He nodded. "Absolutely. So, let's do it. Now."

Marissa took the girl's hand and squeezed it. "Trust us, Dani. We're going to do everything in our power to get these people. Come on, now. I've got you."

"How far is it?" Justin asked.

"You'll see it soon," Dani told hm.

Marissa and Justin followed Dani along the path until she stopped suddenly. "Here. This is it."

Marissa had to look twice at where the girl pointed. What she saw was another thicket of palm and fig leaf trees, with a variety of bushes filling in any spaces. If she strained her eyes, she could just make out stucco walls.

"What are they hiding from?" Justin asked Dani.

"Nothing." She shook her head.

"Dani." He put his hands lightly on her shoulders and turned her to face him. "That wasn't a trick question. And there's no wrong answer. I just need to know if there's something we should be aware of. Why is it so well hidden among all this greenery?"

She looked up at him. "Mr. and Mrs. Morganstern just think its appearance doesn't add to the beauty of the place. They want their guests to see nothing but beauty wherever they look."

"Okay. I can understand that. The door is around on the other side, right?" She nodded.

Marissa looked at Justin. "Dani should ring the bell and answer him. If it's a secure facility he won't open to a stranger, like she said before."

"Right." Justin looked at Dani. "Just tell him you have something to deliver from your boss."

"Okay." Then she let out a long breath. "I can do this. Whatever you need. I want to help you."

"Good girl." Marissa smiled at her. "Now let's get going."

Dani led them around to the front of the building and looked at Justin. He nodded. "Okay, Dani. Hit the button."

A moment later a voice came through the speaker box.

"Who is it?"

"It's me, Luis. Dani, from the kitchen."

"What do you want?"

"I, uh, have something for you from Mrs. Morganstern. Please buzz me in." Marissa looked at Justin and held her breath.

"Okay."

In a moment a buzzer sounded, and a click signaled the disengaging of the lock. Justin yanked the door open but nudged Dani in ahead of them.

"Dani, what do you have—" The man sitting at the chair in front of a huge bank of screens stopped talking in midsentence. "What's going on here?"

He yanked open a drawer and pulled out a handgun.

"Dani." He spoke without looking at her, his gaze fixed on Justin and Marissa. "Take my phone here and call security. What did they do to force you in here?"

Justin held up his hands, palms outward.

"We're not here to do any damage. Please. We need your help."

"Luis." Dani's voice shook. "There are bad men up at the resort with big guns and they are killing people."

The man stared for a moment, then yanked Dani to stand in front of his chair, pointing the gun over her shoulder.

Marissa bit her lip in frustration. Luis Bernal was not at all what she'd expected nor was his setup. She'd been looking for a type of handyman in typical work clothes, in a somewhat dingy mechanical environment. The room they'd walked into looked like mission control. The floor was tiled and along one wall was an array of more than two dozen mega-sized monitors. She had no idea what the images were on most of the screens.

Luis himself was also a surprise. Tall, with dark skin and black hair, he wore tan slacks and black collared shirt with the Rosewood logo embroidered on it.

What had they walked into?

"If you just give us a minute to explain," Justin began.

"Thirty seconds," Luis said. "Otherwise I use the gun."

"Bad men are killing people and they are going to save us if you help us." Dani got the words out in one long sentence without drawing a breath. "Please, Luis. These are not bad people. They got me away before I could be shot. We need to help them."

"Okay." Luis nodded, but he didn't put away the gun. "Talk."

Marissa looked at Justin, signaling him to explain. In concise sentences he told Luis just what was happening and what he wanted to do. What he needed to do.

"My team from the security agency is on their way," he told the man, "but it will be at least another hour before they can get here. I have to do something to throw these people off their game."

"What agency?" Luis asked.

Justin stared at him. "Excuse me?"

"What agency is coming? Who are they? Who are *you*?"

"Let me answer." Marissa turned to the man. "Do you remember when the Morgansterns' daughter was kidnapped and rescued?"

He nodded. "They were afraid they would never get her back."

"Justin is with the agency that brought her home. Please. We need you to trust us."

"And who exactly are you?" he wanted to know. "What are your names?"

"Mr. and Mrs. Kelly."

Luis glanced from one to the other. "You don't have first names?"

Marissa looked over at Justin. "We have to trust someone. That is if we want help."

He hesitated a moment, then nodded.

"Marissa Hayes and Justin Kelly. Justin is an agent with Vigilance. We came here to"—she looked at Justin again—"get away and now we're in the middle of a bad situation."

"We don't have any time to waste," Justin added. "I'm hoping you can help me."

Luis gave them a long, assessing look. Then, as if he'd made up his mind at last, he put the gun down on the long console that ran beneath all the monitors.

"I'm keeping that handy just in case you're screwing with me," he told Justin. "Tell me exactly what's going on."

When Justin had finished anger flashed in Luis's eyes. "Bad doesn't begin to describe this. Okay. What do you want from me?"

Justin looked at the wall of monitors. "I'm going to assume you control the entire electrical system from here?"

Luis nodded. "The security cameras and the electronics, too. Damn!" He sat up straighter. "I had a slight disconnect with the cameras a while ago. Just for a couple of minutes. I was going to radio one of the guards to check it out but then they came right back on."

"My guess? They had a jammer with them. They only needed the system offline long enough for them to get from the hangar to the resort proper."

"I should have had it checked out. Damn!" He slammed his fist on the console.

"Nothing you could have done," Justin told him. "All the guards on duty are dead."

Shock froze the man's features. "Dead?"

Justin nodded. "So, we need to get moving here before any more people die. If that's even possible."

"All right. Tell me what you want me to do."

* * * *

Maes had just had one of Raca's men escort the next person—make that practically carry, the man was so nervous—to the computer when the lights flickered for a moment. He shoved the man into the seat beside Desmet and looked around. The lights flickered again, twice, then went out completely.

"What the fuck?" There was still enough light coming in through the big windows that he could see the room. He strode over to where Walt Morganstern was sitting and yanked him up out of his chair. "What the hell is going on?"

Morganstern stared at him, a look so filled with venom Maes was tempted to have him shot right then and there.

"Sometimes the system has a hiccup. We're isolated from the mainland, so we have to have a self-contained situation. But every now and then, for whatever reason, the system gets a kink."

"Fix it," Maes ordered. "Right now."

But even as he said the words, the lights came back on again.

"Just a minor hiccup," Morganstern repeated. "As I said."

"If it keeps doing that we'll have trouble here. Keep that in mind."

He shoved the man back into his chair and returned to the man sitting next to Desmet.

"You are one of the last people I expected to turn on me, Simon."

Simon Dorne gave him an angry look, albeit one tinged with fear.

"We all have to protect ourselves, Maes. Isn't that what you always preached?"

"But judiciously, Simon. Intelligently."

"So it's both of those things as long as it doesn't affect you? Is that what you're implying?"

"I'm implying that I was the one who protected all of you. Even when the *schoopchino* CIA flexed their muscles and froze so many of my assets, I kept quiet." Maes stared down at the man. "I did so in the misguided belief the rest of you would band together and support me as I set up my new structure."

Dorne looked at him then shook his head. "You're going to, what, take everything we have, and then you'll be satisfied?"

Maes clenched his jaw to hold back the anger that wanted to burst forth.

"I might never be satisfied, but this is a start. Get busy. We have a list of every one of your businesses and accounts, just as we did for Eickner, so don't try to keep anything back." He looked over at the table where one of Raca's men stood, one hand on his assault rifle, the other resting on the .45mm stuck in his belt. "Do you need a little more incentive?"

"What do you mean?"

Maes nodded, and the man put the barrel of his gun against the temple of one of the women who had been sitting next to Dorne.

"No," the woman squeaked. "I'm not his wife. Please."

As if to emphasize what she said, the man next to her tugged on her arm and pulled her closer to his chair. The other woman paled but Maes was dismayed that she showed no fear. He thrived on fear, the greater the better.

Dorne half rose from his seat but Maes put a hand on his shoulder and shoved him back down. The gun barrel was now resting against his wife's temple.

"The quicker you get this done, Simon, the faster that gun will move away from your wife. I'd hate to see her brains splattered all over the dining room because you were stubborn." His lips thinned in a tight smile. "Wouldn't you?"

Swearing under his breath, Dorne pulled the laptop a little closer and began to type. He had just finished when the lights flickered again, this time staying off for more than a minute. Maes looked at Morganstern.

"Just a normal little glitch, is it? For an outrageously expensive resort, you have somewhat shoddy equipment."

Morganstern stood. "I'm happy to go and check on it for you. Make sure it doesn't keep happening."

"Sit down." Maes snapped out the words. "Val, bring up that diagram again."

When they were making preparations for this trip, Val had accessed a detailed map of the island and the resort.

"Got it," he said and pointed on the screen. "Here's the physical plant."

Maes looked at Walt Morganstern. "Is everything controlled from there?"

He watched the man struggle with how to frame an answer. "Well…that is…"

"The truth would be best, Mr. Morganstern. I'd hate to have to shoot your lovely wife because you lied to me."

Morganstern tensed and looked for a moment as if he wasn't going to answer, but then he nodded. "Yes. Everything is there."

Surely there was a workman around to take care of it.

"Who handles repairs for your electrical systems when something like this happens?"

Again, he thought the man was either going to refuse to answer or lie to him. But then he obviously remembered his wife in the hands of a gunman.

"I have an engineer who lives on premises, in the staff residences. When there is a problem outside of regular hours, I call him, and he takes care of it."

"So, he could fix whatever this glitch is?"

"Yes."

"How do you contact him? Is there a house phone system?"

"Yes, but I usually get him on the two-way radio." He looked pointedly at the garbage bag full of electronics. "Mine is in there."

"Get up here and find it. And don't get any big ideas."

Morganstern walked up to where the bag was, fished in it, and finally found what he wanted.

"Call him," Maes snapped. "Now."

Morganstern turned the little radio on and selected a channel. "Luis? Luis, this is Mr. Morganstern. Are you checking the physical plant? There seems to be a problem with the electricity."

Static crackled. Then an answer came back at him.

"I am already here, sir, and working on it."

"What seems to be the problem?"

More static.

"Nothing major. I am working on it right now."

Maes took the radio from him and shoved it in his pocket. He'd keep it in case they had more problems. Then he looked at the armed man closest to him. "Juraj. Take someone and go over there and find out what the fuck is the problem. If you have to shoot someone to get it done, don't hesitate. Just don't kill them because we need them to keep the physical plant operating."

Juraj looked at the screen to orient himself, nodded, and walked out of the restaurant.

Maes turned back to the room. People were shifting in their chairs, and he could see they were getting restless. When people became restless they did stupid things, like trying to rush intruders. He watched Eickner, his face twisted with pain. He'd seen his friend's wife killed and been shot himself, and all his money was gone. He would be a prime candidate to do something. He needed to remind Eickner that he, Maes, controlled the situation, and that it was not a good idea to do something that got people killed.

He looked at Raca who once again fired a burst from his assault weapon into the ceiling, startling the crowd.

"That's to remind you," he said, "in case anyone thinks there is a chance of overpowering us, catching us off-guard, that we are in control here. Anyone who interferes with this process will be shot. I think we've proven that to you. Now." He looked around the room. "Who is next?"

* * * *

"That was good," Justin said after the transmission with Morganstern was complete. "He didn't tell them you were already on duty. By the way, what do you do when it's more than a simple repair?"

"Bring someone over from the mainland. Rosewood has a contract with two different companies, depending on what we need."

"Okay. He didn't let them know that. Good."

Justin was standing behind Luis, eyes moving from one big screen to the other.

"Which screen monitors the cameras?" He pointed. "That one?"

Luis nodded. "Yes. With so few cameras we can have them all up at the same time."

"Can you put up one view and hold it?"

Luis nodded. "Watch." He typed something on a keyboard. In less than a second one image filled the entire screen. Another switch, and it was back to the original setup. "What do you wish to see?"

"I want to know if anyone is heading this way from the restaurant. Right about now Maes should be sending someone to check out the power."

Luis entered a command again, and suddenly, the view of the path from Rosewood filled the screen.

"Thanks. Now I need to get out there before they get here." He looked at Marissa. "You've got this?"

"Yes, but don't you want me out there with you? I can shoot, too, in case you forgot."

He shook his head. "No. I understand you can shoot, but I can't do my job if my mind is on what's happening to you. And it will be. You know that. Besides, I need you in here with Luis protecting this equipment and Dani." He looked over at the girl, sitting quietly in a straight chair. "Dani, your job is to stay here with Marissa and Luis, and watch the screens. If you see anything they miss, point it out right away."

He was sure Luis wouldn't miss anything, but he needed Dani inside and focused on something to keep her mind off what was happening.

If they'd had more time, he was sure Marissa would have argued with him about the arrangements, but even seconds were important right now. As they watched the screen, two of Raca's men in their black shirts and pants, outfitted as if they were ready for war, came into view from the rear of the restaurant.

"Go," she said. "We'll be fine in here."

Luis released the electronic lock on the door, and Justin slipped out. He heard the lock click back into place behind him. He wouldn't have more than this one chance, and he couldn't afford to screw it up.

The area in front of the building was small, by design just enough for one or two people to stand by the door. He had no idea what the shrubs surrounding the building were, just that they were tall and thick, and perfect for his purpose. He pushed his way into them until he had about three feet between himself and the doorway. He took a deep breath to steady himself, focused completely on the door, gun ready. Then he waited.

In what could not have been more than two minutes he heard feet crunching on the seashells in the path and the two men came into view. One of them tried the door, shaking the handle when it did not open. He said something to the other man in a foreign language. Then he pushed the button beneath the speaker box.

"You, in there. Open up for us."

Justin brought his gun up so he had a direct sight on the head of one of the men.

"Did you hear me? I said open up or we will blow the door open."

Justin took a deep breath, let it out slowly, and pulled the trigger twice.

Pop! Pop!

The man fell immediately. Before the second man could react, Justin had moved his hands, sighted again, and pulled the trigger twice more. Two more satisfying pops, and the second man collapsed to the ground. Justin moved out of the shrubbery and pressed the speaker button.

"Marissa? Now I need you out here."

The buzzer sounded but when the door opened it was Luis who walked out to join him.

"Hey, we can do this," Justin assured him. "You don't need to get involved. Things could get messy."

Luis looked at him with eyes so hard and cold for a moment Justin was startled.

"Listen," Luis said at last. "I lived in Cuba until I was eighteen. There's nothing I haven't seen. I'm just damn fucking glad my uncle got me out of there. These guys are heavy. You really want to waste your breath talking? What do you need?"

"Strip them of everything. Clothes, guns, ammo. They said they had explosives so get those and anything else you find."

They worked in efficient silence, and before long they had two piles of clothing, guns, bullets, Semtex, and small radios. Then they dragged the men deep into the thick, high shrubbery, covering them over with some of the broad leaves of the plants.

"Let's get this stuff inside," Justin said.

Luis took a small electronic device from his pocket, pressed it to the lock, and the door opened. Inside he cleared off a small table against one wall, and they placed everything on it. Justin set everything from one pile aside and began stripping.

"What are you doing?" Marissa moved over to stand near him.

"This one guy looked about my size. If you want to blend in with the enemy, you have to dress like them." He gave her a tight grin. "We learned it in Warfare 101."

He folded up his own clothes and put them with everything else. He, Luis, and Marissa began checking the weapons and other equipment. By the time they were finished he was dressed, with the assault rifle slung across his chest, along with extra ammo. One pocket held both pads of Semtex while the radio was shoved into another. His own Smith & Wesson plus one of the H&Ks were tucked into the small of his back.

"Ever fire one of these?" He held up the other assault weapon to Luis.

The man dipped his head once. "I was in the Army when I was younger. We learned to shoot everything."

Justin studied him. "And speaking of all that, you aren't exactly what I expected to find here."

Luis laughed. "Were you looking for a sweaty grunt who ran around with a wrench and a screwdriver?"

Justin's mouth tilted in a rueful smile. "Well, now that you mention it..."

"I could mess with your head and say I'm just dressed up for the day, which isn't too far from wrong. But the truth is, I did a tour in the Army, went to college, and got a degree in electrical engineering. I actually designed the power plant here when Rosewood was being built."

Justin stared at him, dumbstruck. "I'm sorry. Just—"

"No sweat. After we take care of this little problem we've got going on here I'll tell you all about it."

"Deal." He handed the other radio to Luis. "Monitor this. If I'm not here, you may have to fake it."

"Got it."

"Meanwhile, guys," Marissa broke in, "what's next? You said there are almost a dozen guys with weapons in the dining room. We've cut that number down by two and there are two more in the staff quarters. I still don't like our odds."

"The restaurant is the critical area," Justin told her. "We need to winnow their number down as much as we can. Let's see what happens when the two in the bushes don't come back."

The words had no sooner left his mouth than one of the radios crackled. Justin pushed the button to listen.

"Juraj? Come in." The voice was distorted but they could still understand it.

Justin pressed the Talk button. He thought it best to say as little as possible. "Yah. What?"

"Is the electrical under control?"

"Soon. Checking more."

He hoped his phony accent and short, clipped answers would disguise his voice.

"Get back here now. What are you waiting for?"

Justin didn't bother to answer. He had a feeling the man whose place he was taking wouldn't have, either. He was sure Stefan Maes expected unqualified obedience from his troops.

"One more thing." Justin scanned the controls on the console. "I don't know how your light system works. Can you kill the outside lights and leave all the others on?"

"I can. You want that now?"

Justin shook his head. "When Vigilance gets ready to jump, I'll give you the signal."

"Got it. Now what?" Luis asked.

"Now we need to up the stakes a little."

"What can I do?"

"I've been thinking. Let's play with the electricity once more, maybe shut it down for a minute again. Oh, wait." He snapped his fingers. "That will kill the air conditioning, too, right?"

Luis shook his head. "The AC is on its own generator. Both main generators are through that door." Luis pointed to a door to the left of his big console. "That way if we have an electrical failure for some reason, our guests won't sweat to death."

"What about the fire alarms?"

"The same but with battery backup. If we have a blaze the electrical would probably stop working anyway."

"Good. That gives us more than one thing we can drive him nuts with."

"If you want to throw Maes off," Marissa said, "you're going about it the right way. He hates it when things aren't under his control. Or when something happens to throw off his plans."

"We need him to be off kilter," Justin agreed. "That's when people make mistakes." When she still looked uncertain, he said, "Look. You and I both know that after he's taken care of business he's liable to just kill everyone in the restaurant." He rubbed his hand over his face. "I wish I knew how many people he's drained already so we had an idea of how much longer this will go on. Avery said eleven total, since Joubert is out."

At that moment his cell phone, which he'd shoved in the pocket of the pants, vibrated. He pulled it out and looked at the screen.

"Avery." He punched Talk. "The team on its way?"

"It is, but ETA isn't for another thirty minutes yet. Can you hold off until then?"

He snorted. "Do I have a choice? And we have no idea how far down his list Maes is or what he plans after that."

There was a long pause.

"Avery?"

"I'm sorry. Henri Joubert, the twelfth member of the group, had opted out of this trip because he was ill. Maes used that to execute his plan. He sent two goons to Joubert's house to hold his wife and daughter prisoner as long as Henri did what Maes asked. They had him call Rosewood and say he'd be arriving after all. They forced him to use his plane to Nassau and his helicopter from there, only Maes substituted his own pilots. About an hour ago some fishermen pulled Joubert's body out of the Caribbean. One of them caught his hook on what he thought was a big fish."

"Jesus!" Justin pursed his lips in a low whistle. "And the wife and daughter?"

Another pause.

"Brian Gould had someone go check on them. Both dead. Gunshots to the head."

"Oh, my God!" Marissa clapped her hands over her mouth.

"Gould is sending more reinforcements. He reached out to Interpol since Maes is on their watch list. And I just contacted Mike Perez and told him to have the pilot push that helo to its limits."

"It will be dark in another half hour," Luis pointed out. "Can they land in the dark?"

"Mike is going to have them do a HAHO jump. They're equipped for it."

"High altitude, high opening?" Luis raised his eyebrows.

Justin nodded, and held up his hand, mouthing, *One second.* "Have Mike call me just before they jump in case I have to update him on anything."

"Okay. And Justin?"

"Yeah?"

"Maes obviously doesn't know Marissa is there, or he'd have hauled her into the dining room already. But if he's on the warpath and she's spotted, I'm afraid of what he'll do to her. She may wish he'd killed her before it's over."

Justin glanced at Marissa, who had turned as pale as a ghost.

"I'll keep her safe," he assured Avery.

"Okay. Ten four."

Justin shoved the phone back in his pocket and looked at the other two people in the room.

"I have a gun," Marissa reminded him.

"You said that before, sweetheart. But unless I manage to take out all his henchmen before he spots you, it won't do you much good. Promise me you'll stay right in this building with Luis."

"And what if he sends two more guys with Semtex and they do what the first two threatened? Blow out the door?"

Justin took the other assault rifle and handed it to Luis. "Take one of the ammo belts on the table.

Luis took the weapon, checked it over with expert hands, checked the load and nodded. "Good to go."

"Okay, then." He handed the man the H&K .45 mm he'd retrieved from the same body. "Keep this handy, too. Although if they blow that door down and you hit them with the assault rifle, there shouldn't be anything left of them to mop up."

Luis studied the guns. "I wonder how happy Heckler and Koch would be to know how some of their weapons are being used."

"Not too, I'm sure. But once they're sold, the choice is gone." Justin checked his guns one more time. "Okay, guys. I'm outta here. I'm depending on you, Luis. I have to get down to the dock and get the keys from the runabouts, too. And do something about their chopper. That first. We can't give them any way off this island."

"What can I do?" Luis asked.

"For now? Take care of Marissa." He looked over at the girl standing next to her. "And Dani, too. I'll handle the rest."

Chapter 13

Maes glared at Oskar Berglund, sitting at the laptop next to Desmet. The man was sweating up a storm and his hands shook as he tapped the keys on the computer.

"A little faster, Oskar. I don't plan to spend all night here."

"I just want to know what your plans are after you've stolen all our money."

Maes shrugged. "I don't consider it stealing when it was my money to begin with."

Berglund rose from his chair, shaking but defiant. "Only part of it should have gone to you, if any. We still have to provide for our families. Run our businesses."

Maes glared at him. "You dare to even mention that to me? Your businesses?"

"This just proves one thing to me. You haven't changed much since you were a thug on the streets of Zagreb."

Maes took out his pistol, reversed his grip, and hit the side of the man's head. He screamed, fell down into his chair, and clapped his hand to his head. At once, blood ran over his fingers.

"Swine," a woman yelled at him from the table where Berglund had been sitting.

Maes shifted his gaze and stared at her, his hands itching to wrap themselves around her throat. He strode over to the table where she sat and stood by her chair, towering over her.

"I don't think you want to antagonize me, madam. The results will not be pleasant." He nodded to one of the henchman standing near him. "Goren will take very good care of you." He raised his voice a little. "And better care if you behave yourself."

At that moment the lights flickered and went out again.

"Motherfucking son of a bitch."

Maes picked up a water glass and threw it against a wall. The glass shattered, and water dripped down onto the floor. In the dim light he could see everyone watching him, waiting for his next explosion of temper. Temper! Him! Stefan Maes, the epitome of self-control. He needed to take a step back.

"Valentin."

Desmet looked over at him. "Yes?"

"Radio those two men and see what's going on now. Tell them the electric problem is obviously not fixed."

He waited as Desmet called on the radio. When no one answered, his blood pressure began to rise again. What the fuck was happening to him? For decades his trademark had been his icy composure.

"No one is answering," Desmet told him.

"I can tell that for myself," he snapped. Then he took a deep breath and let it out, pulling in the edges of his composure. He pointed at two of the men to his left.

"You and you. Get down there and see what the fuck is going on. If the other two idiots can't take care of things, shoot them. But don't come back until the electricity is working."

They nodded and raced out of the restaurant.

He looked over at where Berglund was sitting next to Val. "Is he finished?"

"Yes."

"Good. Have him escorted back to his seat. Who is next on the list?"

As shaky as Berglund was, he barely made it back to his table. One of the men he was sitting with came forward to help him. Maes wanted to shout that none of these men deserved any help after what they'd done to him, but he kept his mouth shut. He wanted this business finished so he could put an end to it all and get the hell out of here.

As he had been doing all evening he scanned the room, taking the measure of everyone there. There was a restless unease permeating the air. The women were fidgeting, and the men were scowling. If he had to shoot more people, he would. They meant nothing to him. He just hoped he wasn't forced to do anything more until every one of the men had transferred the money. A roomful of dead bodies wasn't necessarily an advantage. If people thought they had no hope of relief, they did crazy things, and he wasn't in the mood for crazy.

If he could just get his hands on Lauren Masters, he'd find out who was helping her. He still had connections. There were still enough people who wanted to curry favor with him out looking for her. She'd been found once. He could find her again.

Meanwhile, he still had important business to transact here.

* * * *

Deny, delay, contain.

Justin repeated those three words over and over silently as he made his way from the physical-plant building. One of the first things you learned when going on a mission where you were likely to encounter enemy combatants.

Deny. Deny the enemy the opportunity to continue their operation as normal.

Check. Interrupting the electricity had thrown them off. Next would come the air conditioning.

Delay.

Delay their actions so they cannot achieve their goal.

He was still working on that, but if he could manipulate the situation with the island's power enough to unbalance them, change things up, he could buy time until the Vigilance team arrived.

Contain.

Prevent them from having a means of escape.

He'd already put the first two in motion. Now he needed to take care of the third.

That meant disabling the helicopter as well as the runabouts at the dock.

He was sure they'd head for the chopper first. It was the quickest and most expedient way to get the hell out of there. It would take more time to get to the boats, at the far end of this side of the island, and it would be more time consuming. So, chopper first. Then, after he checked the situation up at the restaurant again, and figured out how to delay things even more, he'd see about the boats.

It took him longer than he'd like to get to the hangar, what with having to stay off the path to avoid the cameras. He had not seen a man in the dining room who could be the helicopter pilot. All the tables were filled with people who were obviously guests at the resort. In addition, there were Maes, his second in command, and his black-shirt troops. That meant the pilot would be at the hangar, waiting for the signal to warm the chopper for a fast liftoff.

Justin wanted to avoid killing the man if he could. He might work for Maes, but he most likely did nothing but his job as pilot. Still, he had to contain him and do something to the helo. Because he kept himself in top shape, he was barely winded when he reached the hangar, even in the last heat of the day. He could see the chopper, with Joubert on the side in script, sitting on the tarmac. No pilot, so he had to be inside.

Okay, he just needed to bluff enough to get close to the pilot and immobilize him. His black outfit ought to be a good disguise and not set off any alarms. He doubted the pilot had memorized the faces of the thugs, even if he'd flown them before.

He opened the door at one end of the hangar and stepped into blessedly cool air. A man in black slacks and a crisp white shirt was sitting in a chair, his feet up on another one, drinking from a bottle of water. He looked up when Justin came in.

"Is he finished already? He said it would be at least two hours."

"Some things take longer than expected." He walked slowly over to where the pilot sat. "He sent me to take care of something."

"Yeah? Like what?"

"Like this." His fist shot out and connected with the man's jaw. His head snapped back, and he was out cold in an instant. All that kickboxing had perfected his already lethal punch.

Reaching into his pocket, he pulled out the length of duct tape Luis had cut off and rolled for him. Ripping it into the correct lengths, he rolled the pilot to tape his hands behind his back, then wrapped another length around his ankles. He patted the man's pockets, found the outline of a key ring, and pulled out the key to the helicopter.

The man looked over at him, rage in his eyes.

"Sorry about this." Justin gave the duct tape over his mouth one more pat. "As soon as I can get this under control I'll send someone to let you free."

Next were the Rosewood helos. There were two of them in the hangar. He spent precious minutes searching for the keys and found none. He was sure they'd keep them at the office until needed but he'd had to check just the same.

He checked his watch. Ten minutes gone. He had no idea what kind of time schedule he was fighting or what was going on in the restaurant now and he needed to find out. Okay, check the restaurant then head for the dock. He was jogging fast along the path when his cell phone hummed in his pocket. He stopped, pulled it out, and checked the screen. Marissa. God, he hoped nothing had happened in these few minutes.

"You okay?" were the first words out of his mouth.

"Yes, but Luis has been watching the cameras. After that last little flicker of the lights, Maes sent two more goons to check it out. They're on their way now."

"We hoped that would happen, remember? It's easier to pick them off two at a time."

"Are you close to here?"

"Yes, but maybe not close enough. Tell Luis to put on his Army self and get out there in the bushes like I did. I'll take a little detour before heading for the boats. If they get there before I do, he'll have to take them both down."

"Done." Then she added, "Be careful."

He permitted himself a tiny smile. "Always."

He took off running toward the physical plant building, thankful that all the forestation was thick enough to conceal him. He was still a minute or two away when he heard four shots, in clusters of two.

Luis.

He arrived at the spot just as Luis was dragging one of the bodies into the shrubbery. But then he spotted someone dragging the other body and his heart nearly stopped.

"Marissa?" He grabbed her arm. "Are you crazy?"

"No, and I'm not helpless, either. I wasn't going to chance having the second guy shoot Luis. It only took seconds and as you can see, worked like a charm." She dropped the shoulders of the guy she'd been dragging, put her hands on her hips, and glared at Justin. "I am *not* going to put myself in danger. I am *not* going to do anything stupid. But I'm a crack shot, I can kick box, and I am not going to let someone get killed because I didn't help. So, shut up and deal with it."

Her eyes were shooting daggers at him. God, she was just incredible. Once they got out of this mess he was never letting another man near her ever again.

He didn't know whether to throttle her or kiss her.

She did step aside without an argument while he stripped the second man. Then the three of them carried everything into the plant building. They stacked the weapons and the other items on the table along with the remains of what they'd previously gathered.

"I promise you Maes is going insane about now," Marissa told him. "Just like I said before. I know the man. If everything doesn't go like clockwork according to his specifications, he'll kill someone as easily as shaking hands."

"Doesn't surprise me. So, we have to achieve a fine balance here. Okay, Luis, next is the AC. Wait about five minutes then shut it down." He looked at his watch. "I'm surprised Maes hasn't tried again to find out what happened to these other men. He's missing four of his goons. He's not stupid enough to just let them keep disappearing."

He barely had the words out when one of the radios crackled to life.

"Zagor. This is Desmet. What's happening? Did you find the others? What the fuck is going on down there?"

Justin nodded to Luis, who picked up the radio.

"Some problem...equipment. We are..." As he spoke, he continuously pressed the On/Off switch to simulate transmission problems.

"What? Repeat. You're breaking up."

"Trouble with...working...fixed soon..."

"Are you saying it will be fixed soon?" Desmet's voice had a hard edge to it. "Do you even know anything about it? What's wrong with your radio? And where are those two assholes we sent before? Raca will boil their nuts."

"...helping..."

There was a long silence from the other end.

"God damn it, Zagor. Do it and get your fucking asses back up here. And bring those two fuckers with you. You're not supposed to be having a convention down there."

Luis turned the radio off, dropped it on the console, and looked at Justin. "How long do you think before he sends someone else to check?"

"Depends on how long he guesses it will take to fix the power. I need to get up there and take another look at the scene. Figure out where he is in the process. Then I'll take care of the boats."

He started toward the door.

"Wait." Luis held up a hand. He sat down at the console, typed some commands into a keyboard, and a new diagram popped up on one of the screens. "Take a look at this."

Justin moved to stand behind the man. "What am I seeing?"

"A diagram of the electrical workings of Rosewood's main building. Look here." He used an electronic pointer. "On the main floor we left access, so we could work on wiring if we had to without taking the whole system down. See right here? There's a narrow space next to the kitchen and Sunset with a concealed door, just big enough for a man to fit into. If you can get through the kitchen without being seen, the door is right here."

Justin pulled out his phone and took a picture of the diagram.

"Will I fit in there with all this weaponry?"

Luis looked him over. "It will be a tight fit but yes, it can be accomplished."

"Justin." Marissa looked at the assault weapon slung against his chest and the rest of the firepower he carried.

"Don't worry. I'll be careful. I don't plan to open up in a roomful of people, regardless of what Maes does."

Then, despite the presence of Luis in the room, he cupped her face and kissed the life out of her, a hard kiss filled with emotion. When he released her she stared at him, a dazed look in her eyes. Then she skimmed her fingers over his cheek in a light touch.

"Be safe and be careful."

"Always." He winked. "I have something special to come back to."

He made his way to the rear of Sunset. The diagram had shown only one camera along the way, and he was careful to avoid it. He slipped into the kitchen, halting momentarily when he again caught sight of the body on the floor.

Damn it.

Well, there was nothing he could do for her. He had more urgent business. Feeling along the wall, he found the outline of the door, and pressed where Luis had told him the release was. The passage inside was narrow, a tight fit for him and all his equipment, but he made it, closing the door after him in case someone came into the kitchen.

He had just settled himself, one hand on his assault rifle, when he heard a burst of gunfire from the restaurant.

Shit!

He slid along the passage until he found the opening for the dining room and eased it open, just an inch, so he could see what was going on. Maes was standing in the far corner, flanked by two of his thugs. At the table directly in front of him were two men each with a laptop. He was pretty damn sure the one who looked like he'd been in a wreck was one of Maes's targets. The other was Valentin Desmet, Maes's alter ego.

Seated on the floor to the right were the kitchen and waitstaff, looking as if they expected to die any minute. There was a man with obvious gunshot wound, his leg propped up on a chair, and everyone else looked like they were barely surviving. The best he could say was the ugly goons with the assault weapons were four bodies short. But the rest of them still had their guns up and ready.

It was a big fucking mess. He looked at his watch. Theoretically, less than fifteen minutes until Mike and the Vigilance team arrived. Thank God, because no way could he take this army down himself, no matter how good he was.

Double shit!

* * * *

Maes felt his control fraying just a bit, but even that bit was more than he ever allowed himself. The fucking power had the lights flickering on and off and they could go any minute. Then he'd have another situation to contend with, because blackouts turned things upside down. Val was having unexpected trouble with the laptop they were using for the transfer of funds; he couldn't find the problem, and the whole process was taking way longer than he expected. He was on the verge of shooting someone else. Anyone. He didn't care who.

He scanned the room, as he did every few minutes, constantly trying to take the pulse of the situation. Instead of the restlessness he'd sensed earlier, now he read fear on everyone's face. There was no undercurrent of the whispered conversations he'd seen before. Good. That was what he needed. They were still barely halfway through the list at the moment, what with one thing and another.

It didn't help that he had now sent four men to find out about the power and none of them had returned. He was getting a bad feeling about that. It wasn't Rosewood's guards interfering. They were all dead. Someone was doing something, and he had to find out what. And soon.

He cleared his throat, and heads turned toward him.

"I sincerely hope no one is getting bored." His tone of voice was mild although he was feeling anything but. "We still have several more transfers to get through."

Nobody answered, just sat there, watching him. Okay, maybe he could take their edge off a little.

"Raca. Get a couple of the workers up and have them fetch water for everyone." When two of the wait staff, nudged to their feet by an assault rifle, headed for the kitchen, he added, "Do not think you are smart enough to try anything. My men have orders to shoot if anyone gets troublesome. The body lying in there should be enough of a reminder for you."

Both of them swallowed hard, but kept moving through the swinging door.

It would be full dark soon and that in itself presented a problem. He had to find out why his men were missing, finish this up, and get the fuck out of here. He had set himself a time limit, and they were fast exceeding it. Why were people such a pain in the ass?

He looked around the room. Two tables away from him Frank Woford sat next to his wife, his features set in a belligerent expression. Maes pointed at him.

"Frank, my so-called friend. It is your turn up here."

Woford sat up straighter, a scowl on his face. "And if I refuse? Where will you be then? There is no one else here who can access my accounts. No one else who has the passwords."

Maes kept his smile in place, but there was nothing friendly about it.

"You are absolutely right. I would be foolish to put a bullet hole in you before I have accomplished my purpose." He shifted his gaze. "However, your wife is certainly expendable."

The woman next to him clutched her husband's arms and all but crawled into his lap.

"You leave my wife alone," he spat.

"If you think I'm not as good as my word, you have only to look at the body of Van Baer's wife." He waited, but the man did not look like he was about to back down. He nodded to his henchman standing closest to her. The man took out his H&K and shot the woman in the shoulder. Her scream was enormously satisfying.

"Jesus Christ!" Woford shouted.

He grabbed a napkin from the table and used it to tie a tourniquet around his wife's arm. The man on the other side of her ripped the sleeve of her dress, then took his own napkin to press hard against the entry wound. The woman was still shrieking with pain, giant tears rolling down her face.

"You animal," Woford spat. "She needs a doctor."

"The same one can attend to Eickner's leg." Maes looked across the room at the man in question. "If it's still worth saving by the time one gets here."

"Let me at least get her some pain medication. Acetaminophen. Anything."

"Oh. You want a favor? Fine. Come up here and transfer your money, and then we'll see about some pain pills for her." The man still sat there. "Now," he snapped.

Woford stared at him for another moment. Then he leaned over to whisper in his wife's ear, and she nodded. Her screams had died down to moans, but the tears hadn't stopped. Maes had always found that the spouse was the person's most vulnerable spot. They would put their own lives on the line, but not that of a wife or husband.

The belligerence was gone from Woford's face, replaced by a look of pure hate. That was fine with Maes. He wasn't looking to win a popularity contest. He watched the man exchange words with the man on the other side of his wife. Woford stood up, and the other man hitched his chair closer to the wife, put his arm around her, and tried to brace her with his body. To position her in a way where she'd have the least pain.

"Get on with it." Maes nudged Woford with his elbow. "The sooner you finish, the sooner Mrs. Woford can receive some pain medication. If they all behave, perhaps none of the others will need it. "

He had chosen the words carefully, especially the last sentence, and spoken them loud enough for the entire room to hear. He saw a new wash of fear cross the faces of the people nearest him. Good. Being afraid made people compliant and that was what he wanted right now.

He looked over to where the Morgansterns were sitting.

"Raca." The man moved a step closer to hm. "Escort Mrs. Morganstern to wherever she keeps first aid supplies and have her get a bottle of acetaminophen or aspirin. Or whatever she has."

"I'll go." Morganstern stood.

"You will sit." Maes had barely raised his voice yet it thundered through the room. "Your wife will do the honors."

Morganstern looked at his wife. She smiled at him and patted his arm.

"It's okay," she said.

Maes found that for whatever reason she just pissed him off. Maybe he should have Raca or one of the others shoot her just because, after she fetched the meds. No. He was saving her for something special.

The woman rose gracefully from her chair and walked up to where Maes stood.

"I'm ready to be escorted."

Her composure irritated the hell out of him. Why wasn't she trembling like the other women? An unpleasant thought snapped through him. She reminded him of Lauren Masters. Calm, Collected. Unruffled, even in tense moments. He'd asked Lauren to accompany him to some of his board meetings, so she could get a feel for his businesses. The legitimate ones.

His board members were tough. He'd deliberately chosen them that way. At meetings they threw questions at her that a lesser person would have fumbled. Not Lauren. She was cool, collected, self-assured. He had even thought, at one point, she might make a perfect wife for him. He'd lay money on the fact beneath that icy exterior was a hot, passionate woman.

That was why her betrayal had enraged him so much.

He needed to forget her for the moment. Get on with the business at hand.

He nodded at Raca who stepped up, assault rifle at the ready.

"Fetch the medicine and be quick about it," he told her. "No monkey business or you'll come back with a few bullet holes in you."

She looked him directly in the eye. "You have nothing to worry about."

He watched her walk out, accompanied by one of his men, as if she was just going to fetch the mail.

Bitch!

He looked at his watch. His men had been gone too long to fix a simple problem. Something wasn't right here.

He looked at Morganstern, sitting in his chair like a stone statue, his face expressionless. Maes knew the man was worried about his wife, and with good reason. If they didn't fix the fucking equipment, she'd be the next to go.

"Morganstern. Can't you get that fucking equipment fixed? Is your man stupid? And he's got four of my people down there with him."

"I'm sure he's working on it as fast as he can." Morganstern looked at him, his face a mask. "Most of the time it can be fixed in just a few minutes. Maybe it doesn't like you being here."

"Don't get smart with me. I night have to take out a few more of your guests to make my point. And by the way." He turned to Val. "Isn't there a camera down there? Can't you see what they're doing?"

Val tapped the keys on the laptop monitoring the system then shook his head.

"The camera only focuses on the path from the back of this building around to the other side. There's nothing that shows the building where the equipment is."

"Goddamnit, Morganstern." He turned to the resort owner. "Why isn't there a camera down there?"

"The cameras are only for us to keep track of our guests in case they need help. They don't go near the physical plant. Sorry."

If looks could kill Maes knew he'd be dead right now. He opened his mouth to say something but suddenly realized there was a change in the atmosphere in the room. He was stunned to realize he was sweating. When he looked around he saw others mopping their faces or fanning themselves.

Now the damn air conditioning was out? What in the fucking hell was going on?

Someone was going to die for this, just as soon as he figured out who to shoot.

Chapter 14

Marissa paced the control room of the physical plant building, chewing her thumbnail. She kept checking the camera monitors, hoping for a glimpse of Justin, but all she saw was buildings and lush trees and shrubs. It was eerie not seeing people moving about, but everyone was in the restaurant or the staff residence building. The others were all dead.

A shiver skittered down her spine.

From the moment she had spotted Stefan Maes in the dining room she'd been battling a consuming fear. She knew deep in her gut that once he'd accomplished his purpose there was a good chance he'd get rid of everyone else. Right now, the threat of death was keeping them in line. But a half dozen of his men with assault rifles could take everyone out, and no one would break a sweat.

Her cell phone rang, startling her. Justin's name popped up on the screen.

"You're okay."

"I am." Just the sound of his voice assured her. "Tell Luis in three minutes to kill the camera feed again, count off three minutes then restore it."

"Won't they go nuts in the restaurant if that happens?"

"I'm pretty sure they'll think it's just another malfunction. Okay, on my way to the dock."

"Stay safe."

"Always."

Marissa relayed the message to Luis, who started the countdown clock he kept on the console. She watched, nibbling her thumbnail, until it hit the zero mark and he killed the cameras. Then he started the clock again. When it hit zero for the second time she was almost afraid to look. What if Justin hadn't been able to accomplish the task in that little amount of time? But when the screens came to life again all she could see at the docks was the boats. No people. No Justin.

She let out a slow breath. *Thank you, God.*

Two minutes later the buzzer rang, and she heard Justin say, "Luis, let me in."

She opened the door herself, and the moment he was inside, she threw herself into his arms.

He pulled her into a hard hug before letting her go.

"I'm fine," he assured her. "Still in one piece. What's going on?"

"The electric's working again," Luis told him, "but now I've shut down the AC."

"Good. Let's see what that stirs up. I'd guess we'll be hearing from Maes again any minute."

He carried one of the radios the thugs had with them, mostly so when he was out he could monitor anything that came over the air. The rest of them sat in a pile on the table along with the rest of the clothing. Suddenly one of them crackled to life.

"Halsey? Where the fuck are you? Drevna? Toma?" More static. "Damn it. Somebody goddamn better answer me or you'll be planning your own funerals."

"He's losing it," Marissa told him in a low voice. "That's not like him. Taking away his ability to control everything, like the electric and the AC, is getting to him."

"Good. That's when people make mistakes." Justin keyed the radio he was holding. "Working…problems…can't…"

"I don't fucking care what you can't do. Forget it." Maes sounded manic. "Get your fucking asses up here. We'll be through soon, and then they can take care of their own problems."

"Are you going to answer him again?" Marissa asked.

Justin shook his head. "Let's see what he does when now all he gets is radio silence. Maybe he'll be stupid enough to send someone else down here that we can eliminate."

Justin checked his watch again. They were down to five minutes now before Vigilance jumped, if they were on schedule. He had texted Mike the exact location of the best place to land. When he got the signal, he'd have Luis kill the outside lights and the cameras. This had to be timed perfectly.

"Okay. Here's what we'll do. Kick the AC back on now. As soon as I hear from the team, I'll text you. When I do, turn on the fire alarms, wait one minute, and then kill the outside lights. And Luis? This has to be done with precision timing. I need them off kilter in the restaurant, and I want you to be able to see if they send anyone else out looking for their missing men."

"Got it. I'll be ready for your signal." He paused. "And Justin? Good luck."

Justin snorted. "Thanks. I'll need it."

* * * *

"The air conditioning is back on," Desmet murmured to his boss.

"Thank fuck for that." Maes looked at the Morgansterns again. "You think you've seen pain tonight? You haven't seen a hint of what I'll do if we have any more screw-ups. And I'll start with your lovely wife."

He'd be done with the man and this entire resort as soon as the last transaction was completed. He knew the men had Semtex with them. Maybe he'd blow up the fucking resort and anyone not already dead.

"All right, Valentin." He turned to Desmet, sitting at the table. "Who is next?"

Desmet looked at the list. "Georgi Vitale."

"Ah, yes. Georgi." Maes smiled, although it was more of a grimace. Then he motioned to one of his men and pointed. "Please escort Signore Vitale to the table here and bring up his list of accounts."

Georgi was sweating profusely when Raca's man hustled him over to the indicated chair.

"You'll get yours for this, Maes," he growled.

"Really." Maes stared at him. "I don't think you are exactly in a position to be making threats, do you?"

Despite the fact that the man was sweating, that both his shirt and jacket were wrinkled, and his appearance disheveled, he still wore his cloak of arrogance. Maes wanted to smash his fist into the man's face.

"You think you'll keep us all in line by shooting people? Our wives? Killing people in front of us? You may have drained our bank accounts today but tomorrow we'll be back, stronger than ever. Count on it."

"Jesus Christ, Georgi." Simon Dorne stood at his table and shouted at Vitale, "Are you insane? Keep your fat, fucking mouth shut so we can get out of this, or I might shoot you myself."

Maes actually laughed. He couldn't help himself. Dissent in the ranks. He loved it. He might even give Dorne a gun himself.

Vitale swore under his breath, but he sat in the chair next to Desmet, looked at the list of his accounts, and frowning, began to transfer money.

Maes looked at Raca. "We're still missing four of your men. I can't believe they'd have gotten lost here. Something's not right." He looked at Morganstern again. "Does your man at the power plant have a gun?"

Morganstern shook his head. "Why would he need one here? We have no crime on this little island."

"Well, something is fucking off about this whole thing. The only answer is that someone took them out, but who in the hell could it be? It would take a skilled, trained soldier to do this." He looked at Desmet. "Tap into the registrations here and we'll check them against the people in the restaurant. See if there's a loner there."

He looked at Morganstern again, watching the man's reaction. Was that a flicker of something across his face? A movement or expression that would give him a clue?

"Got it," Desmet said moments later.

"Fine." His gaze swept the room again. "We're going to read off each of the names. When yours is called, stand up. I'm sure you have figured by this time I have no hesitation killing anyone who tries to get in my way."

Desmet began the roll call. By the time he reached the end, everyone had been accounted for.

Maes swallowed down his anger. Something was wrong, and he was damn well going to find out what. He looked over at the two laptops and saw that Vitale had finished his transfers. He was so tempted to shoot the man just on general principals. If he did that, however, the last couple of names on the list would balk at making their transfers, sure they'd be killed anyway. Maes knew if you just held the threat of death over their heads, you could get people to do almost anything. He could kill them all later.

"Who's next?"

He waited until the next person was seated before lifting a glass of water from one of the trays and taking a sip. For the first time in more years than he could count, he felt his composure slip a fraction. This was supposed to be a simple affair, well planned and well executed. Things had gone wrong almost from the beginning, and he had the disturbing feelings things were slipping from his control.

What the hell was wrong with the power and utilities on this place? And where were his men? At first, he had assumed there was a bigger problem with the power plant than they wanted to let him know and they were manhandling whoever was in charge to make sure things kept working until they were finished.

But it was taking a damn long time. He looked at his watch. Too long. Sending another man out to check would only compound the problem.

He still had a niggling feeling he was missing something. That someone else was on the island he did not know about. There had to be. And that someone was going to wish he'd never fucked with Stefan Maes.

"Call Zagor again," he told Raca. "Tell him they should just kill the mechanic who can't seem to fix things and get their asses back here. I don't know why they're still there. Do they think this is a vacation? We'll be done soon. We can stand a little discomfort until then. I want them back here at once."

Raca pulled his radio from its clip on his belt and keyed the mic.

"Zagor? This is Raca. Mr. Maes is done waiting. I don't know what the fuck is the problem down there. Just kill the mechanic or whoever is supposed to be fixing this shit and get the fuck back here right now. And bring everyone else with you or just shoot them. I don't care which. If they haven't been able to take care of the problem up to now I don't need them."

Nothing from the radio. No response.

"Zagor? Answer this goddamn radio or I'll kill you myself."

Still no answer. He looked at Maes for further instructions.

"Fucking assholes. Someone else is out there. It's not possible that four men who work for us are so incompetent they can't get this done."

"But who?" Raca asked. "We killed the guards and the employees are either in this room or herded into one room at the staff residence. All except the fucking mechanic who keeps screwing up the electricity."

"There has to be someone else out there. Someone we don't know about. Someone who it seems is not in the computer system." He glared at Walt Morganstern. "You want to tell me who that is, Morganstern? You're the owner here. This place is secluded enough that you don't have strangers just showing up and running around."

Morganstern just stared back at him. "You know every single person on this island by now."

"Boss?" Raca nudged him. "Maybe someone swam here."

Maes stared at his top gun. The man was a stone killer, and he trusted him with his life, but sometimes he was downright stupid.

"Do you know how many miles it is to the closest village? Don't be an idiot. I'll fix this." Maes ground his teeth then grabbed the radio. "I know someone is out there listening and fucking up my project. Whoever you are, you'd better show yourself right now. I am not playing games here. I will kill one person for every minute it takes you to answer me."

He waited, and when there was no answer he depressed the button again and ordered one of the men to fire a shot in the air.

"Did you hear that, asshole? I don't care if I have to kill everyone here, but their deaths will be on your head."

More silence, then the crackle of static.

"Don't kill anyone. I'm on my way."

* * * *

"Don't go. Please, Justin. Think carefully about this."

Marissa was doing her best to hold on to her nerves. She knew when Justin walked into that restaurant Maes would kill him.

"I am, and I have to do this. I can't have the deaths of all those people on my head. You know Maes. Will he follow through on his threat?"

She wanted to say no, but she knew better. Swallowing, she nodded her head. "At least wait for Mike and the team to get here."

"No can do. Think of how many people Maes can kill with each minute that passes." He cupped her chin and brushed his mouth over hers. "And I have to keep him from getting to you. All I need to do is stall until Mike gets here."

"But—"

"No buts. I have to go now. I promise it will be okay."

She wrapped her arms around him, wanting to hold him pressed to her forever, even as she knew he was right. She forgot there were two other people in the room. Forgot everything except the devastation she'd feel if Maes killed him.

"I don't know what I'll do if I lose you." She hugged him more tightly, relishing the warmth of his body and the feel of his arms holding her. "Somehow when I wasn't looking you stole my heart."

"Hey." He cupped her chin and tilted up her face. "That's only fair, since you also managed to steal mine. And I promise you, I'll get us out of this. I want a future with you."

She studied every inch of his face, memorizing it. "You can't promise me that. Maes is—"

He touched the tip of a finger to her lips. "Yes. Whatever you're going to say about him, I'm sure he's that in spades. But I was a SEAL, remember? SEALs are survivors and know a thousand different ways to grab control of situations like this. So, have faith in me."

"I do," she whispered. It was Maes she had no faith in.

Justin cupped her face in his hands. "Mike and the team are due any minute. Listen to me. I need you to be Lauren Masters for a little bit, wearing your CIA hat. I'm leaving the sat phone with you to connect with them. I'm depending on you to get them there in time to save my ass." He stared into her eyes. "But don't go jumping the gun. Mike will get here in plenty of time."

But Mike hasn't even jumped yet. I'll have to handle things. I can do anything as long as Justin comes back to me safe and sound.

She sucked in a deep breath and pulled herself together. She could do this. She'd been in dicey situations in London. This was just different geography. She *had* to do it. For Justin. For both of them.

"Okay." She nodded. "Tell me what you want me to do."

Before Justin could say anything, his sat phone vibrated. He looked at the readout. Mike Perez.

"I'm putting this on speaker." He punched a button. "Mike?"

"Ready to jump. Sitrep. How copy?"

"Copy five by five. Situation has changed."

"What the fuck?"

He gave Mike a brief rundown to catch him up, but even as he did it, the radio spat out static followed by Maes's voice.

"You have one minute to get up here before I pull the trigger and you have yet one more body to deal with. I promise you I am not fooling around here."

"You know he's not," Justin told Marissa. "And he sounds like his nerves are fraying. That's not good." He handed both electronics to Marissa and gave her a hard kiss on the lips. "I gotta get up there. It's up to you now, babe. I know you can do it."

Then he was gone, out the door and racing along the path to the main building.

If only she'd convinced him to wait for Mike, but even as she thought it she knew he'd run out of time.

She could do this, despite the accelerated beat of her heart and the fear for Justin's safety that held her in its grip. Justin was counting on her. She could be again the person who had lived on the edge of danger for three years getting the information to take down Maes. For Justin she could be Lauren Masters again and do whatever she had to do.

She checked the load in her gun again and put it in the pocket of her slacks. Then she picked up one of the handguns the thugs had been carrying, checked its load, and stuck it in her waistband at the small of her back. Despite Justin's orders, she wasn't going to sit around here waiting for Mike and the team. She had a plan. As soon as they were on the ground, which should be any second, she'd put it into play.

* * * *

Justin debated the best way to enter the restaurant, but in the end, decided coming through the main entrance was the best. He also ditched the idea of taping a gun to his back a la Bruce Willis in *Die Hard*. The minute he set foot in Sunset, Maes's men would take charge of him, and the gun would be useless. He couldn't shoot them all at the same time.

Instead he was depending on Marissa, and on Mike Perez, who was unequalled as a team leader, to get there in time to save his bacon. He just had to hold out until the team arrived.

Sure.

Piece of cake.

When he stepped into the restaurant he took in the scene at once. Maes was standing against the window wall to his left, with one of his thugs on either side of him. He had seen pictures of Maes, but they didn't accurately portray the cold cruelty etched in the man's features. His carriage, his attitude, all shrieked arrogance and cruelty.

At the table to Maes's immediate right Val Desmet still sat at a laptop, watching another man typing away on another computer. The rest of the guests still sat at the other tables, looking much the worse for wear. Their expressions were a mixture of fear, despair, and outright terror.

Justin wanted to choke the life out of Maes with his bare hands. Maybe, if things worked out, he'd at least get to break his nose.

He had barely stepped into the room when Maes saw him. His lips curved into a smile that held little humor.

"Ah. Here is the man who has been causing us so much trouble. Raca? If you please."

In seconds the very tall goon at Maes's right was beside him jerking one of his arms behind his back and frog-marching him over to where Maes himself was standing. In the next second he was shoved to his knees.

"Hands behind your back," the thug ordered.

In a moment Justin felt flex cuffs tightening around his wrists. Great. This was not going to be much fun.

Justin complied, not about to antagonize anyone at this point. His job here was to stall as long as he could without inciting any more bloodshed.

"Wait a minute." Maes pulled his cell phone from his pocket, tapped the screen, and pulled something up.

Justin caught a glimpse of the screen and saw it was a photo. Of who? And where was it taken?

Then Maes shifted his gaze back to Justin.

"Son of a bitch." Maes stared down at him. "You are the one in the photo with the bitch." He held it in front of Justin's face. "How did you get her away so fast? My people had just found her. She's here, isn't she? Answer me."

Justin looked at the photo and his heat nearly stopped beating. Fucking A. It had been taken at the Driftwood, when he and Marissa were at lunch with Avery, most likely by the couple whose appearance had started this whole episode. Marissa had been spot-on about them. So now Maes had someone connected to Marissa in his grasp. He could not let Maes believe she was on the island. The man would send one of his killers out to look for her and...

He gave himself a mental shake of the head. *No, no, no, no.*

"Answer me, damn it," Maes barked. "If you are here, she has to be also. A perfect place for you to hide her from me. You must have had her on a helicopter five minutes after my people spotted her."

Justin shook his head. "She's not here. I'm here by myself."

There was little humor in Maes's laugh.

"Really? You expect me to fall for that lie? So, tell me where the fuck she is. I'll overlook the way you've screwed things up for me tonight if you hand her over."

Yeah, right. Like that would happen.

"I told you, I'm here by myself." No matter what, he had to make Maes believe that. It didn't matter if he died. Marissa would get over him. But if he was responsible for her death? He'd never be able to live with himself. Maes could torture him but he'd never confirm she was on Princessa Key. His only hope was that Mike would arrive shortly, and they could take control of things here.

"The Morgansterns hired me to do a security survey of the island. They didn't want their guests to know what I was doing so I'm here off the radar."

"What a crock of shit." Maes's laugh had little humor in it. "Please do not think I am stupid enough to believe that."

Justin clenched his jaw and said nothing. He was better off keeping his mouth shut and letting Maes flap his jaws.

"What a shock it must have been for you both to discover I had arrived here." He frowned. "Just how did you learn of it, anyway, since you didn't come to the restaurant? No one knew we were making this, shall we say, surprise visit today."

Justin used all his training to control his breathing. One wrong step here, and Marissa would be dead. He just stared up at the man in front of him, his face showing nothing. Yeah, he was good at that. He'd had years of experience.

"Still not talking? I know she's here, probably hidden away. And I promise you, I will find out from you where. Then you can watch me kill her one painful minute at a time."

Maes nodded at Raca, who closed his hand into a fist and connected with Justin's face. Justin's head spun, his brain rattled, and he fell to the side. Raca grabbed him by his collar and hauled him back to his kneeling position.

Justin had been in situations like this before. He knew how to control his reflexes and to take himself out of this mentally. Hell, SEAL training was tougher than this, and Mike would be here soon. As long as Marissa was safe he could do this.

"We can do this all day," Maes told him in a measured voice. "Raca is like a machine. But I don't know how much your body can stand. Now. Again. Where is Lauren Masters?"

Chapter 15

As soon as Justin was out of the facility, Marissa began counting down. When she got to two minutes she turned to Luis.

"Whatever you do," Marissa told him, "do not open this door. But in case one of those assholes shows up with Semtex, keep one of those assault weapons at the ready."

"Whatever you're planning," he said in a slow voice, "I don't think I'm going to like it."

"All you have to do is be prepared to shoot Maes or any of his men who come through that door."

"Marissa. You can't leave until Mike gets here. Justin said so."

Dani's soft voice in the corner startled her. She was amazed at how quietly the girl had sat through all of this. She had to be shocked by everything that was happening, especially when Luis and Justin killed the four goons.

"I'll be fine, Dani," Marissa assured her, and tried her best to believe it. "I promise you. You've been great sitting there through all of this. Just let Luis keep protecting you and you'll be fine."

"I won't be fine if you and Justin get killed," Dani protested.

"Not gonna happen." Marissa forced a smile. "I promise."

"You can't make that kind of promise."

"Yes, I can, and you can believe me." If only she believed it herself. But she couldn't sit around here any longer, not when Justin was at Maes's mercy. She was still a crack shot, and she'd learned plenty about stealth in the CIA. Every second they had to wait put Justin in even greater danger.

"Where are you going?" Luis asked. "As if I didn't know."

"Up to the restaurant." She shook her head when he opened his mouth. "Don't try to talk me out of this. I have to make sure Maes doesn't kill Justin before Mike and the team get there."

"And if Maes gets his hands on you?"

She looked hard at him. "I've got two guns. Before he touches me, I'll kill him."

Luis sighed, then buzzed the door open. "Please try not to get yourself shot, okay?"

Her mouth curved in a tiny grin. "I'll do my best. Shut down the lights and cameras now."

"But Justin said—"

"Things have changed. And Maes will think it's the electricity being wonky again. Or if he doesn't, I'll be up there before he can do anything."

She opened the door and slid out into the night. As she did so, the lights went out. Good. No way was she waiting for anything or anyone. She made her way quickly to the main building, the cell phone in her pocket set on Vibrate. She had just reached the back door of the building when she felt it shake against her thigh. She pressed Answer.

"This is Marissa. Status, please."

"On the ground. Where the hell's Justin?"

She had to swallow twice to get the words out.

"At the restaurant. Maes threatened to shoot someone every minute until he showed his face."

"Does he have any way to connect the two of you?"

"I don't think so, but I don't know. Mike, you have to get the team moving. I don't know how much longer Justin has before Maes gets tired of him and just has one of his men kill him."

"On our way. Four minutes until we are in position. No more. Where are you?"

"At the rear of the main building."

"What the fuck, Marissa? I'm damn sure Justin told you to stay put until we landed."

"Yes, well, right now he's in no position to give me orders. Going dark right now."

She knew Mike and his team would be here in scant minutes. These Vigilance teams didn't mess around. All former military, their training was what made them so good at their jobs. There were just seconds for her to make her move. But what if—

She shook her head. Don't go there. Focus. Just focus.

She slipped in through the back door, made her way through the kitchen and up to the swinging doors into the restaurant. She had the H&K ready in her hand, opting for its greater power than the Glock's. When she peeked through the tiny space between the doors, her heart nearly stopped. Directly across from her, Justin was on his knees in front of Stefan Maes. Even as she watched, one of the black-clothed thugs, this one bigger and taller than the others, drew back his fist and punched Justin in the face. Justin fell sideways, and when the piece of garbage hauled him back to his knees again, Marissa got a sideways glimpse of his face and almost passed out. Even worse was the puddle of blood beside him. Had they shot him?

She tried to count down in her head how long since she'd spoken to Mike. They had to be ready now, right? When she realized the man who'd punched Justin had a bloody, long-bladed knife in his other hand, she knew she couldn't wait any longer. Now she knew where the blood had come from. He'd already stabbed Justin once and was getting ready to do it again. She couldn't let that happen. Kicking open the swinging doors, she leveled her gun at the thug and fired off two shots, hitting him in the arm and the hand holding the knife. He dropped the instrument, swearing in a foreign language, which, knowing their background, she figured was Croatian.

Marissa shifted so her back was against the wall, but she still had a good view of everything.

Maes stared at her. "There you are, you goddamn fucking bitch. I knew you were here as soon as I realized this was the man in the picture with you."

She frowned. Picture? What picture?

As if he'd heard her thoughts, Maes held up the phone he still had in his hand.

"This picture. How the fuck did you know we were on to you? Did someone warn you, so you could do that disappearing act almost before that photo reached me?"

Marissa wet her lips.

Never let them see you sweat.

That had been her motto since she entered business school, and it had always stood her in good stead.

"What?" Maes raised his voice again. "Nothing to say? It's your face Raca should be rearranging. You ruined everything."

"Apparently not enough." She swept her gun back and forth, trying to keep everyone on the goon squad in sight.

Just as she was trying to figure out who to shoot next, the sound of breaking glass filled the air and the Vigilance team smashed into the restaurant. She heard the rapid chatter of assault weapons and the crack of handguns. When she looked she saw the Vigilance agents spreading out everywhere in the restaurant, pushing people to the floor as they downed one tango after another. Women were screaming, men shouting, more gunfire.

Marissa was focusing on Maes and saw one of the Vigilance agents grab him. Maes managed to pull away from the man trying to flex cuff him. He yanked a small handgun from his pocket and aimed it at Justin. Marissa reacted at once. She fired two shots again, in rapid succession, hitting Maes's hand and arm.

"You fucking bitch," he yelled again. "You think you're rid of me now? Forget it. I'll get out of this like I do everything else. Then I'm going to hunt you down and dismember you one limb at a time."

He was still screaming epithets at her, cradling the arm and hand against his body, when she felt arms around her and a hand closing over her gun.

"It's me, Tiger," a familiar voice murmured in her ear. "Bad guys are all taken care of. You can stand down."

She stared at Maes, now being wrestled from the room by one of the largest Vigilance agents she'd ever seen.

"Pay no attention to him," Mike Perez said. "This is the last daylight he'll see for a long time. Maybe forever. He's got a lot of crimes to answer for and Interpol is anxious to get their hands on him."

She tried to pull away. "I have to get to Justin. He's been stabbed and there's blood all around him."

"One of my guys is taking care of him as we speak. Look over there. See? Come on."

She handed him the H&K and hurried over to where Justin was now stretched out on the floor. When she got a look at his face she had to swallow back the nausea. Taking a deep breath, she knelt on the side opposite from the man treating him.

"Justin? I'm right here." She put her mouth close to his ear, and would have reached for one of his hands except the guy working on him nudged her arm away.

"Justin?" Mike asked. "Can you hear me, buddy?" He looked at the man working on Justin's knife wound. "Sitrep, please."

"It's not good. That blade is more than twelve inches and he shoved it in sideways. It got a lot of the blood vessels and I have no idea how many organs are compromised. Right now, I need to stop the bleeding, or at least slow it until we can get him to a level one trauma center."

"What can I do? Please let me do something."

"Here." He handed her some gel packs. "Keep these on his face while I work on the wound. We'll pack them against him when we get him in the chopper."

She was only vaguely aware of what was going on in the restaurant. The Morgansterns were moving from table to table, soothing their guests, and checking everyone's needs. Little by little they were being escorted out of the restaurant. Marissa was sure none of them would sleep easily tonight. Nor would they forget what had happened here.

She studied Justin's face. "He's not conscious, is he?" Statement, not question.

"No, but in a way, it's a blessing. We don't have to depress his vitals with pain meds." He wrapped another row of wide tape across Justin's chest and stood up. "Okay, we're gonna boogie. Stand back, please."

"We're going to transport him to the chopper right now," Mike told her. "Come on. They need to get him on the litter."

"I'm not leaving him," she insisted.

The other agent frowned. "I don't—"

"It's okay." Mike helped her to her feet. "She can go with him in the chopper. Marissa, I sent one of the guys back to the helo to warm it up. They can load the stretcher right into it. Just let us get him set. The owners have a couple of trucks they keep on the island for moving big items around. They had someone bring it around for us. Come on."

Yeah, let's get to it," the other man said. "We need to leave five minutes ago."

She stepped to the side only long enough for two men to move Justin to the makeshift stretcher. Then she hurried out to the truck with them. One man climbed in the back next to the stretcher and someone else helped Marissa up into the cab where another agent was behind the wheel.

"Hold him steady," she called to the man in back.

"Yes, ma'am. We'll take good care of him."

She was a nervous wreck until they got to the place where a large helicopter sat, lights on, waiting, the rotors already idling. As soon as they had the litter strapped down, an agent beside it, tucking gel packs around Justin's badly swollen face, Mike helped Marissa in.

"You can sit up front in the copilot seat," he told her.

She shook her head. "I'm riding with Justin."

"Joe's got it. Justin's in good hands."

She shook her head again. "Help me into the cabin."

"Mike," the man beside Justin began. "I'm not sure…"

"It's all good," Mike told him. "Just get going."

"Got it."

"You're not coming with us?" she asked him.

Mike shook his head. "We have a lot of cleanup to do. And, we'll help the Morgansterns take care of the guests here. Two people are wounded. There's a medic on one of the choppers coming from Gould. Plus, Avery said Gould wants us to help his guys debrief the men who were the targets of all this. They should be getting here..." He looked at his watch. "Any minute now. So get going."

"Will he—" She stopped and wet her kips. "Will he make it?"

"Yes. At least I'm pretty sure. He's a tough guy, Marissa. My money's on him."

"Thank you."

"Okay. You're good for liftoff. Radio with an arrival time when you're on your way back," he told the pilot.

"Got it."

He slid the cabin door closed and banged on it to let the pilot know they were all set. Seconds later they lifted off.

Marissa was sitting cross-legged beside the stretcher, holding Justin's hand when the agent monitoring him cleared his throat.

"Uh, Marissa? You might want to ask the hospital if they've got some scrubs you can change into when we get there."

"What?" She frowned.

He gestured at her clothing. "It's a little, um..."

She looked and was startled to see big splotches of blood on her blouse and slacks. God. So much blood. Again, nausea threatened but she swallowed it back. She had to stay focused. For Justin.

The trip seemed interminable. Joe, the agent in the cabin with them, kept checking Justin's pulse and making sure the field dressing was okay. About twenty minutes into the flight he changed it from the kit beside him. Marissa felt ill when she saw how soaked it was with blood.

"He's okay," Joe tried to assure her.

"But so much blood can't be good," she whispered.

"He's not hemorrhaging. It looks worse than it is."

If only she could make the helo fly faster. With every passing moment, Justin's situation became more critical. She crouched on the floor next to him the entire time, holding his hand and praying. She heard the pilot on his radio every so often. About the time she was sure she would explode if they didn't get to a doctor, the pilot hollered back that they were coming in for a landing.

She gripped Justin's hand even harder, and she noticed Joe was paying careful attention to the stability of the stretcher until the touchdown. Then the pilot slid open the cabin door and gently but firmly nudged her away from Justin. Strangers' hands helped her out and eased her to the side as they lifted him out of the helo. She looked around and saw men and women in scrubs waiting with a wheeled stretcher. In what seemed like seconds they had him settled and were rushing him through the open rooftop door.

She ran after them, heart beating wildly.

"Wait! Where are you taking him?"

"Surgery," someone called back to her. "Waiting room on the third floor."

"Marissa?" Joe touched her arm. "Go on. Here's Avery."

She looked, and sure enough, there was Avery hurrying through the door. The first thing she did was wrap her arms around Marissa. Then she waved at Joe, who climbed back in the helo. Seconds later, it lifted off.

"Thank you for being here," Marissa told her as Avery guided her into the building.

"Well, of course. Where else would I be, but here with two of my favorite people?"

Marissa blew out a breath. "You have no idea how hard it was for me when he decided to go up to the restaurant alone."

Avery took her hand. "From what Mike told me, I don't think he had a choice. Justin would never have been able to live with himself if he let Maes shoot all those people."

"I know. I keep telling myself that. Then I keep asking what unbelievable fucked-up fate had Maes coming to this place he'd never been to before when I was there hiding from him."

Avery snorted. "If you ever find an answer to that, let me know. We have situations like that all the time. It's one of the reasons Vigilance is always so busy." Then she smiled at Marissa. "I did get word, though, that you managed a few well-placed shots. Good girl."

"I'd have been there sooner, but I had to wait for Mike and the team."

"As well you should. No hotshots in this rodeo. You did good, both of you. And he's going to be just fine. Now come on. Let's get to the third floor. And you need to change your clothes."

That was the last thing on her mind at the moment. All she could think of was the image of Justin lying on the floor bleeding out, his face battered and swollen, his pulse so weak.

"Avery, how soon do you think we'll know anything?"

"That's hard to say. But we've got one of the finest surgeons working on him. And he made it from Princessa to here so that's good."

Marissa looked around. "Where exactly is here?"

"Memorial Hospital in Sarasota. They have a level one trauma center and I wanted the absolute best care we could get." She lifted the little tote bag she'd been carrying. "Meanwhile, you might want to change out of those clothes and give them to me to burn."

Marissa let out a sigh. "I guess. But I don't want to miss the doctor."

"I promise you, there's plenty of time for you to clean up and change. There's a ladies' room right across the hall. Do you need me to come with you?"

"No. Thanks." She managed a tiny smile. "I think I can do this by myself."

"Okay." Avery handed her the tote. "But holler if you need me."

In the restroom Marissa took a good look at herself in the mirror and wanted to throw up. Her makeup was smeared and underneath everything she was paler than a hospital sheet. She had left without her purse. That had been the last thing on her mind at the time.

Well, she'd just have to do the best she could. She yanked off her ruined clothes, stuffed them in the trash, washed her face and hands, and pulled on the jeans and T-shirt Avery had brought. What she really wanted was a long, hot shower, but that would have to wait until she knew what Justin's condition was.

"Much better," Avery told her when she walked back into the waiting room. "At least you won't frighten the nurses anymore."

She dropped into the chair beside Avery. "You know it's my fault he nearly died."

Avery stared at her. "Are you crazy? Where did you get that insane idea?"

"Facts are facts. He was at Princessa Key because of me. And he was protecting me when he went to the ballroom and nearly got himself killed."

Avery sighed. "Marissa, that's his job. He took the same risks when he was a SEAL. Even if you weren't there, Justin would be protecting everyone else."

"But if Maes wasn't chasing me we wouldn't have been—"

"Enough." Avery turned in her chair. "Marissa, look at me. Justin takes those kinds of risks every day. The same situation could have happened on any assignment. So, I don't want to hear any more about feeling responsible for any of this. The only one responsible is Stefan Maes."

"This might help settle your nerves."

Someone held out a go-cup of coffee. She looked up and recognized the man she'd met at lunch what seemed a lifetime ago.

"Blake. Right?"

He nodded. "My wife and I happened to be in Avery's office when Justin called for reinforcements. My wife has worked on assignments with him a few times and knows him well. She wanted to come here to see what his condition was and maybe give you a little moral support." He nudged the cup at her. "Here. It beats anything the hospital provides."

Marissa wrapped her fingers around it, absorbing the heat and wondering if she'd ever feel warm again. But when she sipped the liquid, she blessed the heat spreading through her.

When she looked up to thank Blake she realized his wife was with him. "Thank you both for coming. Sam, right?"

Sam Quenel Morgan smiled. "Yes. I'm surprised you can remember anything in this situation." She sat down beside Marissa and took her hand. "I heard you say you feel responsible. Trust me, this one is not on you. From what I understand, it was the coincidence of the century that the men he was after picked this weekend to be in the same place where Vigilance tucked you away. Probably wouldn't happen again in a million years."

"You can't control everything," Avery reminded her. "Would you feel better if you were still hiding and he'd been shot breaching the room?"

"Yes. No." She shrugged. "I don't know."

"Right. So what you have to concentrate on right now is sending positive healing thoughts to Justin so he'll recover fast. Now drink your coffee before it gets cold."

Marissa had no idea how long they sat there. Blake Morgan and his wife spoke in low tones, but she was too numb to listen. All she could do was pray. And hope.

It felt as if they'd been sitting there for a week when a woman in scrubs came to the waiting room door.

"Family of Justin Kelly?"

Marissa wanted to leap from the chair, but she was frozen in place, trying to decipher the expression on the doctor's face.

"That's us," Avery said, urging Marissa from the chair. "You're Dr. Thornton?"

The woman nodded, and smiled. "And I have good news for you."

"Is he going to be all right?" Marissa could barely get the words out.

"Yes, he is." The doctor heaved a little sigh. "I have to say it was touch and go for a while. The knife hit several blood vessels and nicked a lung and his spleen. We were able to repair the damage, although we had to remove the spleen. He has a long recovery ahead of him, but I expect in the end he'll do just fine. He's in excellent condition."

"But there was so much bleeding," Marissa told her.

"As I said, it hit a lot of veins. The thrust of the knife must have been particularly savage. But whoever field dressed the wound did a great job. Probably saved his life. We also addressed the wounds on his face."

"What about his face?" Avery asked. "Any broken bones? And is there a head injury?"

"He won't be beautiful for a while," the doctor answered, "but he should heal nicely. We had a team of doctors working on him. His cheekbone was fractured, but fortunately still in place. He also suffered a broken nose and a dislocation of the jaw. Again, we were able to stabilize everything. He was lucky the mandible wasn't broken, or he'd have his jaw wired for four to six weeks."

"Yeah." Avery snorted. "That would have really been a problem with him. No other damage? Not that this wasn't enough."

Dr. Thornton shook her head. "While we had him under we did X-rays to make sure there was no skull fracture, no spine or brain damage."

"And those were all negative?"

"Yes, thankfully. I know this will sound strange, but he was really very lucky. Those were some powerful blows he suffered."

Every bit of energy drained from Marissa's body as relief swept over her. If it hadn't been for Blake's arm around her, holding her up, she was sure she'd have collapsed.

"When can we see him?" she asked.

Dr. Thornton looked at her watch. "Not for at least an hour. He'll be in recovery that long. Then he'll be moved to a room. I understand all the paperwork was taken care of before he got here, so just see the front desk if you want to make any special arrangements for his room."

"All taken care of," Avery assured her. "Thank you so much, Doctor."

Marissa stumbled back to her chair, dropped her head into her hands, and let all the tears she'd been holding back flow unimpeded.

Chapter 16

Marissa was sure the following couple of days were the longest she had ever spent. Avery and Sam, and Avery's sister, Sheri March, took turns bringing her food and forcing her to eat. At night she slept in the big chair she'd dragged over next to Justin's bed. She left the hospital only when Avery insisted on driving her back to Arrowhead Bay to shower and change. She fidgeted during the hour-long drive, and after packing a bag with enough things to tide her over for a few days, insisted on being taken right back to the hospital.

Justin woke up only for short periods of time. The nurses, as well as the doctor when she made rounds, assured Marissa he was doing just fine. That they were keeping him sedated until his body began the healing process, and he was getting plenty of nourishment intravenously. She was torn between wanting him to sleep through the worst of it, and needing him to be awake, so she could truly believe the doctor's prognosis.

Despite the many assurances by the medical staff, Marissa was afraid to leave his side for fear he wouldn't still be alive when she returned. Except when the nurses were changing his dressing, or bathing him, or checking his medications, she held his hand as if she could infuse him with the strength to recover.

"If you don't start taking care of yourself," Avery told her, "we'll need a hospital bed for you, too."

"I'm fine," Marissa insisted.

"Tell me another story." Avery snorted. "Listen, if you run yourself into the ground, what good will you be to him when he does wake up?"

But she couldn't make herself leave again, fearful of a change in Justin's condition while she was gone. The rest of the time she spent in the big chair, which after a while became surprisingly comfortable. And she prayed, more than she ever had in her life.

"I have news," Avery told her, coming into the room the next morning. "Good news."

Marissa was just coming out of the bathroom where she'd washed, brushed her teeth, and changed into one of the fresh outfits she'd brought from her house.

"Great. I could certainly use some."

"I also brought you goodies."

Marissa had zilch appetite, eating the hospital food only so she wouldn't get sick. But the coffee from Fresh Roasted and the chocolate chunk muffins from Fresh from the Oven actually made her taste buds wake up. She took a sip from the cup Avery handed her and hummed with pleasure.

"You are a goddess."

"Sit," Avery ordered, placing the disposable food carrier on the bedside table. "Eat and drink while I give you all the details."

Marissa took another sip of the coffee, and a large bite of the muffin, then sat back. "Okay. Let me have it."

"First, an update on Stefan Maes. Interpol initially had him locked away where he had no contact with anyone. Forget about everything else on their list. They had to settle all the jurisdictional problems before they could do anything else. The woman he had executed was from Belgium and they want their pound of flesh. With the testimony from the guests at Rosewood, they have enough to put him away for two lifetimes."

"Yeah, right," Marissa snorted. "He'll weasel out of that like he has everything else. Even after sweeping his money the CIA didn't have enough evidence with his personal fingerprints on it to put him away. They had to be satisfied with cutting him off at the knees."

"Maybe so." Avery nodded. "However, it seems he's also wanted on several murder charges in Croatia. People who were terrified to testify before have come forward now that his team is decimated. There was a dustup over who had jurisdiction first, but Croatia isn't quite as democratic as Belgium. Maes screamed blue murder as he was dragged on to a private plane with officers of the Criminal Police Directorate. The *Ravnateljstvo Policije*. I doubt if we'll ever see or hear from him again."

"Good. He should be torn limb from limb then shot in every piece of his body."

Avery laughed. "I had no idea you were so bloodthirsty."

Marissa leaned forward. "Avery, he ordered a woman shot because she was trying to send a message for help. Killed her. Shot others just because he could and because he wanted them to know that he could. I have no doubt that if the Vigilance team hadn't arrived, after all the money was transferred he'd have killed everyone in that restaurant."

"Well, good riddance."

"Amen to that." Marissa bit off a piece of muffin and chewed thoughtfully. "What about his men?"

"Three dead at Rosewood, shot by my men. The rest also back to Croatia. There seem to be a number of people now in important positions who have grudges against them. And Croatia is one of the last places I'd ever want to be on trial. Finally and forever, Stefan Maes is shut down and done."

Marissa felt as if a heavy weight had been lifted from her body.

"That's the best news I've had in forever."

"I'll bet it is. What do you think you'll do now that you have choices?"

Marissa shrugged, chewed on another bite of muffin. That was a good question. She had the opportunity now to live her life without hiding, without disguise or camouflage. She could do whatever she wanted. Go wherever she wanted.

"What I do *not* want is do is another job for the CIA. I'm done playing superspy. The price has been too high."

"You could go back to the world of finance, the environment you were recruited from," Avery pointed out.

Marissa shook her head. "No, I think I've lost my taste for it. In spite of the reasons that brought me here, I really enjoy living in Arrowhead Bay and running the gallery. I've gotten such pleasure from discovering new local artists and helping people choose the right art pieces for themselves. And by the way, you can pass the word to Blake Morgan that I'm sorry he and Sam didn't get to come by the gallery before I had to go into hiding. I'd be happy to meet them there when I can and help them choose some pieces."

"You know," Avery said in a slow voice, "you don't have to leave. You could stay here. Keep the gallery open, even go on being Marissa Hayes, unless you have another life you want to get back to."

She shrugged. "Not really. There's nothing anywhere I have the least desire to go back to."

Both her parents were dead, and any friends she'd had were lost in the void of the last five years. So there really was nothing to go back to. No pieces to pick up. And staying here, in this sleepy Southern town, was so tempting.

"Marissa, you look like you're trying to solve the problems of the world." Avery finished her own coffee and tossed the cup in the trash. "You don't have to decide anything right now, you know."

"That's good, because all I can focus on is Justin and wondering how soon they'll reduce his meds, so he can wake up for more than a few seconds at a time. And that only happens when his dressings are changed, or they need to do something else to him. I have to see his eyes open, hear him speaking to me, before I can draw a full breath."

"Honey, Dr. Thornton told you more than once they're keeping him heavily sedated because they had to do so much digging around in his body. On top of that, our bodies are wonderful things. They can shut down rather than deal with pain, until it becomes tolerable. Thornton says he'll be just fine, and I believe her."

"I know." Marissa reached between the rungs of the side rail and took Justin's hand in her own. "I know he takes chances like that as part of his job, but it's just so hard seeing him like this day after day. Even the few minutes he's awake now and then, he barely says more than one or two words." She held up a hand. "And before you go there, I know he's dealing with a dislocated jaw. But if he'd just wake up and talk to me…"

"Don't…talk so loud…and I will."

Marissa jumped, shocked at the sound of his voice. And she realized she was not just holding on to his hand, he was squeezing hers in response.

"J-Justin?"

"Don't know…who else would…be in this bed."

His words were slurred and his voice low, but it was the most wonderful sound she'd heard in what seemed like forever. She rose from her chair and bent over the rail, touching his face with her free hand. She scarcely noticed the tears running down her cheeks.

"It's about time you woke up," she told him.

"Hurts." The word came out in a guttural tone. "Where am I?"

"Memorial Hospital in Sarasota," Avery told him. She'd come to stand at the other side of the bed. "You gave us all a damn good scare."

"Sorry…about that."

Marissa pressed the call button for the nurse. "I need to let them know you're awake."

"Okay."

He squeezed her hand, hard, and she knew it was a reaction to the pain he was feeling.

The nurse hurried in, smiling when she saw his eyes open. "That was some nap you took, Mr. Kelly. Glad you're awake."

"Hurts," He repeated the word.

"And I have just the thing for you. Let me take your vitals and I'll get it."

Five minutes later, the pain meds now circulating in his bloodstream, he eased his grip on Marissa's hand.

"Better." He let out a slow breath.

"I'm going to set this up for you." The nurse came back, rolling in a piece of equipment. "You can push the little button when you need something for pain. It's regulated so you don't get too much."

"Thanks."

"Well." Avery smiled at him. "As long as we're sure you're going to be among the living, I'm going back to the office. We have a number of situations in play. I'll keep checking on you but you're in good hands." She nodded at Marissa.

"Best hands ever," he agreed, just before he closed his eyes again.

"I'll leave you to it," Avery said. "Just keep me in the loop. I'll stop by whenever I get a chance."

"Thank you so much for everything." Marissa hugged her. "Without the Vigilance team I know things would have been a lot worse."

"I just wish we'd had the information before we sent you off for what we thought was the perfect hideaway."

Marissa shook her head. "What is it you're always saying to me? Shit happens?"

"That's right."

As soon as Avery left, Marissa sat back down in the chair. But she slid her hand through the side rail again to wrap her fingers around Justin's hand. She couldn't take her eyes away from him, watching his breathing ease and some color return to his face.

What would happen next with them? In the midst of death and danger, she'd fallen in love with him. Totally. Completely. She didn't want to imagine a life without him. Sure, they'd said a lot of things to each other, hovered around the edge of making promises. Enjoyed the most spectacular sex of her life. Had that all just been a product of the situation they were in? She'd heard danger could be great for creating artificial situations that disappeared in the aftermath.

She knew other Vigilance agents had married, despite the uncertainty of the lives they lived. Would Justin, once he recovered, reconsider everything he'd said to her and decide his existence was too chancy to share with someone? She could deal with it, but would he insist on not dragging her into it?

Heaving a sigh, she curled herself into a more comfortable position in the chair. The peak of her anxiety receded. Justin had awakened and fallen back into a more natural sleep. Everything would be all right. She would be here every minute until he was well enough to be on his own. Then, when he was more coherent and on the road to mending, maybe they could have a talk, so she could figure out what to do with her life.

* * * *

"Where is she?" Justin demanded.

He'd called Avery at eight-thirty that morning and barked that Marissa was missing. The afternoon before, while he'd been napping, Marissa had slipped out of the room. No note. No nothing. And she hadn't been back.

"She's not missing," Avery told him. She had run out of the office when Justin threatened to walk out of the hospital and go look for the woman himself.

"Then where the hell is she?" He was almost shouting, or at least as much as his condition allowed.

A nurse came rushing in, her forehead ceased in a frown. "What's going on in here? Mr. Kelly, please lie down. If you move around too much, you'll pull your stitches."

"I don't care about the goddamn stitches. I have a problem. I have to get out of here."

"Yeah, that's not happening." Avery looked at the nurse, who was adjusting the IV line. "Right?"

"Indeed. Mr. Kelly, you are only six days out of surgery, and some damn complicated surgery it was. You wouldn't make it as far as the elevator."

"Watch me."

He moved as if to push the nurse away and lower the guardrail, but Avery put a hand on his shoulder and shoved him back on the bed.

"If you try one more time to get your ass out of this bed," she told him, "I will have the nurses bring in restraints and tie you down. You know I'll do it."

"I'm good at that, too," the nurse added.

"There you go." Avery looked at Justin. "Will you be good?"

"Will you tell me where Marissa is and why she's not here?"

She nodded. "If you'll behave."

"Whatever," he grumbled. Swallowing a groan, he lay back against the pillows.

* * * *

When Avery had texted Marissa earlier to ask if she wanted to go home for a bit, rest, change her clothes, and maybe get some real food to eat, she had said yes. The truth was, she had no appetite and she wasn't sure when she'd be able to sleep again. But she had to get out of the hospital. Justin's color was better, and it looked like he was on the road to recovery, albeit a long road. And she wanted to sneak out while he was still asleep.

"Rhonda Morganstern packed all of your things herself while Mike's team and Brian's guys were cleaning up the mess in the ballroom. Mike brought it back with him when the chopper returned for him and his guys."

"That was very nice of her. I'll have to write her a thank you note." She stared out the car window. "I'm sure they had their hands full taking care of their terrified guests, especially the wounded ones, not to mention the man whose wife was killed."

"Rhonda is nothing if not efficient. She and Walt both. They got it taken care of."

"Some of their own people were killed, weren't they?" She had just remembered the guards.

"Yes." A look of sadness washed over Avery's face. "Nice men doing a job in a place that should not have had any threats. Walt and Rhonda are taking care of their families, but that's small consolation."

"So much death and pain in a place meant for pleasure." Marissa felt sick. "Those poor people."

"Let's not go overboard," Avery told her. "Keep in mind the targets of Maes's visit were involved in his criminal enterprises. They weren't so squeaky clean, despite the front they put on."

"I know." She sighed. "But everyone else was caught up in the terror of the situation for no more reason than they happened to be guests at that particular time."

"Yes. Everyone will be a long time getting over this."

Marissa rubbed her forehead. "It makes me sick to know how many people were partnered with Maes and made money on the blood of others. If I'd had a little more time, I know I would have uncovered all of that."

"Yes, I believe you would have. In any event, it's someone else's mess now. Forget about it and get some rest."

Her car was in the driveway, and Avery handed her the keys.

"I know you're perfectly capable of driving yourself back and forth," she said. "Still, call when you want to go back to the hospital. Less hassle for you."

Marissa was silent for a long moment, figuring out how to phrase what she had to say. "Avery, I'm not going back to the hospital. At least for now."

Very little ever got a reaction from Avery but her eyebrows rose almost to her hairline. "You're not? I can't imagine why. It's obvious there's something good going on between you and Justin. Why would you turn your back on him?"

"I'm not." She nibbled on her thumbnail. "Well, not exactly."

"Well, then, what, exactly?"

She hadn't meant to dump it all on Avery, but the minute she opened her mouth, there it was, like an unstoppable waterfall. Everything. Their feelings for each other. His commitment to Vigilance. The possibility that his career would be a stumbling block to a relationship. For him, not her.

Avery was silent for a long time.

"It's really not up to me to convince either of you one way or another. I'll just say two things. One. I've seen many relationships like this work very well as long as both parties have a strong commitment. I see it in Vigilance. And two, don't make decisions for Justin. Go back to the hospital. Talk to him. Figure out if what you have is real."

"I'm just being sensible," she insisted. "I don't want him to feel any sense of obligation. Putting any pressure on him while he's just at the beginning of the healing process is a bad idea. I thought I'd wait until he was a lot more recovered."

Avery shook her head. "This might be the very thing that helps him heal faster. Will you at least think about it?"

"Yes. I'll think." She opened the car door. "I promise."

"That's good enough for me. At least for the moment."

Marissa closed the door, climbed the steps to her little porch, and walked into her house. She was so weary she could hardly move. The air was musty and stale, so she opened some windows to let in the fresh breeze. She had little in the house to eat, but food was the last thing on her mind at the moment. She was more tired than she could ever remember being.

She stumbled into her bedroom threw off her clothes, and climbed into bed. And prayed for sleep.

* * * *

"What do you mean wants to give me time? Time for what?" Justin was sure his blood pressure had just kicked up twenty notches. "She has to come back."

Avery chuckled. "She doesn't have to do anything."

"Yes, she does."

He waved the hand with the IV in it, wondering how long they were going to keep pumping him full of antibiotics this way. He'd insisted they stop the intravenous pain meds. The level of pain had receded, and he had a high threshold anyway. Now he wanted off this stupid IV setup. Why couldn't they just give him a couple of pills? This morning he'd complained so much about it the nurse threatened to bring back the catheter if he didn't quit his bitching. He knew he was acting like an idiot, but he didn't care. Now Marissa had disappeared, and he wanted her back. He had no idea why she'd taken off the way she had, before they even had a chance to talk.

Avery chuckled. "She's only been gone three hours, Justin."

"Feels like three days. Did she say why she left? I know you drove her home because she didn't have her car here. She must have said something to you." When Avery didn't answer, he added, "Well? Give it up, Avery."

"I have no idea how I got into the role of relationship counselor and I'm getting out of it is fast as I can. Okay. Here it is. I don't know what happened between the two of you at Princessa Key, and I don't want any details. I do know that I saw something growing between you guys before that." She paused.

"Well?" Justin prompted. "Don't stop there."

"She's aware things escalate during danger. People say and do things that change when the danger is passed, and she doesn't want you to feel any obligation to make a commitment to her."

His eyes widened. "What the fuck? Jesus, Avery. I said things to her I've never said to another woman. Nothing's changed about that. At least for me. I figured we'd have a chance to move this thing forward once the danger was past. I didn't think some fucking asshole was going to rearrange my face and try to slice up my organs."

"I believe she's worried about compromising your career. That you'll make sacrifices to—" She stopped because Justin was shaking his head.

"Have I wondered if I had any right to ask her to share my life with me? Damn straight. Anyone in my position has those misgivings. You know that." He rubbed his hand over his still discolored face. "I never thought I'd meet anyone I felt that way about. But shit. From the minute I met her we had this invisible connection."

"Wow!" Avery grinned. "Look at you, being all touchy feely."

"Yeah, right." He'd managed to push down the edges of the physical pain. That was something he'd done way too many times. But not this emotional pain, which was so foreign to him.

"Others make it work. We can, too. That's all the stuff I wanted to talk to her about. And Marissa has a greater understanding of my job, which should make it easier."

"Or harder," Avery pointed out. She cocked her head and studied his face. "I have to say, Justin, you surprise me."

"Why's that?"

"You've always been so self-controlled emotionally. So immersed in your missions. Even during your recreational off times, you were friendly and certainly had your share of women. But it's like you never wanted any of them to get beneath the top layer."

"You're right," he agreed. "But I enjoyed Marissa the times we were thrown together. Maybe because I sensed she kept so much of herself beneath the surface, too."

"So what changed?"

He had to search his mind for the answer, since he hadn't really stopped to figure it out.

"I think when she started taking the kickboxing lessons. There was something simmering beneath the surface, and it wasn't just the physical attraction. When you sent me to Rosewood with her, I took a chance because I thought she felt the same way."

Avery's lips curved in a tiny grin. "And I'm guessing it worked."

Heat surged through him as he remembered exactly how well it had worked. But he wasn't about to give Avery any details.

"Yes. And that's all you need to know."

"Okay, here's my take, for what it's worth." She leaned forward. "I think she's worried you'll be distracted thinking about her when you're on a job, or weigh options differently in certain situations. She doesn't want you to feel an obligation to her and—"

"An obligation?" he almost shouted the words.

"Cool it, or you'll split your stitches."

"This is my fault. I figured we'd have plenty of time to talk and move this thing between us forward after the Maes situation was resolved. And if that bastard hadn't stuck me with his knife, we would have. But I—" He stopped. "Never mind. Saying this to you does me no good. I need to talk to her. You're good at getting people to do things. How about getting her back to the hospital so we can talk?"

"I'll try."

Justin shook his head. "No trying, only doing. The sooner the better."

"All right. I guess my business can run without me for a couple more hours while I play matchmaker."

At that Justin laughed, albeit a rusty sound. "Don't give me that. You can run that business from a rowboat in the middle of the ocean with a cell phone."

A wry smile played over her lips. "Thanks for the vote of confidence. All right, let me see what I can do."

"I want results," he called after her as she walked to the door.

She just shook her head and flapped a wave at him.

* * * *

Marissa was sitting out on her tiny patio with a cup of coffee, trying to figure out the rest of her life, and wondering how she was going to fill the hole in her heart, when her cell rang.

She looked at the screen. Avery. She was tempted to let it go to voice mail, but then she couldn't be rude to the woman who had been nothing but nice to her.

"Morning," she greeted her.

"I come without muffins," Avery told her, "but if I need to bribe you ,we can always take a detour through town and pick them up."

"Bribe me for what? Oh, wait. Where are my manners? How about a cup of coffee?"

"No, thanks. I'm coffee'd out for the moment." Avery dropped into the other chair at the table. "I just came to chat a little."

Marissa frowned. "But we already talked this morning when you brought me home. What else is there to say?"

"Apparently a lot, so I'm here on a mission, and I want you to listen to everything I say before you make a comment."

She talked, and Marissa listened, more astonished at every sentence that came out of Avery's mouth. When the other woman finished, she sat there, not quite knowing what to say.

"I guess I just figured it was the situation prompting everything that happened. That once things were back to normal, he'd just remember it as a nice interlude." And how often had she thought that to herself?

Avery stared at her. "If that's what you think, then you don't know Justin Kelly very well. Look. I can't force you short of taking you at gunpoint, but I think you owe it to both of you to get to the hospital as fast as you can and work this out. Happiness is too fragile to let it slip through your fingers, especially when it could just be a stupid misunderstanding on someone's part."

"You mean my part," Marissa said.

"If the shoe fits and all that." Avery rose and picked up her keys. "Now it's up to you, kiddo. Make the right choice, for both of you."

Marissa barely remembered the drive to the hospital, thankful for all the prominent signs along the interstate and in the city. Her brain was on autopilot. She'd been so determined to give Jason time to make sure how he felt. Time to analyze how a relationship between them would work, but she was out of practice in that area.

Don't get your hopes up, she kept repeating to herself. *Maybe he just wants to make sure we're still friends.*

The only empty spaces in the parking garage were on the top floor, and the elevator moving downward seemed to be stuck on a very slow pace. At last she was on his floor and hurrying down the corridor. Just before she reached his room she paused, gathering herself.

Holy shit, she thought. *I didn't even put on makeup or anything. Oh, well. I guess this is the chance to see if it's the real me he wants.*

Letting out a slow breath, she pushed on his partially open door and walked into the room.

If she'd had any misgivings at all, they disappeared the moment she saw Justin sitting up in bed. There was no mistaking his grin or the light in his eyes.

"Come here, woman," he growled, albeit in a slightly subdued voice. "Right now. I want to touch you. If I get out of this bed, I'm liable to rip out all my stitches."

"They've had you up for a short time for the past couple of days," she reminded him.

"Yeah, but right now I might not be able to take it slow. Come on, Marissa. Come closer." He paused. "Please."

"All right."

When she was near enough that he could reach her, he grabbed one of her hands. "Marissa."

Her name sounded like a caress the way he said it. And just that simple contact sent both chills and heat through her system, and her pulse thrummed a steady beat.

"I-I'm sorry I ran out while you were still sleeping. I just—"

He touched two fingers to her lips. "Ssh. Me first." He caressed her knuckles with his thumb.

The need she was trying so hard to tamp down spiked. How had she thought she could walk away from him, even for a little while?

"I figured we had plenty of time to talk after the Maes situation was resolved. I always expected it would be taken care of soon, just not the way it happened."

"But good riddance," she interrupted.

"I agree. Only with the way things happened I didn't have the chance to tell you how I feel." He stroked his thumb over her hand, which he still held. "Those things I said at Rosewood? That wasn't just the heat of the moment, or the edge of danger situation, or any of the other things that might be running through your mind."

"I just wanted—"

Again, he touched her lips with the fingers of his free hand.

"Not finished. You don't know me well enough. Yet. But I'm not a guy who throws words like that around. And I didn't even get to say the most important ones."

"Most important?" She quirked an eyebrow.

"I love you. And I want a relationship with you. A permanent one. Let's go from there."

"But I explained to Avery about—"

"Not your turn yet. Anyway. I'm not in the most stable business. If anyone knows that, it's you. But I don't take unnecessary risks. I'm not a danger junkie. Even when I went up to the restaurant at Rosewood, I knew Mike and the team were arriving any minute."

"Please let me say something," she broke in. "Before you go any further. I'm not worried about how you do your job. Three years undercover taught me that life is full of risk. That you have to grab what you can when you can."

He looked bewildered. "Then what's the problem?"

"I was afraid you'd think better of the things you said and decide your life was too risky to make me a part of it. Or that I'd be too much of a distraction."

"Distraction? Really? Is that how you see the kind of discipline I have? I must be doing something wrong."

God, this was just going sideways. She was doing it all wrong.

"That's not what I mean." She tried to find the right words, but her brain seemed to have a kink in it. "Yes, I've seen the kind of discipline you have. I just…the risks…I don't want to affect how you do your job."

"And if I said yes, I'm in a business filled with risks, what would you say?"

She studied him, looking for clues. Maybe he wanted to hear it from her first.

"What would I say? Okay. Here it is. Justin, it's just like I said. Life is full of risks. You could get killed crossing the street. After everything I've been through, I can handle anything as long as I know you love me."

"I love you."

She stared at him, stunned. "Just like that?"

He nodded. "Just like that. Marissa, we have something very special going here. We agreed on that before all hell broke loose. I want a chance to make that grow. To plan a life together. Here. Or anywhere you'd like to go. With Maes out of the way, your options are unlimited, and I can live anywhere."

She linked her fingers with his and watched him while she let it rattle around in her mind. But she already knew what her answer would be.

"I know we can go anywhere, but I want to stay in Arrowhead Bay. I love it there. The town, my gallery, the people. We have friends there. Would you be good with that?"

"Whatever works for you works for me. As long as I know you love me, all is good."

She smiled at him. "I love you."

"Come here." He let go of her hand and opened his arms.

"We have to be careful of your stitches," she reminded him.

"My stitches are fine. Everything's fine as long as I can hold you."

Because the rails were now down in the bed she was able to get close enough to him that he could put his arms around her. She hugged him, being very careful of his wound. He tipped her face up with his fingers and placed a soft kiss on her lips. Heat surged through her and the last bit of tension left her body.

"Maybe." He winked. "When I get out of here, I'm going to take you away someplace secluded, so we can concentrate on each other, make love, and talk about our future. How does that sound?"

"Sounds great to me. But please. No secluded Caribbean islands, okay?"

Justin burst out laughing. "That's a deal."

After that there was no more talking for a long time.

Meet the Author

Desiree Holt is the USA Today bestselling author of the Game On! and Vigilance series, as well as many other books and series in the romantic suspense, paranormal and erotic romance genres.

She has been featured on CBS Sunday Morning and in The Village Voice, The Daily Beast, USA Today, The (London) Daily Mail, The New Delhi Times, The Huffington Post and numerous other national and international publications. Readers can find her on Facebook and Twitter, and visit her at www.desireeholt.com as well as www.desiremeonly.com.

Hide And Seek

In case you missed it, keep reading for an excerpt from book one in the Vigilance series

Anything can happen when you let your guard down . . .

After receiving a violent threat on the heels of her father's disappearance from the town of Arrowhead Bay, Devon Cole fears for her life—until Vigilance, a local private security agency, steps in to shield her from danger. Although she isn't usually quick to surrender her freedom, she has no problem stripping her defenses for her new sexy bodyguard . . .

Tortured by the painful memory of lost love, Logan Malik is determined not to fall for a client again. So when he's tasked with watching over Devon day and night, he's focused on doing his job. Day is no problem, but as tensions rise at night, nothing can protect them from giving in to unbridled passion . . .

A Lyrical e-book on sale now.

Learn more about Desiree at
http://www.kensingtonbooks.com/author.aspx/31606

Prologue

Graham Cole clutched his cell phone, barely restraining himself from throwing it against the wall. Where the hell was Vince? Everything was falling apart and they needed to get the hell out of Dodge.

How had they even gotten to this point?

A drug cartel. He was laundering money for a drug cartel.

It had all started so slowly.

"We think if you changed these suppliers, you'd help your bottom line."

"If you switched distributors for these products, you'd be in a lot better shape."

"These people are the cause of all that red ink. Get rid of them."

When Graham had discovered the true source of the funds he'd used to save his business, and wanted to pull out, Vince had convinced him it was too dangerous. Vince had been right. No one ever walked away from a cartel.

Still, he'd been determined to see if there was a way out of the chokehold. Somehow—he had no idea how—word had gotten through to Cruz Moreno, head of the vicious Moreno cartel, that Graham wanted out. He was told to take his money and shut up.

"They could go after Devon, too," Vince had told him.

God! On top of everything else he'd made both Vince and Devon targets of these miserable assholes.

In the end, the only answer he'd come up with was to disappear. Maybe without him there, they'd leave Vince and Devon alone. Giving up the lifestyle he'd worked so hard to build wasn't even a factor. If he stayed, things would be a lot worse. If he was arrested, Moreno could use a threat to Devon to keep him from testifying. If he was gone, he was no longer a threat and she'd be safe.

He hoped.

El Jefe had laid it out plain and simple. *"We own you, compadre. Never forget that. And don't screw me over."*

So he'd made his plans, quietly and under the radar.

He leaned back in his chair, rubbing his chest, feeling the acid burn of indigestion. He hoped to hell he wasn't having a heart attack.

As always, the television in his office was on so he could skim the day's headlines, keeping an eye on the financial reports for anything that might affect the conglomerate. Old habits die hard. Now, a running news story caught his attention.

"That's all the information we have at the moment. Repeating, Vincent Pellegrino, vice president of corporate finance for Cole International, has been found dead in his car on Interstate 75. It appears he swerved for some reason, crashed through a barrier on a curve, and went over the side. Authorities are calling it a one-car accident but they are still investigating. We'll bring you more information as it becomes available."

Vince dead?

Jesus Christ on a crutch.

Beads of sweat formed all over his body. He rewound the story twice, but the details never changed. What the hell had happened? Had Moreno somehow found out what he was planning and killed Vince as a warning? For the first time in a long time, he knew real fear. What had once seemed like the answer to a prayer now felt like an octopus wrapping its tentacles around him, choking the life out of him. They could be coming for him any minute. Who knew that when he attempted to repay the money, he was inviting a possible death sentence?

Now he needed to get the fuck out of here before Moreno's men showed up at his doorstep. But he was damn sure taking all the evidence with him. He might need a bargaining chip.

He checked the desktop computer one more time for the feed from the security cameras. Nothing. He'd triple-checked that the alarm system was still on before getting ready. Also good to go.

Satisfied he was still safe, he unplugged the external hard drive from his desktop computer and stuck it in his briefcase along with the laptop and the portfolio. Then he opened the tower, removed the internal hard drive, and shoved it into his briefcase, too. When he got to sea, he'd deep-six the internal one along with the laptop. Even if he wiped it, a good technician could restore everything, and who knew what would lead them to him. As long as he had the external he was all set. He was almost ready now, heading for the one person he could trust, to a place where he could set himself up with a new computer and figure out how to best use this stuff as leverage.

He sent a quick text to a prearranged burner phone, then took a moment to restore his phone to factory settings. His briefcase was locked, so he stuck the phone in his pocket. He was planning to toss it anyway. As soon as he was away from the harbor, he'd chuck it overboard. Anyone trying to find him with a GPS locator would have a hell of a hard time doing it. Let them stick that up their collective ass. He'd be long gone by then.

If he had one regret, it was for Devon, the daughter he was leaving behind, and the damage he'd done to their relationship. He considered leaving a note for her or sending her a text, but he didn't want anything that could connect her to this. Too dangerous. Still, it saddened him greatly that he'd probably never see her again. He hadn't been the best father in the world the past couple of years. Once he got to his new location, he'd keep track of her through the internet, Googling her name, and checking the newspapers as well.

He thought again of Vince's so-called accident, and nausea bubbled. But right now he needed to get the fuck out of here. Blotting the sweat on his forehead with the sleeve of his shirt, he unlocked a drawer in his desk and pulled out a slim portfolio. Then he grabbed his Glock 9mm from another drawer and stuck it in his pocket. He didn't have much time, needed to move right now.

He lifted the briefcase and headed for the garage. A sound caught his attention as he opened the inside door. It sounded like it came from the kitchen and his stomach knotted. No, no, no. Impossible. There was no one here. He was imagining things. He'd given the housekeeper and groundskeeper the week off. The alarm should let him know if someone was trying to break in.

I'm imagining things. That's what happens when you put yourself in a dangerous position, screwing over dangerous people.

He needed to calm down or he'd stroke out before he even got out of here.

Then he heard it again. A squeak, as if someone walked on the highly polished hardwood floors. He held his breath, straining to hear. Was that yet another one? His heart pounded so hard he thought it would beat itself out of his chest, his fear so strong he smelled it.

He hadn't seen anything on the security cameras, but why hadn't the alarm sounded? No, he was imagining things. It was his state of mind. Edging up to the door, he peeked out into the hallway, looking one way, then the other. At this time of day, the house was filled with sunlight. Surely he'd see anyone if there was someone to see.

I'm driving myself nuts. I need get the hell out of here. I'm running out of time.

Letting his breath out, he turned once more toward the garage door, stopping when again he thought he heard another sound. He grabbed his gun and started to turn around, but a hard, muscular arm locked itself around his neck. A hand yanked the gun from his grip as if it were nothing more than a feather duster and pressed it into the small of his back.

Fuck! Double fuck.

His legs had turned so rubbery he wasn't sure he could stand if the man released his hold. If only Vince hadn't cried wolf so many times before, Graham would have paid more careful attention to his warnings. If only he'd left earlier. If only he'd been more careful. If only a lot of things.

"Going someplace?" A guttural voice ground out the words in his ear, hot breath singeing his skin.

Real fear crept through him, paralyzing him. He hadn't made it. His escape was so close but exactly what he feared had happened. His timing sucked. Was this it? Was this how it was all going to end for him?

"H-How did you get in?" What had happened to his high-priced alarm system?

"You're not quite as safe as you think you are, asshole. A strong radio frequency can knock out even the best alarms."

"You're choking me." Graham could hardly get the words out as the stranger pressed harder on his windpipe and dragged him along the floor. He was sweating so badly now he could smell it on his body. How would he ever get out of this? He'd been so close, so very close.

"We're going to take a little trip, you and I," the man went on, "along with whatever is in that briefcase. Mr. Moreno says you're unhappy, *amigo*. He wants to meet with you and make sure you understand nothing is to change. Your friend, Vincenzo, tried to run, too. Unfortunately in his haste he met an untimely demise before he could give us all the information we want."

Vince. Goddamn.

"Let's move." The man urged him forward, still exerting the pressure on his neck and nudging him with the gun.

He couldn't let Moreno's thug get him past the front door. Graham dragged his feet and looked around wildly for something, anything, any option to get him out of this. Whatever it was, he'd have only a few seconds to make it happen. Then, in the hallway, he spotted something that gave him a faint ray of hope, if he could get hold of it.

"I—I can't breathe." He made his voice as faint as possible, and sagged against the man behind him.

"Too bad."

"If you deliver a dead body," Graham gasped, "Moreno won't be very happy with you."

He could have sworn the man growled, but he finally loosened his hold. Knowing he'd have scant seconds to do anything, Graham yanked on the man's arm and ducked beneath it. In one desperate movement he spun around, grabbed a bronze statue from the hall table, and hit the man over the head. For an endless moment nothing happened, and he was afraid he'd misjudged. Then the man toppled to the floor, nearly taking Graham with him.

He had no idea if he'd killed the man or merely knocked him out, but he didn't stop to find out. If the man was dead, in a few days his housekeeper would find the body, somewhat rancid by then. If it was the latter, he was short on time to get the fuck out of here.

He picked up the gun and the briefcase that he'd dropped and raced for the garage. He was sweating profusely and shaking so much he bumped into the car, the briefcase slamming into the fender. He yanked his keys from his pocket, hoping he was steady enough to drive. He jumped into the most innocuous of his vehicles, a gray Mercedes, and hauled ass down the driveway to the road.

When he made the turn onto the highway, he spotted a black utility vehicle parked near the trees with a man in the front seat.

Fuck!

The driver, spotting Graham's car, pulled out onto the road just as his partner, wobbling slightly, came racing down the driveway.

I should have hit him harder.

Lucky for Graham, the few seconds the driver stopped so his partner could jump in gave him a miniscule lead, but not much. Graham punched the accelerator and hauled ass down Seacliff Road. He had a small window of opportunity to get the fuck out of here, and he wasn't wasting any of it. That SUV would be on his tail any minute.

Faster! Faster!

He glanced at the speedometer and saw he was doing a hundred. He hoped he didn't wreck the car and kill himself just when he was nearly out of here. He was so focused on reaching the marina that it wasn't until he touched his pocket that he realized his cell phone wasn't there. Fuck again! What the hell had happened to it? If the wrong person found it and managed to restore it, his ass would be grass. Of course, first they'd have to find him. Right?

Breathe, he told himself. *Just breathe. Almost there.*

All the way to the harbor he kept checking the rearview and side-view mirrors. The road twisted and turned around the shoreline so at times his view of the rear disappeared. There. Was that a black SUV? No. No, it was a pickup and it turned off into a strip center before it caught up to him. He was definitely going to vomit first chance he had.

Jesus, Graham, don't lose it now.

Or any more than he already had. He just had to get to the boat before they caught up with him. Then he'd be safe. He always kept the smaller of his two boats provisioned and ready for anything, as part of his emergency plan. Just in case. He also made sure he had all the equipment on board he'd need.

Don't think about it. Don't think about it. Too late now.

He rounded a curve in the road and there was the marina up ahead. He could see *Princess Devon* now, its twin hulls bobbing in the water at its berth. Almost there. Still no SUV in his rearview mirror, but it could appear around the curve at any moment if those two guys had gotten their shit together.

At last he was parked and headed down the pier where the boats were docked. All he needed was another few minutes. A few more steps…

Chapter 1

"Your father is missing."

Devon Cole tightened her grip on her cell phone and tried to make sense of what Sheridan March had just told her, as fear swept through her. Maybe she hadn't heard right.

"What do you mean, missing?"

"The Coast Guard found the *Princess Devon* drifting five miles offshore early this morning," the Arrowhead Bay chief of police explained. "But there's no sign of him anywhere. And no clue to anything in the house. We went through every inch of it. The alarm was fried, probably needs to be replaced, but otherwise the place was clean as a whistle."

Devon clutched the phone. "Was there anything on the boat? Something he might have had with him that could give us a clue?"

"Nada."

"Where's the boat now? Would the Coast Guard hold on to it?"

"In its slip at the Bayside Marina. After the Guard went over every inch of it, they had one of the men on the cutter bring it back in and berth it. I have the keys."

Devon swallowed to ease the tightness in her throat. "When was the last time anyone saw him?"

"Sunday," Sheri told her. "As soon as I got the word from the Coast Guard we began checking with his friends. The last time anyone saw him was when Cash Breeland had lunch with him at the Driftwood."

"That's the same day I talked to him." She rubbed her hand nervously on her jeans. "He didn't say a word about going anywhere. Did the Moorlands say anything about seeing him?"

Ginny and Hank Moorland owned both the Driftwood Restaurant and Bayside Marina.

"Hank was in Miami for a couple of days but Ginny was there. She said she never laid eyes on him."

"And Gary at Bayside? Did he see anything?"

Sheri made a rude noise. "I talked to him myself but he's usually so off in his own world a marching band could have taken off and he'd never notice. I swear I don't know why Hank doesn't can his ass. Besides, it was a Sunday, so the marina was jammed with people arriving and leaving and some just working on their boats. He did say a couple of guys were asking about him, but he thought they were just friends."

"Did you talk to anyone who has a boat in a slip near his?"

"The ones we could find."

"God." Devon tamped back the rising fear. "I can't believe this could happen. He's an avid sailor and very, very safety conscious."

Her father had been sailing for as long as she remembered. When he still lived in Tampa he was out on the water every Saturday, sailing down the coast, sometimes with business associates but more often with her mother. That was how he'd discovered Arrowhead Bay. But he almost never went out during the week. Saturdays were his days on the water. And, after her mother passed away, sometimes on Sundays. It was something both her parents had enjoyed, and Devon often thought it was a way for him to recapture her presence.

"I know," Sheri agreed. "Everyone knows that about him."

"And the other boat?" Devon asked. "The *Lady Hannah*?"

"Still here. There's not even a sign anyone was on it." She paused. "We know he's an excellent sailor. The Coast Guard thought maybe he'd fallen overboard, but—"

"I guess that's possible, except he was a nut about water safety. He'd be careful."

"That's what I told them," Sheri agreed.

"The Coast Guard started searching immediately, right?"

"Yes, but it's a big ocean. They brought in another cutter to search as well as one of their Dolphin helicopters. I promise you it's a full-out search and rescue operation. And there's another thing."

"What?" What else could there be?

"I don't know if you caught it, but there was a story on the national news yesterday that Vincent Pellegrino, one of your father's vice presidents, was killed in a one-car accident."

Ice chilled her blood. "Are you saying the two things could be related? That my father didn't just fall overboard?"

"I'm saying we have to look at all possibilities. This is too much of a coincidence to ignore."

"Did you call his office? Ask his admin if he'd decided to take an unannounced vacation?"

"I did, but she knew nothing. And they are all in a turmoil over Pellegrino's death."

"But who would want to kill him?" Nausea bubbled up in her throat. "Either of them?"

"We don't know, and that may not be it at all. I'll just have to connect all the dots."

"Holy crap, Sheri."

"One other thing. His house was meticulously clean, as if someone had gone through and sanitized it. But—this is weird—his computer was on his desk but the internal hard drive has been removed."

"What? What the hell?"

"My thoughts exactly."

"What about the external hard drive? It should be right next to it."

"Nada," Sheri told her. "Gone, gone, gone."

Even as she tried to dial back the sick feeling creeping through her, Devon was already dragging her suitcase out and pulling things out of her drawers and closet. She ran through her mind all the projects she had in process, which could be put on hold, who she needed to try to renegotiate deadlines with.

"I'm coming down there right now. I can't just sit here and wait around. I'll finish packing as soon as we hang up and be on the road right away."

"Good. I think you need to be here. Corporate is sending some people down here and I know they'll want to talk to you, too. Call me or come see me as soon as you get here." Sheri paused. "We're all over it, Devon. I just wish we had more to go on."

"I know. It's just…" Just that she'd already lost one parent and didn't know if she could deal with losing another. "I think I'll go to the house first and take a look around."

"Sounds good. I'll wait to hear from you."

The minute she hung up from Sheri's call, she packed the suitcase and threw it and her computer stuff into her car. Less than thirty minutes later she was headed south from Tampa on Interstate 75. She alternated between the threat of tears and full-blown panic as the conversation replayed like a looping tape in her head as she ate up the miles.

While she drove, she kept trying to reach her father. She had both the cell phone and the house phone on speed dial, but she got nothing. Where the hell was he? She'd been on the road for about an hour when her cell rang. The readout showed Sheri's name so she pushed the remote button to answer.

"Have you found him?" she asked, forgoing any kind of greeting.

"I wish. No, I just wanted to give you a heads-up."

Now what?

"What's going on?"

"We've got a couple of reporters sniffing around here, asking about your father's disappearance."

"How did they find out so fast?" Devon asked.

"A million ways. This is the age of the internet. Maybe they were after your father to ask him about the death of his executive. I wouldn't put it past them to rent a boat and go check on the search."

"Damn, damn, damn." Devon pounded a fist against the steering wheel.

"You said it," Sheri agreed. "Anyway, I'll bet anything the first story will hit the newspaper tomorrow and they're looking for more details."

"Oh, my God. Sheri, I can't talk to them now."

"Don't worry. I'll keep them off your back. But it's possible if they give it a big play, someone seeing it might remember something."

"You're right," Devon agreed. "I'm just not good with stuff like that and right now my mind's in too much of a whirl to even speak coherently. I'll probably say the wrong thing and make the situation worse."

"I understand. We can't shut them out, and but I will do my best to keep them off your back for as long as I can."

"Thanks." Devon blew out a breath.

"If they catch you, the best thing is to tell them no comment. I'm sure they'll hit the Cole International offices in Tampa. Just let the people there make any statements."

"Sounds good to me."

"Don't forget. Call me or come by as soon as you get here."

"I will."

She disconnected the call and stuck the phone in the console.

Great. Just great. Reporters, looking for juicy scandal about the disappearance of a business giant.

Oh, Dad, how could you do this to me?

The fact was, she'd been worried about him for the past several months. Her mother's death five years ago had thrown him for a loop. Piled on top of that were problems with Cole International. He didn't discuss them with her but there was a hint here and there, and he was constantly on edge. Then, suddenly things seemed to be better.

She'd missed him when he moved to Arrowhead Bay, but she understood him wanting a change. The house was filled with too many memories of her mother. Plus her father said he was tired of city living.

On the trips to the little town while he was still living in Tampa, he met people. Made friends. The times she sailed down there with him she'd gotten to know people, too, and fallen in love with the small, sleepy Southern town. He was as happy as she'd seen him since her mother died.

She'd met Sheri March at one of the many festivals the town held and they'd connected at once, becoming good friends. Through Sheri she'd met a lot of other people, including the chief's sister, Avery, who ran a private security agency. With friends to hang with and her father almost himself again she'd begun to look forward to visiting him. He loved hearing about the growth of her graphics design business and praised her for what she accomplished.

Then he'd stopped asking her about it except on rare occasions.

She tried to pinpoint just when that had all started. *Almost two years ago*, she thought. The tenor of the visits had changed. *He* had changed, becoming more tense, edgier, sometimes even withdrawn. When she asked about it, he just brushed it off. She missed their tight relationship. They had always been close, so it bothered her more than she let on.

He was abruptly more preoccupied with the business than ever, even obsessed with its financial situation. It never made sense to her because Cole International was worth millions. Whenever she asked him what was wrong, he assured her everything was fine. Just some pesky business details, he told her, that were taking a little more of his attention.

She'd continued to make sporadic visits, hoping to recapture the tight sense of family they'd had. After all, it was just the two of them now. But no matter how hard she tried, she'd felt them drifting apart more and more. There was a wall of some kind around the man she just could not breach.

When she noticed the change in him, she tried to question Cash Breeland about it. Cash was the president of the locally owned Arrowhead Bay Bank. Devon didn't know him all that well, but he and her father had become friends even before the big move. In fact, it was Cash who had introduced her father to friends of his and drawn him into their social circle. But Cash just downplayed her questions.

"I know your daddy's been preoccupied some," he drawled when she asked him to meet her for coffee. "He's just working through some knotty business problems. With all this overseas competition, some of his units aren't performin' the way they should. He'll pull out of it as soon as there's an uptick in trade."

But he hadn't and now he was gone.

Missing.

The word gave birth to a lot of speculation and none of it good.

She spotted the highway signs for Arrowhead Bay and gave herself a mental shake. She needed to clear the garbage out of her head until she could find out for sure what was going on.

She took the farthest exit for the town, the one that took her to the road where her father's house was. He had built at the far end of town in the area known as Seacliff. More land, larger homes. He liked space, he'd told her. Cole International board members and executives routinely visited him there. And from his side patio he had a magnificent view of Arrowhead Bay and the harbor.

His house was the next to last one on Seacliff Road, and in minutes the familiar gateposts came into view. She gave silent thanks that there were no reporters around. They must have taken Sheri literally. She pulled up in the driveway and shoved the car into park, then stared at the house for a long moment. Automatically she reached into the half-empty bag of red licorice bites on her console and popped a couple in her mouth.

Sitting there now, chewing on the candy, she remembered the last time she'd seen him, a little more than a month ago. Their brief conversation played out in her head.

"You're leaving already?" He had looked up from his desk when she stopped in the doorway to the den.

"You're busy and I have work back in Tampa to take care of."

"I thought you brought your laptop with you."

"I did, but I think I'd be more comfortable at home."

For a fleeting moment, a pained expression crossed his face, one almost of sorrow.

"We should spend more time together."

She'd nearly snorted at that. They'd always been so close, especially after her mother died, but he'd withdrawn from her.

Still, he was her father and she loved him.

Was it possible this was voluntary? Had her father chosen to disappear so completely? No. *Too outrageous*, she thought. He was the epitome of the corporate icon. A mover and shaker. Winner of awards. Profiled in magazines. Business school graduates used him as their aspirational model. What on earth could make a man like that choose to vanish as if he'd never existed?

Even with his changes in personality and behavior, she could say this was 100 percent unlike him. What if he'd been grabbed by someone? But who? It could be a competitor, a disgruntled employee, someone on the bad end of a business deal. She knew very little about his business dealings. Would there be a ransom request? Would they contact her or his corporation? How would she get the money if the call came to her? How—

No. Sheri hadn't said anything about a kidnapping.

Another thought stabbed at her, one that chilled her. Had someone killed him and dumped the body overboard? But who? And why?

She would ask Sheri those questions as soon as she spoke to her again. Meanwhile, back to square one. If neither of those things turned out to be a reality, why had Graham Cole disappeared? What was going on with him?

Stop!

God, she was driving herself crazy.

She felt an unexpected rush of tears and a tightening of her throat. Despite the state of their relationship, he was her father. She still loved him and his disappearance frightened her.

Enough, missy. Get your ass into the house.

But the moment she climbed out of her car, a sudden chill raced down her spine and an ominous feeling gripped her. She stood there, gathering herself. Could a house be menacing?

Ridiculous. Stupid.

She wasn't the type of woman given to feelings like that. She was down to earth and practical. *Some might even say hardheaded*, she thought with a tiny smile.

Okay. I'm here. I should go inside and see if I can find anything the police might have missed. Or that would give me some kind of clue as to what had happened, something that would mean something only to me.

Go on. Don't be a chicken.

It was just bricks and stucco. What did she think was inside? A body? Not likely. The police had already searched the house. When she was sure she had herself under control, she hiked up the steps to the front door, for the moment leaving all her stuff in the car. As she slid the key for the front lock into place she wondered if it still worked. When the key turned and the lock clicked open, she breathed a sigh of relief.

Automatically, she reached for the alarm panel in the front hall, then remembered Sheri said it wasn't functioning. That a whole new one would need to be installed. How very weird. It was always on.

At least the air-conditioning had been left on, a blessedly cool change from the furnace that was Florida heat in the summer. Jingling the key ring, she walked through the house, looking around, although she had no idea what she expected to find.

The house was open and airy, with a wall of windows the length of one side that looked out to the lawn and beyond that to the bay itself. Her father had hired a decorator and given her free rein. The result was a tastefully decorated home that was open and welcoming.

As she walked from room to room, the same eerie feeling that gripped her when she'd stood in front of the house swept over her again. As if something very bad happened here. The chill racing over her skin had nothing to do with the artificially cooled air. She sensed a presence of evil in the air, and kept looking over her shoulder, as if expecting someone to pop out of a closet.

Stupid, stupid, stupid. I've been watching too much television.

She wandered into his den, seeking any kind of clue. Framed photos of herself and her mother and the three of them sat on the credenza but the desk was uncharacteristically bare. There was nothing on it, not an open book, a stack of papers, nothing. No sign of any activity, yet this was the room where he spent much of his time. How strange. Except...

Damn. Sheri was right. The computer was on his desk but the hard drive was gone. She checked all the drawers, although she was sure the police had already done this. No hard drive, internal or external, and no laptop. She'd forgotten to ask about that. Would he have taken all that with him? What did he plan to do with all his information if he'd decided to disappear? Could he run his business if no one knew where he was?

Again that icy feeling raced over her skin, the kind you got when people told ghost stories in the dark. As if strangers had been here, and not the ones investigating Graham Cole's disappearance. Could evil leave a sense of its presence?

Evil? Really?

Dramatic much, Devon?

She just couldn't shake the feeling something was off.

If only she'd forced the issue, made him talk to her. Fixed whatever barriers had been thrown up between them. Maybe she'd have a clue as to what was going on.

For a moment she considered the B and B in town, but why spend money she didn't have to? A house couldn't harm you, right?

A loud noise from the kitchen made her pulse leap and her heart thump. She grabbed a golf club leaning against the wall, tiptoed down the hall, and peered into the room. Nothing. No one. Should she step inside? What if someone was hiding in the alcove? With the alarm system not working anyone could come into the house.

Then the noise repeated, and she blew out a breath when she realized what it was. The icemaker in the refrigerator was disgorging cubes into the container.

Devon sat down at the breakfast bar, hands still shaking, and tried to steady herself. Maybe staying here wasn't such a good idea at all. Was she crazy to think someone had left an imprint here and it wasn't her father?

There's nothing here. Give your imagination a rest.

The landline on the kitchen wall rang, startling her. Who would be calling? Most of her father's calls had come in on his cell phone. Automatically she reached for it.

"Hello?"

Dead silence.

She waited, then, "Hello? Is someone there?"

Still silence. Why did the words *dead silence* come to mind? Then she heard it, the faint sound of someone breathing.

"If someone is there, speak up, or else I'm hanging up this phone."

When there was still no answer, she replaced the receiver, irritated. And troubled. She wanted to believe it was kids making prank calls, but with her father's disappearance it took on a more ominous feeling.

Right, Devon. Make this into some big deal. A lousy phone call. Probably just some wrong number and they were too embarrassed to say anything.

Maybe. She was not someone given to flights of fancy or premonitions. If anything, she was solidly grounded and practical to a fault. Only nothing had felt right to her since she walked in the front door, and the phone call had just added to the feeling of unease. She had a sudden need to get out of there, be with noise and crowds. Her stuff could wait until later. Right now she needed to be with people. A lot of people.

She had just headed out of the kitchen when the phone rang again. With a mixture of impatience and dread she picked up the receiver.

"Hello?"

Silence again.

"Listen. Whoever you are, either talk to me or I'm hanging up. If you call again, I won't be here."

She slammed the receiver back in the cradle. That did it for her. She needed to get out of here and find Sheri right away.

Her stomach chose that moment to grumble, reminding her she also needed food. She'd left Tampa two hours ago with only a large Starbucks in her stomach, and said stomach was now sending her signals. She remembered the housekeeper kept the fridge and the freezer stocked with basics so she could just fix herself something if she wanted to. But the eerie feeling wouldn't let go.

Sheri had said to call or come by as soon as she got into town, and right now seemed like a very good time to do that. Going straight to the police station seemed the best thing to do. She'd feel better seeing Sheri, anyway. Maybe she could help Devon put her feelings in perspective. The police had gone over the house thoroughly. Surely if something was out of whack, they'd have found it and told her. Something besides the jacked alarm system.

I'm just letting my mind play tricks on me. That has to be it.

Okay. That was it. She was getting out of here for a while. She'd head right for the police station and try to find out where things stood. She should have gone there right away. And she wanted to know what the latest was with the Coast Guard. The whole thing was still so unreal to her.

She walked through the house to the garage, still carrying the golf club and peeking around doors and walls. And feeling like an idiot. She found the extra remotes for the garage door and grabbed one, then hurried back through the house and out the front door. Without understanding why, she checked three times to make sure the front door was locked. She also looked carefully around as she got into her car, as if expecting to see someone peeking at her from behind the garage or one of the many massive trees that dotted the place.

Damn. If reporters might be hanging around, she'd better get that alarm fixed in a hurry. Anyone could get onto the property if they wanted to.

She wasn't easily frightened but the whole situation spooked her. Maybe she *should* stay in town at the B and B until she figured out if she was needed for anything. Still, she'd be damned if she'd let anyone chase her out of her father's house.

Seacliff Road was sparsely populated, the homes built much farther apart than those in town. There was only one house on the road past her father's and after that was a dead end. The lack of traffic made her nervous, as did the thick growth of trees that lined the side opposite the houses. Probably no one was lying in wait for her—where had *that* thought come from?—but she'd feel a lot better being part of a crowd. She kept looking in her rearview mirror.

"Just in case," she whispered.

But in case of what? Besides, who even knew she was in town? She was letting the entire situation spook her. What she needed to do was get into town and talk to Sheri face-to-face. Once she got a better read on the situation, she'd settle down. At least she hoped she would.

Just as she came to a slight curve in the road, she glanced in the rearview mirror and her heart nearly stopped beating. A black SUV that seemed to have come out of nowhere rode her bumper. Oh, God! Doing her best not to panic, she gripped the wheel and pressed down harder on the accelerator, but no matter how fast she went the car kept pace with her.

She navigated the next turn, hoping she could pick up a little speed and put distance between her and whoever this was. But then she felt a jolt as the SUV hit her rear bumper, just enough to scare her. Her engine was built for economy, not speed, and no matter how hard she pressed the accelerator she couldn't seem to outrun the vehicle riding her back end. Praying for someone to show up and help was useless. This was a thinly populated road where half the residents were snowbirds. Getting help right now was in the region of impossibilities.

In the next moment the other vehicle bumped her again, much harder, causing her car to lurch to the side. Suddenly she was losing control, no matter how she wrestled with the wheel, and she veered off the road. She came to a stop in the deep ditch that ran alongside the road. The SUV bumped her once more before it pulled up and stopped in front of her at an angle, blocking her, even if she could move.

What the hell?

The first thing that popped into her mind was Vincent Pellegrino's so-called one-car accident. Was this what happened to him? She was equal parts scared and pissed off. Scared because it was obvious whoever this was meant her no good. Pissed off because her day just kept going downhill and she was sick of it. She grabbed her cell phone, but dropped it because her hand was shaking. By then a man had climbed out of the SUV and was instantly at her side of the car. Another man appeared at the passenger side, boxing her in.

The one next to her knocked on her window, startling her so she dropped her cell phone again. She reached down to get it, but the man on the driver's side banged on her window once more.

"Open the window," he barked in a harsh voice.

She shook her head, double-checked to make sure the doors were locked, and reached down again for her phone. The next thing she knew something hit the passenger window, hard. The window cracked and shattered into what looked like a million pebble-sized chunks that flew across the seat. Startled, she let out a little scream and pushed back as hard as she could against the seat.

The man on the driver's side knocked on her window again.

"If you don't want me to break this one, roll it down," he growled.

Devon shook her head. She knew she should probably be cowering in fright, except that wasn't her style, even in a dangerous situation. Surely someone would come along on this road, right?

She closed her eyes for a moment and when she opened them, the man on her side knocked on the window again and held up an iron bar.

"I'm not going to kill you, bitch." His voice was a low monotone, slightly accented. "Not yet. This was just to get your attention. Next time it could be your legs. Tell me where he is and I'll leave you alone."

"Please. I—"

"Do you hear me? Where has he gone? When you talk to him, tell him we'll be happy to have you as our guest until he shows his face. We know where to find you."

Devon slid her gaze from one to the other. The two men looked as if they'd kill her before breakfast and still eat a hearty meal. She opened her mouth but no words came out. She pushed back against her seat again as the man on the right started to reach through the broken window to unlock the door.

At that moment a four-door pickup zipped around the curve behind them and slowed, the driver obviously spotting the tableau on the side of the road. The truck passed both of their vehicles, then pulled over across the road and stopped. Was this backup for the two men already bent on terrorizing her or could fickle fate be sending her a savior?